THE FIRST DEA

Staring through t
not been mistaken. It was *he*—a figure emerging from the past through the snow-filled evening. Golding's heart pounded in his chest. He could feel the cold, the hunger, the fear, and the revulsion he had not felt for more than thirty years.

The two men faced each other through the door. Golding's hatred mounted to the point of overwhelming him. The man smiled at him. It was a crooked, vicious smile. His right arm moved. There was a shattering of glass.

When Steven Golding arrived several minutes later, there was a crowd in front of the door.

Morris Golding lay motionless amidst the broken glass. Arms outstretched, left leg folded under him, his lifeless eyes stared at the ceiling. A large red stain covered the left side of his shirtfront and spread to a puddle of blood gathering beneath him. His life was gone, but the fear and the hatred remained on the cold blue face.

After thirty years, the malignant spirit of Dachau rises again. . . .

THE JUDAS GENE

ALBERT and
JO-ANN KLAINER

A DIVISION OF CHARTER COMMUNICATIONS INC.
A GROSSET & DUNLAP COMPANY

Published by arrangement with Richard Marek Publishers, Inc.

First Charter Printing May 1981
Published simultaneously in Canada
Manufactured in the United States of America

2 4 6 8 0 9 7 5 3 1

To our children, Peter, Lori, and Traci—three of the most important chapters in our lives.

To Claire Smith—for her encouragement, patience, and friendship.

To Helen and Louis Showstack—for their love and understanding.

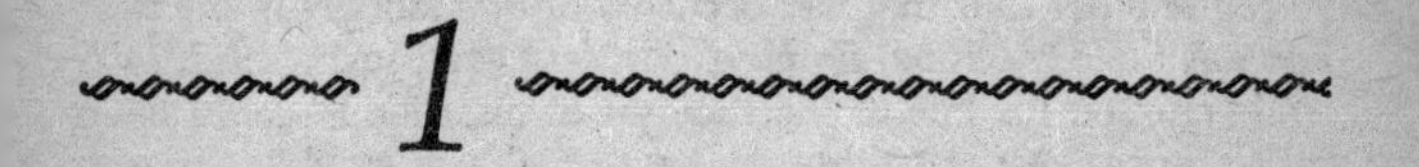

The breathing and the telltale rattle in the throat ceased abruptly. Except for the hiss of the oxygen escaping around the edges of the celluloid mask, there was only silence. Mechanically, because it was an instinctive action, Asher Ben Levi brought his hands to the stethoscope hanging loosely about his neck and started to place it in his ears; but he stopped and instead reached to turn off the valve on top of the steel cylinder. There was no need to listen. He had seen death often enough to recognize it, and the absolute quiet that now permeated the hospital room was witness to its presence.

Reaching down, he unfastened the oxygen mask, removed it gently, and bent forward to close the eyelids. Then he sat down on the edge of the bed to regain his composure. Shaking his head in disbelief, he wiped his palms across the front of his khaki shorts and shuddered.

Death did not always affect Ben Levi this way. Usually he was frustrated and angry when a patient died because he knew that he might have done more if he had had the modern equipment of institutions like the Massachusetts General Hospital, where he had taken part of his training, or the major hospitals in Jerusalem, Tel Aviv, and Haifa; but he could cope with these feelings. The decision to return as the only physician on his kibbutz had been his own, and he never regretted that he had come back.

The death he had just witnessed, however, was different—as were the other four that had occurred on the kibbutz in the past few days. No machine, no physician, not even Joshua Fields—a smile crossed his lips at the thought of his friend—could have saved those lives; and although that in itself was troubling, it was the autopsy findings that frightened him most.

He stared a the dead man's face before covering it. The man had been in his early seventies, but he had borne his age well. The leathery skin was well-tanned and wrinkled with deep lines on the cheeks and forehead and smaller ones about the eyes that gave it a weathered but pleasant appearance even in death. A beard of thinning grayish curls wet with sweat and matted from the recent pressure of the oxygen mask framed high cheekbones, a large nose, and generous lips that bespoke his Eastern European origin. But Ben Levi could see beyond the features; he could see the muscles devoid of tone, the drooping mouth, the sagging jaw—the remnants of a shattered nervous system. . . .

Taking one last look at the form beneath the sheet, he walked to the window and peered out across the lush farmland disappearing in the distance at the foothills of the mountains. The earth had been good to the Israelis; it appeared that God had indeed kept His promise to return this land to His chosen people. Ben Levi's thoughts braked. Were these deaths another trial to prove them worthy? Scolding himself for being philosophical at such a time, he turned back to face reality: the man on the bed . . . the four who had died before him . . .

The empty sensation that enveloped him was more than fear; it was a response to death he had not experienced since he was in training. He had learned then that a physician who could not detach himself from the deaths of his patients died a little with each one; it was this conditioned, unpassioned objectivity that now deserted him, for the man beneath the sheet and the four who had preceded him were more than patients—they were friends. He had lived and worked with them; he had cared for them and their children since he returned to the kibbutz; he had delivered the grandchildren of one and had helped to bury the wife of another; they had been his family since—

"Asher!" The orderly burst into the room. At the sight of the covered body, his voice dropped to a whisper. "Another one has just been brought in. Please come!"

The woman was sixty-eight; her name, Shannah Greenberg. She and her husband had been members of the original group that had settled the kibbutz. Her story, told in slurred, barely audible words, was the same as that of the other five: she had been in reasonably good health until about a month ago when she began to experience periods of headache, loss of memory, numbness and weakness in the hands and feet that progressed to the arms and legs; then some difficulty with vision . . . She could tell him no more—speech was gone. She just stared at him with terrified, beseeching eyes as he began his examination.

With the memory of what he had seen in the others clearly in his mind, Ben Levi worked quickly and efficiently. Shannah's blood pressure had dropped precipitously to the brink of shock. Her pulse raced and then slowed; finally, only an occasional run of dysrhythmic beats was palpable. Her breathing, at first rapid and shallow, quickly deteriorated into gasps separated by lengthening intervals. The accelerating destructive process in her nervous system that was causing every other organ system to fail defied explanation. Hearing and vision faltered; then sensation waned, followed by the loss of motor function; with the latter, the muscles of her thorax could not support respiration, and breathing stopped. For an interminable moment she existed as no more than a mass of cells without purpose or function. And then she was dead.

Asher Ben Levi felt himself pale. The six people who had died on the kibbutz in less than a week had had the *same* symptoms, the *same* signs. All had had the numbers on their left forearms. But it was the scar on the left flank of each . . .

It was time to seek help. *He had to see Joshua Fields!*

Thaddeus Reichmann drained the last remnants of wine from the goblet, swirled it leisurely over his tongue, swallowed, inhaled slowly through his mouth to accentuate the bouquet, and then dabbed the corners of his mouth with a linen napkin. Standing up, he brushed a speck from the front of his black smoking jacket and paused to choose a cigar from the hand-carved box on the sideboard beside the glass doors that led to the terrace. Glancing back at the dinner table, he decided to let the maid clear it in the morning. Usually he stacked the dishes in the washer himself—the mess disturbed his sense of orderliness—but tonight he had more important things to do than to bother with the chores that living alone demanded. Viewing his reflection in the glass doors, he adjusted the ascot at his throat and turned his head to the side. The gray at his temples was becoming more prominent; but this, he felt, added to rather than detracted from his attractiveness—many women equated maturity with sexual prowess. He laughed aloud. If one could strip away the romantic facade, most women probably gave themselves to older men to fulfill their subconscious longings for their fathers. Although he preferred mature, married women, it was not for any Freudian reason; it was simply that they were unlikely to reveal the identity of their lover. He smiled sardonically. He had used them and abused them and then discarded them as he had his mother.

He bit hard on the cigar. It had taken him years to outlive the stigma of his parentage. The son of a Munich baker was not readily accepted at Heidelberg, especially to the faculty of medicine; but he had been and still was a skillful opportunist. The price for admission to medical school had been a reasonable one in his estimation: as a member of the Hitler Youth, informing on his parents' lack of appreciation for the New Order had been a responsibility rather than a hardship. Their demise had left him a ward of the state, and the state had seen to it that his leaning toward medicine was fostered.

Pushing aside the doors, he stepped out onto the terrace, refreshed and invigorated by the cold wind that bit at his cheeks. Snow was forecast for tomorrow. Plunging his hands into the pockets of his jacket, he surveyed the dark shadows of the New York City skyline surrounding Central Park. He felt a sudden surge of power, and his lips twisted. He turned quickly, walked inside, closed and locked the doors behind him, and carefully drew the curtains across them. His time had come. He had known it would; it was all a matter of being patient.

He poured a brandy and was about to sit down, but stopped as he glanced again at the dishes that marred the otherwise stark, meticulously clean atmosphere he had created for himself. He knew he would be unable to work well until he had cleared them.

As with everything else in his life, tidying up after meals was reduced to a quick and efficient system. It was a bothersome nuisance, but living alone was an absolute prerequisite for maintaining the secrecy of his identity. At least he was fortunate enough to be able to afford the luxuries that made his self-imposed isolation bearable. When he was at home, he ordered all of his meals—including the finest wines—from some of New York's best restaurants and had them delivered to his door. The maid came every day but Sunday, arriving immediately after he left for his office and departing just before he returned, with the understanding that his dinner was to be set out and waiting for him. She took care of all his needs. Well, not *all*. He grinned. She was a buxom, olive-skinned exile from Cuba. He had often wondered if the Cuban women were as good as their cigars. She was certainly far more attractive than the first woman he had interviewed. He frowned. There had been something about her . . . At first he had thought an older German woman would be an ideal maid for him; but the one thing he did not need was a damned Jewess. Her name, Eva Schonberg, meant nothing to him; but he sensed he had seen her before. Forgotten faces and identities could come back to haunt you, and he was unwilling to take even the slightest chance.

He washed his hands and combed his hair, reproaching himself for dwelling on the past; it was time to concentrate on the present—and the future. Returning to his desk, he unlocked his briefcase and removed a manila folder containing two sheaves of papers neatly stapled together. He picked up the first and read:

Autopsy No.: MECNY 1337

Name	: Jacob Bronstein	Birthdate	:	August 9, 1907
Address	: 412 E. 69th St. N.Y.C.	Birthplace	:	Russia
		Nationality:		American
Race	: Caucasian			
Religion	: Hebrew			

Clinical Diagnosis: Overwhelming nervous system degeneration, unknown etiology, unknown type

He seemed pleased with the diagnosis and continued reading:

		ANATOMIC DIAGNOSIS
Cardiovascular	:	Coronary atherosclerosis, moderate; left ventricular hypertrophy
Respiratory	:	Pulmonary edema, bilateral
Gastrointestinal	:	Agonal hemorrhage, stomach
Liver and gallbladder	:	Fatty metamorphosis of liver, mild . . .

The major abnormality was of the nervous system:

Nervous System	:	Acute degeneration, diffuse, involving all levels, central & peripheral

He reread this diagnosis and then went on:

Clinical History: Elderly Jewish man living alone discovered by neighbor in next apartment. No known significant past medical history except for mild hypertensive cardiovascular disease (on hydrodiuril 50 mgm./p.o./b.i.d. and potassium supplement prescribed by patient's son, who is physician, Dr. Morton Bronstein, Ft. Lauderdale, Fla.). No recent trauma, surgery, travel, or exposure. Patient retired garment-store owner. Friends and neighbors contacted mention that for approx. past two months patient had been complaining of intermittent headaches, blurred vision, lapses of memory, weakness in arms and legs, and generalized paresthesias. Otherwise able to care for self adequately. Could not contact patient's son.

General Inspection: The body is that of a well-developed, well-nourished white male who appears his stated age. The body measures 1.75 m. in length and weighs about 80 kg. There is no jaundice or edema. Numbers (21306) resembling those utilized in the Nazi concentration camps during WW II are indelibly etched in the skin of the left forearm. The pupils are round; the right measures 3 mm. in diameter; the left, 5 mm. The right eye is lower than the left; there is right proptosis. The nasal septum is deviated to the right. The hair is scant and gray. There is moderate dependent lividity. There is a 12 cm. well-healed horizontal scar 3 cm. below the left costal margin extending around the left flank.

Primary Incision: The body is opened with the usual Y-shaped incision. Upon removal of the sternum, about 100 ml. of clear yellowish fluid is noted in each pleural cavity. The abdominal organs are in their normal situs. . . .

He scanned the description of the individual organ systems, frowned at the mention of the dimple on the lateral surface of the spleen, and then smiled when no comment followed. When he came to the section concerning the nervous system, he read more slowly, paying careful attention to each word and phrase.

Nervous System: The brain weighs 1130 gm. There is extensive degeneration of the brain, spinal cord, and peripheral nerves. The intracranial sinuses are free of thrombi. The convexity of the brain is normal. The arachnoid vessels are congested. There is slight molding of the cerebellum. The ventricles are dilated. Serial sections of the pons and medulla show diffuse destruction. The internal capsules are destroyed. The pituitary gland is normal.

ADDENDUM: Careful examination and dissection of the left subcostal scar reveals no obvious reason for its presence; grossly it resembles a surgical scar, but no evidence of a surgical procedure in the area was observed.

MICROSCOPIC FINDINGS

Multiple sections of the various organs have been examined, and the microscopic findings are included in diagnostic terms on the first page of this autopsy protocol. Sections through the left subcostal scar and the underlying tissues reveal no abnormalities and no findings of an unusual nature.

The microscopic pathology of the nervous system is of particular significance. There is acute severe glial cell degeneration, demyelinization, and moderate perivascular cuffing with nests of mononuclear cells. There is acute degeneration of all peripheral nerves without evidence of an inflammatory infiltrate.

COMMENT

This patient died of an acute diffuse degenerative process of the nervous system resulting in cardiorespiratory incoordination and failure. Neither the gross nor microscopic findings is diagnostic of any known disease, but there are some suggestions of an acute meningomyeloencephalitis, although a greater inflammatory response should be seen in this entity. A more definitive diagnosis may be apparent after special studies are completed.

The left subcostal scar remains unexplained. It is obviously surgical rather than traumatic in origin, but nothing in this post-mortem examination reveals that a surgical procedure was performed in this area; sections have been submitted for special stains and studies.

Satisfied, Reichmann began to read the second autopsy report. Other than the fact that this patient was an eighty-one-year-old Jewish woman, the clinical history, the gross and microscopic findings, the diagnosis, and the comment were almost identical to the first, including the numbers on the left forearm, the unexplained scar on the left side, and the acute degeneration of the nervous system. The lack of a specific diagnosis in both cases excited him.

His hands trembled slightly as he put back the two reports into the manila folder and returned it to his briefcase; he experienced a sense of vigor that he had not felt for over thirty years. It was as if the invisible wall that separated past and present had suddenly been razed—the glory and the fame that had eluded him so long ago were within his reach. The thought sobered him. He chided himself for his premature euphoria. It was reasonable to have aspirations, to be optimistic, to forge ahead, especially when one already had a glimpse of success—the two autopsy reports had provided him that; but one courted disaster if one allowed the first taste of victory to dull the senses sufficiently to render them incapable of winning the battles that remained.

He unlocked the center drawer of his desk, removed a small black leather notebook, found the page he wanted, and ran his index finger slowly along each line as he read. The data about the two men whose names were underlined and about a third whose picture was encircled on a newspaper clipping taped to the following page convinced him that each was a major threat not only to his survival but also to the fulfillment of his dream of power and recognition. They had to be eliminated! He would have to kill them himself; he could not chance the involvement of others until he was certain of success.

Collecting data about persons, places, and events that might relate to him was a long-standing habit that had ensured the security of his position. Although maintaining active and reliable sources of information in many parts of the world was enormously expensive, the more than thirty years he had spent in the United States without being exposed or apprehended had convinced him that intelligence was a necessity as long as there was the possibility that any trace of his past still existed.

Scowling, he closed the notebook, replaced it in his desk, and leaned over to remove a steel box from the bottom drawer. He unlocked it and painstakingly examined the contents. Satisfied that the Luger was still in good working order, he set the box carefully in his briefcase. Pausing to review his plans, he could find no flaw and decided he deserved a second brandy before going to bed.

As forecast, it was snowing—not hard, but enough to cover the sidewalk and the street and to slow the rush-hour traffic heading west on Forty-seventh Street.

Buttoning his overcoat, Morris Golding squinted through the glass door, looked to the right, and glanced at his watch: 5:20. Stephen was probably caught in traffic. The underground garage was only two blocks away, but getting across town at this hour was a problem even in good weather. They still had plenty of time; his brother Avram's plane was not due at Kennedy for two hours.

It was early for snow in New York—the first storm rarely came before Thanksgiving—but it was fine with him. Snow brought on an early Christmas spirit, and that meant better business. Actually, it had been a banner year; jewelry, especially the unique and expensive kind in which Golding dealt, was becoming a more attractive investment to those who could afford it. The holidays were still the most profitable time; and the earlier the spirit began, the better.

He looked again, first at the double row of bumper-to-bumper cars and then at his watch. Where the hell was Stephen? He should have gone to the garage with him, but his son always insisted on saving him the walk. Sitting down on the bench opposite the elevator, he unbuttoned his coat and lit a cigarette.

It would be good to see Avram again. How long had it been? Buenos Aires, 1973, at Sophie's funeral. He had tried then to convince his brother to give up the diamond exchange in Argentina and to join him and Stephen in New York, but Avram would not hear of it. "Why should I give up a million-dollar business and move again? I was an immigrant in 1946—a poor, penniless Jew from the concentration camp. Never again! Besides, should I give all this up just because my wife died? I have roots here. A business, a home, friends. So Sophie and I didn't have children. Does a man need to have a family next door to survive? Of course not! If I need you, I can afford a telephone call, believe me. You go back to New York, Morris. *This* is my home."

Now he was coming to join them. Golding shuddered. The accelerating wave of anti-Semitism in Argentina since the spring of 1976 mirrored much of what had occurred in Germany in the 1930's; over thirty years after the fall of the Third Reich, neo-Nazism flourished. Swastikas and pictures of Hitler had been brought out of hiding. Unlawful detention, torture, and unexplained death were no longer horrors of the past—they were realities of the present. Those who had survived the Holocaust vowed they would not endure another. They left while it was still possible to leave.

"Jesus!" Golding swore aloud; it was 5:30. He ground out his cigarette in the floor receptacle beside him and walked to the door. The traffic was moving a bit faster, even though the snow was beginning to accumulate. "Must be slippery," he mused as he watched a heavyset man in a trench coat maneuver on the opposite curb as if searching for a safe place to cross. He glanced down Forty-seventh Street to look for his son's Volvo in the line of cars; but the snow had reduced the visibility to a few feet, so he turned back to see if the man had been able to make it across the street.

There he was! Golding felt himself stiffen. Beads of sweat moistened his forehead. He was suddenly hot, and a painful emptiness struck at his stomach. His shirt seemed tight; as he ran his finger around the inside of the collar to loosen it, he found his hand shaking. Fixing his gaze on the figure coming toward him, he tried desperately to make out the man's features through the snow. The man was almost across. Golding could see him more clearly now. He was short—probably a little over five-foot-five—and stocky, but the coat made him appear even heavier. The snow, the darkness, and the wrinkled felt hat pulled down over his brow hid most of his face except for the tip of the broad nose above thick lips that disappeared gradually into a tight double chin. He stepped onto the sidewalk directly in front of Golding.

Staring through the glass, Golding knew he had not been mistaken. It was *he*—a figure emerging from the past through the snow-filled evening. Golding's head hurt; his mouth was dry; his heartbeat pounded in his chest; the scar in his left side throbbed; he could almost *feel* the numbers etched on his left forearm. He could feel the cold, the hunger, the fear, and the revulsion he had not felt for more than thirty years.

The two men faced each other through the door. Golding's hatred mounted to the point of overwhelming him. Memories that had long ago been buried suddenly burst forth in an uncontrollable rush; faces that had been erased from all but an occasional nightmare flooded his thoughts. But the hatred—the searing, burning, unbearable, all-consuming hatred—was the most real of all.

The man smiled at him. It was a crooked, vicious smile. His right arm moved. There was a shattering of glass.

When Stephen Golding arrived several minutes later, there

was a crowd in front of the door. Parking his car at the curb, he made his way through the throng to find his father.

Morris Golding lay motionless amidst the broken glass. Arms outstretched, left leg folded under him, his lifeless eyes stared at the ceiling. His coat lay open; a large red stain covered the left side of his shirtfront and spread to a puddle of blood gathering beneath him. His life was gone, but the fear and the hatred remained on the cold blue face.

Smiling politely, Asher Ben Levi handed his passport to the officer behind the glass partition and watched him closely as he noted the country of origin. There was no change in the man's expression; he asked the standard questions.

"Purpose of travel?"

"Business."

"What kind?"

"Medical conference."

"Where?"

"Columbia University." As he answered the questions, Ben Levi measured the man carefully: the florid face, the blue eyes, the square jaw, the remnants of red in his hair; probably Irish, but . . . could be of northern European origin. . . . Ben Levi felt himself tense. He had given too much information already; he would have to be more careful. He wanted no one to know too much about his itinerary for the next few days.

"Duration of stay?"

"About a month." He wanted no implication that his business in the United States was urgent.

The agent looked up for the first time and eyed the Israeli curiously.

Suddenly realizing that his attempt at caution had cast suspicion on his answers, Ben Levi countered the man's unasked question with a hurriedly devised explanation: "I spent four years in the States during my internship and residency. Massachusetts General Hospital in Boston. I plan to visit friends there and in New York after the conference."

Nodding blandly, the agent stamped the passport and returned it with an icy stare.

Ben Levi walked through the gate into the baggage area, but it was not until he had passed through customs that he felt the tension begin to wane. He put on his overcoat and scanned the multitude in the El Al arrival area but found no one paying particular attention to him. No face stood out from all the rest. The noise, the excitement, and the crush of people gave him a sense of security; and the sights, sounds, and smells of Kennedy International Airport brought back memories of the good times he had spent in the United States. As his fears slowly dissipated, so did the premonition of impending doom. The thought of seeing Joshua Fields again exhilarated him. Picking up his bag, he hurried to look for a taxi.

There was a large crowd at the curb; and although a supervisor did his best to keep the line of cabs moving, tempers began to flare. Ben Levi allowed himself to be carried along by the momentum of those around him; it was like riding the New York subways in the old days. A woman in front of him, struggling with her bags, glared at him.

"It's crazy." A stocky man in a trench coat and felt hat shrugged his shoulders apologetically as the crowd pressed him against the Israeli.

"Damn! Watch where you're going!" the woman in front of them shouted indignantly over her shoulder. She turned abruptly, prepared to hurl whatever abuse she could muster at the man who had pushed her; but her angry scream caught in her throat.

Asher Ben Levi lay at her feet. A red stain spread rapidly in all directions from the two large holes in his back. His last word was lost in the blood that oozed from the corner of his mouth. "Josh . . ."

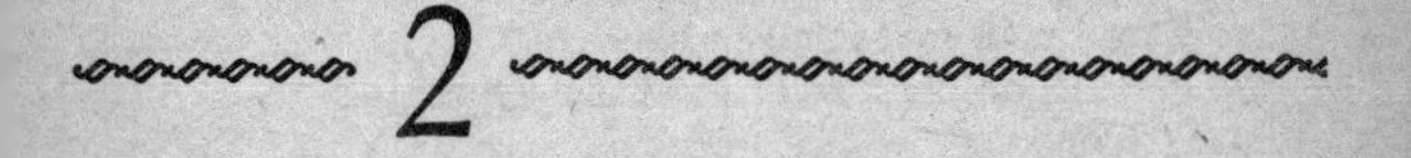

2

Peter Juno felt his impatience turning to annoyance. It was just after four P.M.; his and Renée's appointment with the police commissioner had been scheduled for three. True, the man's position endowed him with the privilege of a certain leeway in keeping others waiting; but *this* was ridiculous! Choosing another magazine from the table in front of him, he began to leaf through the pages in the hope that he would attract the attention of the secretary in the corner of the waiting room; but she continued typing, undisturbed, as if ignoring those around her was an integral part of her job.

"Today of all days!" He slapped the magazine down on the table and threw up his hands.

Patience was never one of Juno's virtues; and at the moment, he was inundated by an overwhelming workload. In addition, this was the night that he was to have dinner with his brother; and that was an appointment for which he was never late.

Tall, with a powerful frame, Juno at once commanded respect from men; but it was his dark, penetrating eyes, his aquiline features, and the deep cleft in his chin that made him appealing to women. The commissioner's secretary, however, was unmoved by his charms; she responded to his outburst with an icy glare.

"Relax, Pete. When you get to be the police commissioner of

the city of New York, you can keep the peasants waiting, too." Renée Tracy squeezed his knee without looking up from the newspaper she was reading.

"When I get to be . . ." He smiled broadly.

"Now read your magazine and behave."

"Lieutenants do not take orders from sergeants."

"Male chauvinist."

"Bullshit! It's called rank."

"Bullshit yourself." She picked up the magazine he had been reading, flipped to a page showing a model in a string bikini, and pressed it firmly into his lap, her grin showing him that she was fully aware of the exact spot where her hand had landed. "Now study this and cool off."

Without looking up, he watched her out of the corner of his eye. It was hard to believe that this enticing, outspoken woman next to him was his partner on the force—and a sergeant at that. Although not strikingly beautiful, she was attractive in a sensuous way and exuded an air of self-confidence. Short-cropped dark brown hair framed an oval face with large brown eyes that were somehow serious and seductive at the same time; she had a pert, slightly pug nose that was indicative of her Irish ancestry, and full moist lips that were a bit too inviting.

The buzzer at the secretary's desk startled him.

"The commissioner will see you now."

"Our master calls. Let's go." Renée started for the mahogany door to her right.

"Sorry, but I haven't finished my magazine; he'll have to wait." Laughing, Juno stood up.

The police commissioner's office told of the time when the city was not under a sentence of financial death. A large room with paneled walls, wall-to-wall carpeting, and tasteful furnishings, it had actually been refurbished the previous year with carefully chosen hand-me-downs to suit its new tenant without offending the banks and the unions. The man behind the desk continued to ignore his visitors as he signed one after another of the letters stacked in a neat pile before him.

Trying to decide whether to interrupt him, Juno followed Renée's cue and sat down in one of the brown leather chairs arranged in a semicircle in front of the desk. Despite his respect for the office, Juno was not particularly fond of the man who filled it. Winthrop Davis was, by his own admission, an administrator, not a cop; he viewed his position as merely a political stepping-stone. Even the commissioner's special task force was plagued by politics. Established to deal with difficult and/or sensitive cases whose solutions demanded freedom of action by people who could function independently outside the usual bureaucratic structure, the force had unlimited potential. As a member of this team, Juno found the challenge stimulating and rewarding but loathed the need to ingratiate himself to those above him.

"Relax, Pete." Davis made a point of keeping on a first-name basis with the men and women on his special task force. "You should learn to be calm like your pretty partner." He signed the last of the sheets in front of him and looked up. "You two been busy?"

Renée and Juno exchanged knowing glances. They could hear it coming. Winthrop Davis knew damned well that they were up to their ears in work, because it all came from his office. He personally assigned their cases, followed their progress, and evaluated the results.

"Very busy, sir," Renée answered.

"Well, I'm afraid I've got another one. A real stinker."

"We're already *drowning* in a sea of stinkers," Juno said. "How do you expect us to do any more than a half-assed job on any of them if you continue to pile it on?"

"That's what I like about you, Pete; you say what's on your mind. But this time it doesn't matter what either of *us* feels about the situation; the mayor says this case is *priority one!*"

"And what priority do we give the others? . . . The rape of that congressman's daughter . . . the attack on that union boss . . . the three assaults and robberies at the UN. Are they any less important than this new one? We can't function effectively if you and the mayor keep overloading us; you're defeating our very purpose."

"I've told the mayor that, but he's adamant about this one."

"Why?" Renée asked the question more to stop her partner than to obtain a specific answer.

Ignoring her question, Davis leafed through a pile of manila folders, chose one, and began to summarize its contents. "One Morris Golding, president of the New York City Professional Jewelers' Association, was shot and killed in the lobby of his office building in the diamond district late yesterday afternoon, sometime between five-thirty and six. This is the sixth major crime—of which only one has been solved—involving diamonds in the past two years, and we're getting a lot of flak about it. The jewelers are threatening to form their own vigilante group unless we can show them concrete results."

Renée sat forward in her chair. "Then you think there's a conspiracy against the diamond merchants of New York and someone wanted Golding eliminated because he was the cohesive force—"

Juno's laughter cut her short. "After being the partner of—and I quote you—'the most cynical Greek since the Trojan War' for nine months, you still have a lot to learn. Your logic is admirable; your credulity, amazing. But the commissioner hasn't answered your question. Why, when the special task force has not previously been invited to participate in the resolution of this situation, are we to be given the privilege of being assigned to *this* case?"

"Your sarcasm is noted but not appreciated," she snapped. "Okay, smart-ass, why?"

"Because, if you read the newspapers, you would know that Mr. Golding promised and delivered the overwhelming support—financial and otherwise—of the jewelers of our city when the mayor was running for office. If I remember correctly, a photograph of Mr. Golding with the mayor appeared in *The New York Times* several months ago; the picture was taken at a dinner given by his honor to express his appreciation to those who had supported his campaign. In fact, if you want to see it, I'm certain the commissioner has the clipping there in his file." Juno smiled with satisfaction. "Am I right?"

"You *are* a sneaky bastard." Davis took a newspaper page from the folder and handed it to Renée.

"So you see, Sergeant," Juno went on, "the mayor *owes* the jewelers. I'm sure he promised Golding and his colleagues protection in return for their votes and their influence. Obviously, whatever he's done up to now hasn't been enough; and considering that Golding himself was the victim this time, the mayor's decided to go with his first team." He paused and glared at Davis. "Which brings me to my main reason for objecting to this assignment—besides the extra work, that is. One of the major guidelines upon which you established this task force was that it would be free from political influences. Does that still stand?"

"Yes, it does."

"It doesn't sound like it."

Davis walked around to the front of his desk, perched himself on the edge, and looked directly at Juno. "You don't like politics, do you?"

"Not when it intrudes where it doesn't belong."

"What you're saying is that you don't like politics when it extends beyond what *you* think are its proper bounds. I said the task force would be free from political influence. It is. But you don't see it that way, because I follow orders from my boss—who happens to be an elected official, a politician—the same way you do. That's not political influence; it's the order of things in any organization. When, on the other hand, elected—or appointed—officials apply law and order differently to the members of one political party than they do to those of another, or when they use it to further their own goals or those of their party to the detriment of others, *that* is political influence."

Davis slid off the desk, returned to his chair, closed the folder, and folded his hands over it. "I've never forced anyone who works for me to do anything he really didn't want to do, and I won't start now. I'd like you to think it over. You can let me know in the morning." He pressed the intercom button again. "Where is that damned secretary?"

Juno got up to leave. "Coming, Renée?" He was tired and frustrated, and Davis's recitation of his political dogma to explain away decisions that might not be otherwise justified had irritated him more than it usually did. There were days when he wanted to give up the whole business.

"Who is in there with the commissioner?" Joseph Mann turned suddenly to face the secretary.

"Lieutenant Juno and Sergeant Tracy."

"How long will they be? I am busy."

"They should be out shortly. And may I remind you that Commissioner Davis is also busy."

"The commissioner and his special task force! I am sick of it! You would think no one else does anything important in the police department. We all know Juno is his fair-haired boy. It would not surprise me if he appointed *him* the chief medical examiner; I am only the *acting* chief, you know." Checking the time on his pocket watch, Mann grumbled unintelligibly and resumed his pacing in front of the commissioner's door. "Do you know why the commissioner wants to see me?"

"Something about the Golding murder case."

"I see. That must by why Lieutenant Juno is here." Mann tried to make his statement sound more like fact than query.

"I think so."

Without further comment he took a seat near the door; he needed a moment to think.

At last the door opened.

"Good evening, Sergeant Tracy, Lieutenant Juno," Mann said. "I understand you, too, are here about the Golding case. Have you come up with anything?"

"I haven't even decided if I'll take it. Now if you'll excuse me . . ."

"If you do, come see me. I have some ideas that might help."

"If I do, I'm quite capable of handling it." Juno grasped Renée by the arm and hurried her through the reception room. He did not see the look of satisfaction on Mann's face as they left.

When they reached the elevator, Juno hit the down button with the side of his fist. "He's all I needed right now. Shit!"

"Who put the hair up your ass?"

He ignored her question. "What are you going to do tonight?" he asked as they got onto the elevator. "I'm having dinner with Josh."

"Dammit, Pete! You have the nastiest habit of changing the subject!" She sighed. "I'm going to make myself a toasted cheese sandwich, wash my hair, and work on some reports. Okay? Now that I've answered your question, answer mine!"

"Well, Davis started it, and that arrogant bastard Mann

finished it." He took a deep breath to regain his composure. "I understand that the commissioner has to follow the mayor's orders. But, goddammit, he knows we've got more important things to do than investigate the murder of another fat cat. Do you remember that congressman's daughter? Twenty years old, pretty, intelligent, her whole life ahead of her; now all she's got to look forward to is years of plastic surgery and psychotherapy. We should be spending our time catching the bastard who beat and raped her instead of looking under diamonds for someone who didn't like Golding's choice of profession."

"I know all that; but what do you want Davis to do? Tell the mayor to stick it in his ear?"

"No. I just want him to cut the bullshit . . . to tell it straight: 'I want you two to take this case because the mayor owes a political favor and I owe the mayor.' All right, let him put his money where his mouth is. Tomorrow morning I'm going to call his bluff. I'm going to tell him I really don't want the case."

"And what if he won't be bluffed? What if he says, 'Okay, Pete; I'll give it to someone else on the task force or assign it through the regular homicide channels.'?"

"Then Mr. Winthrop Davis will go up a million percent in my personal popularity poll; and you and I will get back to the guys with the perverted pricks." He paused. "And what will you do—one way or another?"

"We're a team. Where you go, I go. If I'm destined to walk a beat with some stubborn, pigheaded, misguided Greek, so be it."

"Screw you."

"Sorry, you're having dinner with your brother."

"I'll be home early; he likes to be in bed by eleven."

Laughing, they walked out of the elevator and headed down the ramp leading to the underground parking garage.

"If you really want to keep me as a partner, there is a way . . ." She smiled.

"Yeah? What? Bribe the mayor? Marry you?"

"Neither, although I might give the latter some consideration." She became serious again. "Take the case. We'll have it solved in forty-eight hours."

"You never give up, do you?"

"Not when I think you're wrong. . . . No, not wrong, just precipitating a showdown about something that isn't worth it."

"That's your answer every time Davis gives us shit. You have to take a stand sometime."

"You're as bad as Davis." She pouted. "And what about Dr. Mann? Is he a tool of the politicians, too? You certainly gave him the cold shoulder."

"I wasn't in the mood to listen to him. It's always the same: either he knows the one fact that will solve your case, or he whines about not being appointed chief medical examiner; it's bad enough he's the *acting* chief." At the mention of the pathologist's name, Juno felt the muscles in his neck tighten; he tried to force himself to relax, but the ache persisted and started to spread downward across his shoulders. Certain people and situations triggered this response in him. Josh had likened it to a severe tension headache. "Better you should have a headache than an ulcer," his brother had said. "All of us know some people who give us a pain in the neck."

"I just don't like the bastard; he's a pompous ass. You keep telling me, 'If you can't say anything nice, don't say anything at all'; and when I follow your advice, you want to know why. Typical feminine logic."

Renée smiled, put her arm through his, but did not respond. It had been a rough day, and there had been enough talk. She did not speak again until they had reached her car. "Say hello to Josh. I'll be waiting up for you." She winked, kissed him playfully on the cheek, and drove off.

Reichmann watched Rolfe Penzel test the weight of the Luger in his palm.

Penzel was tall and muscular with a powerful body that moved like a silent, well-oiled machine. He was a handsome man with closely cropped blond hair, piercing blue eyes, and well-tanned skin that made him appear younger than his stated age of thirty-nine; but his face was totally lacking in warmth or emotion. His expression varied little as he examined the gun, and his replies to Reichmann's questions were curt and direct. His dossier characterized him as a compulsive man with a keen mind, an obsession with details, a penchant for leaving nothing to chance, total disregard of fair play and human life, and blind loyalty and obedience to the Party. He seemed especially fit for the tasks Reichmann would require of him.

"I'm a little uncomfortable with a Luger. Do you think it's wise to use a weapon that's characteristically German? I'd prefer a Smith and Wesson or a Beretta."

"At this point in my life, killing an enemy is more than a necessity; it's the fulfillment of plans laid long ago. It's time we stopped hiding. Let them know who pulled the trigger!"

"At the right moment, yes. Now it's a risk I prefer not to take."

"Now *is* the right moment!" Reichmann restrained himself. He had contemplated carrying on alone, but the rapidity of events and the mounting demands he had made on himself since he had had the first glimpse of success had convinced him that he could not. He had been apprehensive at first, but Penzel's qualifications had allayed his fears. Still, none of the new breed could really understand. Theirs was a cause inherited from another generation; when some of their own blood had been spilled, they would not speak so glibly.

Penzel eyed the older man cautiously. "But how do *I* know that?"

"You do not have to know; you only have to follow orders!"

"Only up to a point. I have no intention of committing suicide because you have visions of grandeur. Several of my colleagues made that mistake, and they're dead because they listened to the promises of feeble old men who were convinced that their moment had come." Penzel paused to assess Reichmann's reaction. The older man was still in control. That was good. Those of the old guard who responded to challenge irrationally could not be trusted to know when the time was ripe for bold acts. "On the other hand," he continued, "I would give my life willingly for the Party if the goal justified the risk."

Reichmann's rage at the younger man's unexpected impertinence dissipated rapidly. Someone capable of handling himself so adeptly in the present situation was likely to succeed in other tight spots as well. For the present, Reichmann decided, he would have to trust him; but he would not hesitate to eliminate him, too, if he failed to live up to his expectations.

With a minimum of details and explanation, Reichmann

summarized the events of the past several days and their potential significance to the future of the Nazi Party and the Fourth Reich.

"Now will you follow my orders?"

"Of course!" Penzel almost clicked his heels.

"Peter Juno, an exceptional detective, will be in charge of the Golding investigation. If anyone could cause us problems, it's he and his bitch of a partner."

"Where do you get your information? I've never met anyone so well-informed."

"I have my sources."

"In the New York Police Department?"

"Yes. And in the UN and the United Arab Republic and the Israeli Cabinet. . . ." Reichmann smiled complacently. "One doesn't survive as long as I have by guessing where and when threats will arise—one has to know in advance what his enemies will do. Any more questions?"

"No, Herr Reichmann."

"Good. Then listen, and do as you're told! Your first assignment: *kill Peter Juno!*"

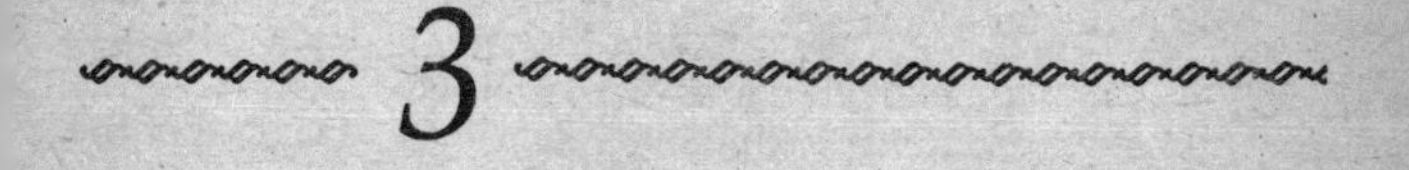

Unbuttoning his coat, Juno rested his hands on top of the steering wheel and leaned back against the headrest as he waited for the light at the Eighth Avenue intersection to turn green. Ordinarily, westbound rush-hour traffic on Forty-second Street pushed his patience to the limit; but tonight the forced inactivity was almost a respite.

He had been on the New York police force for twenty years, fifteen with the homicide division, the last on the commissioner's special task force; and although he had been intimately involved in the investigation of approximately seventy murders during that time, he had yet to become accustomed to killing. Perhaps it was because, as a child, he himself had been affected by violent death; perhaps it was because he had been raised to be a man who respected and cherished life. Whatever the reasons, he perceived life as a commodity of inestimable worth, and murder as a sacrilegious waste of it. Although he could not accept the commissioner's unstated premise that one life was worth more than another, he was not so inflexible as to refute the corollary that someone had to take the Golding case; reality and principle were not always mutually exclusive.

He started to think again about his meeting with Davis, but then decided not to let it spoil his evening. He looked forward to the second Wednesday of each month when he and Josh got together for dinner. Other than Renée, Josh was the only true friend he had.

Sitting back, he relaxed his grip on the wheel as he watched for Fifty-seventh Street to take him across town to Park Avenue and Josh's apartment. He smiled. Joshua Melton Fields—Melton had been his mother's maiden name—was one of the real people in this unreal world. Actually the only unreal thing about him was his last name: it had been Feldstein, but his father had changed it after the war. "A Feldstein could never have gotten into Harvard Law School," Saul Fields used to laugh and say, "but then again, neither did a 'Fields.'"

Joshua Fields was now Professor of Medicine at Columbia University College of Physicians and Surgeons—a formal and formidable title, Juno thought, for a very informal and unassuming man. That was one of the things he liked best about Josh: despite the well-deserved fame that had come to him as one of the world's foremost geneticists, he had never forgotten that he was a simple Jewish boy from Chelsea, Massachusetts. More importantly, he never forgot who his friends were.

They went back a long time together.

He was five years old, frightened and alone except for the tall, good-looking American army captain with the curly hair, the big nose, and the strong hand that held his securely. The soldier who had found him lost and wandering the streets scavenging for food in a small town outside of Athens had cared for him well: he had plenty of good food, a warm bed, and even two used comic books. Peter Juno did not understand the soldier's language, but Saul Feldstein did not have to speak Greek; he spoke with his large brown eyes and accentuated the unspoken words with the bushy eyebrows above them and the broad smile below. All Peter knew or cared about was that this man who always comforted him when he cried was going to take him to America to live with him, and there was nothing he wanted more than that. The American had a son about Peter's age—he had shown him a picture from his wallet. His name was Joshua, "like the man who blew down the walls of Jericho with bugles and trumpets," the captain explained later when Peter knew some English. Joshua's mother, Deborah, could not have more children; he would be Joshua's brother.

Once in America, a close bond developed between Peter and Joshua. When the prejudice that accompanied the immigrating Jews who had survived the Holocaust affected the Feldsteins, especially Josh, in any way, Peter was always there with his fists to protect his new family; there were times he felt he could even kill for those he loved.

When the Feldsteins changed their name to Fields and the question of formal adoption had to be settled, it was Joshua who insisted that Peter keep his own name so that he could give it to his next generation.

As boyhood gave way to young adulthood and then to manhood, their love and friendship continued to grow; but individual abilities, needs, and drives caused each to go his separate way. They kept in touch with letters and calls but only saw one another when the holidays and the death of Deborah Fields called them home to the house on Gardner Street.

Last year when Josh joined the faculty at Columbia Medical School, they decided it was time to renew and strengthen old ties, if only for one night a month.

"Hi, fuzz!" Joshua Fields opened the door and embraced his brother. "It's good to see you again. How's Renée?" Fields's eyes twinkled. "When are you going to marry that girl?" He smiled at Juno's "Please-don't-start-that-again" expression as he pulled him into the foyer. He took Juno's coat and held him at arm's length. "Very dapper. Maybe one of these days you'll give me the name of your tailor."

"I'm afraid you'd give him heart failure." Juno laughed good-naturedly and feigned a critical look at Fields's slight form.

Joshua Fields was a head shorter than his brother, with long arms and legs that looked like they should belong to someone a good deal taller. He had brownish curly hair that hadn't changed a bit, Juno thought, since the first day they'd met. The bushy eyebrows, the lively brown eyes, the large Semitic nose, and the wrinkles on his forehead when he smiled were definitely his father's; but the small mouth and the smooth, slightly protruding chin clearly were his mother's traits. The sleeves of his striped shirt were too short; and the collar was considerably out-of-date, as was the cut of the wrinkled gray flannel slacks that barely reached the top of his loafers.

Juno settled himself into a black leather chair and looked around. Fields's apartment resembled a page out of some interior decorator's handbook. Chrome and glass; black, white, and blue; every piece of furniture in the correct place, and every detail perfect.

"I never cease to be amazed by you." Juno took the drink offered to him.

"Why?" Fields sat down on a white crushed-patent-leather stool near the fireplace and sipped his sherry.

"Look what you can do with an apartment, and yet you can't match a sport coat and a pair of slacks without setting men's fashions back twenty years."

"If you like it so much, why don't you two move in?" Josh put up his hands in front of him as if to ward off an imaginary blow. "I was only kidding. . . . On the other hand," he held up one finger and changed to a heavy Yiddish accent, "I am not around much. I voodn't infringe on your—"

"You'd cramp my style." Actually Juno had thought about moving in with Josh a number of times before he met Renée; but his brother would have insisted on paying the rent, the utilities, and the food bills. He had made up his mind the day he left Boston for New York that he had taken enough from the Fieldses and that it was time to pay his own way. He changed the subject. "Still got that cleaning lady working for you?"

"Sure. Want to borrow her? She's free on Thursdays."

"Maybe. Renée is pretty busy these days; she could use some help once in a while." In truth, they couldn't really afford a cleaning woman. He didn't know why he'd asked. He decided that it was because every once in a while his three-room walk-up with the secondhand Danish modern walnut furniture with the worn brown-and-turquoise cushions got to him, and he needed to fantasize a bit to make it more bearable.

As usual, the dinner was superb; Josh was an excellent cook. After dinner, they sipped brandy and talked about old times. They were both concerned about Saul, living alone since Deborah Fields's death; and both felt guilty about not visiting him more often. They argued good-naturedly about who was Saul's favorite until it was time for them to leave for Lincoln Center—this month it was a concert of the New York Philharmonic; they alternated the choice to satisfy their widely different tastes in music and the arts.

"Just about ready?" Josh drained his glass. "Don't want to miss the Haydn."

"God forbid!" Juno laughed.

"Wise-ass!" The phone behind Fields rang. "Damn! I told the hospital I didn't want to be disturbed." He picked up the receiver. "It's for you. A Dr. Sin Wah Joy. Since when have you been moonlighting at the Chinatown Clinic?"

Juno leaned forward and took the phone. "He's with the medical examiner's office, ding-a-ling. What the hell does he want at this hour?"

"Juno?"

"Speaking."

"This is Dr. Joy, downtown. Commissioner Davis asked us to keep you informed about the Golding case, so I thought you'd like to be brought up-to-date on the medical examiner's report. What's more, I have messages for you from the crime lab and from Ballistics. The boys evidently knew this was your night off and thought we'd bother you only once." There was a weak laugh and a pause.

"Thanks. Very thoughtful of all of you." Juno was fuming. That settled it! Davis had gone too far this time. He would tell him just that in the morning, even if it cost him his job. Still, Juno thought as he rubbed his chin, Davis was no fool; he wouldn't have had the pathologist call him unless there was something in the autopsy report that would work *for* him, not against him. His curiosity began to subdue his anger. "Go ahead."

"Golding received three bullets accurately placed into the left precordium—that's the left side of the chest. One penetrated the ascending aorta; one, the left ventricle; and one, the interventricular septum. In other words, he was shot in the heart and died almost instantaneously from the heart wound and massive, acute blood loss from the punctured aorta. The boys at the crime lab say he was shot at extremely close range—almost face to face—through a glass door from the outside."

"How do they know that?"

"From the pattern of the slivers of glass buried in the victim's clothing, skin, and hair and the fact that there were no powder burns on either his clothes or his skin. There appears to be little doubt about it: Golding was standing inside the door, and his killer was outside and fired at him point-blank. It's all in their report. You can read it in the morning; they've left a copy on your desk."

"Fine. You said you had something from Ballistics?"

"Yes. Bullets came from a Luger. World War II vintage."

"Anything else?"

"A lot of material documenting their conclusions. Want me to read it to you?"

"No, thanks." Juno thought for a moment. The whole thing didn't make sense. There had to be more. "Dr. Joy? You still there? . . . Good. Listen, did *you* find anything else of interest? Anything out of the ordinary, I mean?"

"Indeed so. . . ." Juno could hear papers being shuffled at the other end of the line. "Ah, here it is. A number was tattooed on the left forearm; the victim must have been in a concentration camp." Another pause. "Oh, yes, there was what appears to be a surgical scar on the left side just lateral to the spleen—unlike any I've seen before. . . ."

"Maybe he had an operation."

"Obviously. But there were no signs of surgery internally. The scar extended through the skin, the subcutaneous tissue, and the muscle and fascia. The spleen was okay except for a small wedge-shaped dimple beneath the capsule—probably a small splenic infarct; not so remarkable in a man his age. Everything else was normal. Maybe I'll learn something more from the microscopic exam."

Although Peter Juno did not fully understand the medical jargon, the pathologist's apparent inability to explain his own findings bothered him. He had to admire Davis's guile: he had used the information in the medical examiner's report to bait him.

"Thank you, Dr. Joy. Good night." He hung up.

"You look troubled," Fields said. "Anything wrong?"

"I'm not sure. A sixty-two-year-old jeweler was shot yesterday in the diamond district . . ."

"So what else is new? This is New York. Happens all the time."

"Ballistics thinks the bullets came from a World War II-type Luger."

"So?"

"When a Jew who was in a concentration camp is shot with a Luger, my neck starts to hurt."

"Tension headache. I've told you that a dozen times. Why don't you come down to the hospital and let me get some tests and an X ray just to be safe?"

"Radiation is bad for you. Don't you know that? Besides, since when does a professor like you need all of that to diagnose a tension headache?"

"I don't. I just want to rule out degenerative arthritis or cervical spondylosis."

"Save the big words for your colleagues." Juno stood up.

"What's bugging you? Anything I can do to help?"

"Yuh. Dial the phone for me, will you?" Juno gave him the number.

Fields pressed the buttons. "The sum total of my athletic abilities." He handed the receiver to his brother. "I presume this means no concert."

Juno shrugged. "I'm not sure." He listened to the ring. "Ballistics? This is Lieutenant Juno, NYPD. Glad to see you guys working so late. Who am I speaking to?"

"Roger Baldini. How are you, Pete?"

"Fine. Listen, Roger, I need some information."

"Shoot."

"How often is a Luger involved in a shooting in our jurisdiction? Just a ball-park figure."

"Maybe once or twice a year. Funny you should ask, though."

"What do you mean?"

"We just had *three*—all killed yesterday. Your man Golding . . . Didn't you get the message? I asked Joy in Pathology to give it to you . . . a guy named Goldstein, and some Israeli."

"Yes, I did. Thanks. Tell me about Goldstein and the Israeli."

As he listened, Juno felt his pulse quicken and his palms begin to sweat. Avram Goldstein, an elderly Jew, had been killed by a single gunshot wound in the chest; his body had been found in a men's room at Kennedy Airport. The Israeli, Asher Ben Levi, had been shot twice in the back while waiting for a taxi outside of the El Al arrival area.

Juno motioned to his brother that he'd take a brandy and downed it in one swallow as Roger Baldini finished speaking. "Thanks, Roger. Switch me to Pathology, will you?"

Joy told him that Dr. Mann had performed the autopsies on the other two Luger victims.

"You're kidding!"

"Well, he did not actually do the entire autopsies; he had one of the junior men assist him. But at least he was there and got his hands dirty. Perhaps he thinks this sudden show of interest will get him his promotion."

"Possibly. The commissioner and the mayor are taking a personal interest in the Golding case. There seems to be some relationship . . ."

"Would you like to speak to Dr. Mann? He's in his office."

"This late? He really is getting religion." Juno hesitated. He never liked talking to Mann, but he wanted the information. "Put me through."

It was a few moments before Mann came on the line. "Good evening, Lieutenant Juno. How nice to speak to you again. So you need some help with the Golding case after all."

Juno felt his annoyance growing. "I still haven't made a decision. Commissioner Davis asked that I be kept informed. Just tell me what the autopsies showed on the other two Luger victims."

"Goldstein and Ben Levi?"

"Yes."

"Did the commissioner ask that you be kept up-to-date on them as well?"

"No, but . . ."

"Then please go through the regular channels. I am very busy. Good night."

Juno slammed down the phone, swore, and dialed again.

Joy informed him that Dr. Ritchfield had assisted at the two autopsies. Ritchfield wasn't available, but his notes were. Joy read them. When he finished, Juno put down the phone slowly, the ache in his neck acute.

Fields stood behind him with his jacket and coat held ready. "Figured you'd want to leave." He smiled and led Juno to the door. "Don't forget next month. I like seeing you. One of these days, when you can tear yourself away from your busy schedule, maybe you'll come in for a physical exam and a film. Meanwhile, try heat and aspirin for that neck of yours."

Juno grasped his brother's hand with both of his. It was small and fragile with slender fingers that seemed lost in his own strong, meaty grip. "Be careful," he said.

As he headed toward the elevator, he had a sudden, inexplicable urge to turn and go back; but it was getting late, and there was a stop he had to make before he could go home to Renée.

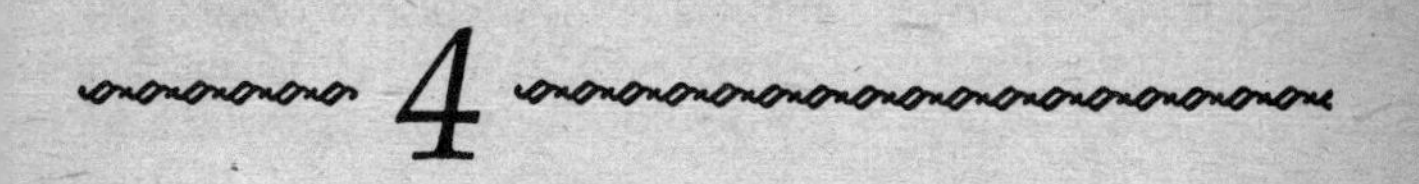

Tsve Shem and Mordecai Grossman filled out the registration cards and returned them to the clerk. They found their room, bolted the door, set up security precautions, and began to unpack. They had been thoroughly briefed about the nature and importance of their mission: to investigate the death of Asher Ben Levi and to maintain strict surveillance of Joshua Fields. Their instructions were clear: to avoid overt encounters at all costs. But as they removed identical Lugers from carefully concealed, X-ray-opaque compartments in the walls of their respective suitcases, each knew that as a member of the Mossad, he had license to kill in any matter pertaining to the security of the state of Israel.

Juno entered the time in the register and nodded to the white-coated orderly who had assisted him in viewing the bodies of Golding, Goldstein, and the Israeli physician named Asher Ben Levi. Although he had seen many murder victims, Juno was struck by the look imprinted on the faces of Morris Golding and Avram Goldstein; never before had he seen such intense fear and hatred persist after death. Ben Levi had no such look—he had probably not seen his killer.

What did these three men from three different continents have in common that led to their deaths on the same day, in the same city, and probably at the hands of the same killer?

Shaking his head as he walked briskly toward the exit from the morgue, he decided the answers to these questions could wait until morning. Right now, all he wanted to do was to get home to Renée. It was almost eleven o'clock; she would be waiting for him.

"Lieutenant Juno!"

Swearing softly, Juno turned slowly and saw Joseph Mann lumbering down the corridor toward him. The pathologist was dressed in an immaculate green scrub suit covered by a crisp white laboratory coat. It was the first time Juno had seen him dressed in anything but a formal business suit.

"Please, Dr. Mann. I'm tired and in no mood for another argument."

"But that is why I wanted to talk to you—to apologize for my behavior. It was rude of me to hang up on you. I know you were only trying to do your job as I try to do mine. I am sorry." He held out his hand.

Reluctantly Juno shook the pathologist's hand. He was struck by the firmness of the grip.

"Is there anything I can help you with?" Mann laughed. "There I go again."

Juno nodded. "Tell me what you wanted to tell me this afternoon."

"You are taking the Golding case?"

"I really haven't decided, but I'd like to hear what you have to say."

Leading Juno to a corner, Mann lit a cigar, puffed thoughtfully for a moment, and then spoke. "This man Golding was shot with a Luger—"

"I know that."

"Did you also know he had been in a concentration camp during the war?"

"Yes. I saw the numbers on his left forearm."

"Bastards! They did it to all of us." He pushed up his sleeve, exposing the blue figures partially hidden by the coarse graying hair, and then quickly rolled it down. "Do you think there could be a connection?"

"I've given that possibility some thought."

"And?"

"I'd need some more time and more information before I'd be willing to speculate further."

"Of course. But if you do take the case, please let us work together. I know some of you find me difficult—it is the German in me—but I will try to let only the Jewish part of me get involved in any future discussions."

Juno parked his car in the underground garage several blocks from their apartment and used the walk home to try to put the events of the day into perspective. In light of the information he had received from Pathology and Ballistics and from what he had seen on viewing the bodies of the three Luger victims, the murder of Morris Golding no longer appeared to be just one more New York shooting.

By the time he reached East Seventy-sixth Street, he was convinced Joseph Mann was correct: there had to be more of a relationship between the victims and the murder weapon than appeared on the surface. Tomorrow he and Renée would start collecting evidence to prove it, but tonight . . .

Renée let him in with a kiss.

"How's Josh?"

"Fine. Sends you his love. Still wants us to move in with him." Juno loosened his tie, removed his jacket, and collapsed into a chair. As he watched her pick up his discarded jacket and hang it in the closet, he realized that despite his fatigue, he wanted her. Her negligee clung to her. From behind, her body was supple and straight, with small shoulders, graceful arms, a slender back, and a tiny waist that flared into well-rounded hips and buttocks. She was the most alluring woman he had ever known.

Closing the closet door, she turned suddenly, causing the bottom of her robe to separate and billow. Juno stared at her with increasing longing.

Noticing the direction of his eyes, she stopped; and with no attempt to close the robe, she winked, ran her tongue over her lips, put one hand on her hip, the other behind her head, and thrust her chest outward. "Do I still suit your taste?"

Juno swallowed hard. His fatigue and the ache in the back of his neck dissipated as her hand moved from her head to the top button of her robe. Walking slowly toward him, she dropped the robe, paused for a moment to stand before him, and then fell into his outstretched arms.

Juno smiled contentedly as he watched her move gracefully about the kitchen to prepare breakfast. The smell of coffee and bacon filled the room; sunlight filtered between the curtains framing the window above the sink; the table was set for two. As she whisked by him on her way to the refrigerator, he reached for her. Slapping his hand playfully, she kissed him lightly and straightened her skirt.

Juno pulled her to him and ran his hands over her hips. Slipping onto his lap, she put her arms around his neck, kissed him hard, and then let her lips rest against his ear. "What are you going to tell Davis?"

"Bitch. And all the time I thought you were just hot for my body."

"I am. But if I can ensure my position in our professional partnership while getting my rocks off, why not?" She ran the tip of her tongue along the inner curve of his ear. "Are you going to take the Golding case?"

"Sure! Why not. Might as well get a little extra ass and keep my job, too."

"Bastard!" She squinted at him suspiciously. "When did you decide?"

"Last night . . . *before* I came home." He laughed.

"You miserable son of a bitch!" She pulled away and pushed his hand from her thigh. "So you finally admit I'm right. How come? I'll bet Josh talked you into it."

"No. But if you'll feed me some breakfast, I'll tell you about it."

As they ate, Juno related what he knew of the other Luger killings. She remained silent until he finished describing what he had seen at the morgue and his conversations with Joy, Baldini, and Mann.

"Are the bullets all from the same Luger?" she asked.

"Ballistics is still working on it."

"Then why try to tie them all together until you know for sure? It's possible they're unrelated, and—"

"Possible but not probable. *Three* Luger killings in one day?"

"Then where do we go from here? I think we should discuss it with Davis."

"Later. Right now I'll just let him know that we'll take the case. That ought to make his day."

"Then what?"

"I've been over the initial reports of Golding's murder. Golding had a son. He lives in New Jersey. We'll start with him."

Although the snow made driving difficult, they made good time; and by 12:15 they were in Morristown. Stephen Golding met them at the door with a polite hello and a reserved smile. He was dressed in black slacks, a dark flannel shirt, and slippers—slippers, Juno remembered, were a part of the traditional attire worn by Jews during the week of mourning. He had a pleasant face, but it was obvious that his father's death had taken its toll: the dark-rimmed glasses could hide neither the remnants of puffiness about his eyes nor the fatigue and the sorrow reflected in them.

"How's the driving?" Golding helped Renée off with her coat.

"Getting nasty." Juno looked around in admiration at the spacious foyer.

"Forecast is for heavy snow for the rest of the day. Hope you won't have any trouble getting back." Golding led them through a set of louvered doors into a large, well-lit country kitchen. "Have a seat." He motioned to a breakfast nook. "Coffee?"

They nodded.

"You'll have to forgive my wife. She was up most of the night with my mother, so I decided to let her sleep."

Golding poured the coffee; then, sitting down, he lit a cigarette and leaned back. "Go ahead and ask your questions. I'll answer them to the best of my ability, but there isn't much I haven't already told the police."

"I'd like to hear the story in your own words," Juno said.

"I left my father at the office a little before five and went to get my car from the garage about two blocks away; he lives . . . Excuse me . . ." His voice wavered and he swallowed hard.

". . . *lived* about a half-mile from here, so we'd drive to and from work together. We'd been doing it for several months now since Nancy—that's my wife—and I moved into this house; actually, I've been in the business since I finished college five years ago. Dad was fine when I left him. It took me a while to get back because of the snow and the damned traffic. When I finally pulled up at the entrance to our building—Dad always waited at the door for me so I wouldn't have to park—there was a crowd gathered. . . ." He inhaled deeply on his cigarette and stared at the floor. After a moment, he cleared his throat and continued. "I was so upset and confused by Dad's death that I forgot about my Uncle Avram until late in the evening. Maybe if I'd sent someone to pick him up earlier, I might have prevented his murder." Golding choked back a sob.

"Your uncle was also murdered last night?" Juno's eyes widened.

"Yes. My father's brother. His name was Avram Goldstein. I assumed you knew."

"Avram Goldstein?" Juno shouted the name.

"Brothers? With different names?" Renée asked.

"It's really quite simple. After the war, the Jews emigrated to many places: the United States, South America, Australia, Palestine. Although most families stayed together, some ended up scattered all over the world. The immigration authorities tried to process them as quickly as possible. When it came to completing the forms, they filled them in with the first thing that sounded like the names they heard. So in New York, Goldenschweig became Golding; and in Buenos Aires, Goldenschweig was baptized Goldstein with a flick of a pen. Since these documents were their only means of substantiating their identities in their new homelands, the immigrants had no choice but to adopt the new names."

As he listened to Stephen Golding, Juno found his shock beginning to subside. Myriad thoughts raced through his mind: the fact that Golding and Goldstein were brothers and that both had been in a concentration camp and had been killed by a Luger not only linked the two deaths together but established a relationship between the victims and the murder weapon that could not be ignored. He turned back to Stephen Golding.

"Golding and Goldstein were brothers, and they're both dead," Juno repeated.

"Yes." Golding's voice trembled. "They'll be buried side by side as soon as the police release the bodies."

"What else do you know?"

"Only what the police told me—that my uncle was found shot in the chest in a men's room at Kennedy Airport. He was coming from Argentina to live with my parents and to join the business . . ." Golding's voice trailed off.

"Don't blame yourself. I doubt that you could have done anything that would have made a difference. It appears that it had all been carefully planned."

"Why?"

"Tell you what—you answer our questions first; then we'll try to answer yours."

"Of course."

Opening a worn notebook, Juno turned to the page he wanted. "Your father and uncle were in the camps during the war?"

"Yes but—" Golding was surprised by the question.

"Which ones?"

"They were both in Dachau. They had spent five years there when the Allies came in 1945. They lost their mother, father, two sisters, and a brother there. They were the only members of their family who survived."

"Did your father talk much about it?"

"Almost never. Once in a while, like on Passover when he'd had too much wine, he'd mention it. Most of what he said was aimless rambling, almost as if he were trying to rid himself of the guilt."

"Guilt?" Renée interrupted.

"Sure. Everyone who survived felt guilty about it."

"I'd have thought they'd have been thankful as hell."

"That's just it. They felt guilty about being alive and being glad of it when millions of others had died."

"Did anything extraordinary happen to him at Dachau"—Juno chose his words carefully—" other than the horror we know went on?"

"Not that I know of; but as I told you, he rarely talked about it. What are you getting at?"

"The scar on his left side. Did he get it there?"

"I think so, but I'm not certain. I asked him about it once; he became very agitated, cut me short, wouldn't discuss it. . . . I did mention it to my mother, and she said that he had the scar when she married him. She, too, had asked him about it; but he wouldn't talk about it even to her."

"Had he had any surgery to explain it?"

"To the best of my knowledge, my father had *never* had an operation. Not even tonsils."

Juno made a short note. "Did he have any enemies?"

"I'll make it simple for you, Lieutenant. I've given it a great deal of thought. My father was a pretty normal human being. He came to this country in 1946 as a poor Jewish immigrant; he worked hard, built himself a nice business, and raised a decent family. He smoked a little too much, drank only on Jewish holidays and at bar mitzvahs and weddings, never gambled, never ran around, and paid his taxes. Sure, he probably antagonized a few business associates and pissed off a few members of the temple when he thought they were acting like pompous asses. He was a great supporter of Israel, but he was smart enough to realize that the Arabs couldn't be ignored. He was a good husband, a better-than-average father, and a kind, gentle man who loved life. No one except a psychopath could have hated him enough to shoot him."

"He was shot with a Luger." Juno watched Golding blanch. "It seems to me that the only thing in your father's past that might tie into his murder is the fact that he was in a concentration camp. It's possible that the make of the gun means nothing. The killer could have had it as a souvenir or bought it from a pawn shop. For the sake of discussion, however, let's assume it belongs to someone also connected with Dachau. At least that narrows down the possibilities."

"Another inmate?" Renée asked.

"Possible, but not plausible. I can't believe that two prisoners from one of those camps, both fortunate enough to have survived, would carry *any* grudge for over thirty years, for whatever reason, and then suddenly decide to kill."

Golding frowned. "Maybe they just hadn't run into one another before; and when by chance they did, the hatred exploded."

"There's the key point; it *wasn't* by chance! Not unless the assailant made a habit of carrying a loaded gun every day for years, just hoping that someday he'd run into your father. Besides, a Luger of the caliber used isn't light, and it's not easily concealed. You carry it only when you *plan* to use it. I'm convinced that whoever killed your father *knew* he would be in the lobby of your office building, and he went there for the express purpose of killing him.

"And *that* narrows it down even more. The killer was someone your father feared and hated so vehemently that even death could not erase its intensity from his face—I saw it when I viewed his body. No, I'm convinced the killer had a very specific reason for wanting your father dead."

Stephen Golding shook his head in disbelief. "I saw that look on Dad's face, too. . . ."

Juno picked up his notebook. "I'm going to read you a list of names; listen to them carefully: Wiesenthal, De Vito, Allen, Pupko, Schiano, Korman, Perlmutter, Kremer, Whitelaw. Have you ever heard of any of these people? Did your father ever mention them?"

"'Wiesenthal' rings a bell. Isn't he a Nazi hunter?"

Juno nodded.

"Some of the others are common Jewish or Italian names, but they don't mean anything special to me; I don't remember my father speaking of them. Who are they?"

"They're *all* Nazi hunters. Wiesenthal, of course, is the best known. Is it possible that your father was murdered because he was involved in exposing some Nazi war criminal, perhaps one who had been at Dachau?"

"I doubt it. A few years ago, we read in the newspaper that they deported some Ukrainian who had been a guard at Dachau—I forget his name and most of the details, but he had been living in Miami. I asked Dad about it. He said it was time they closed the book—they couldn't go on turning over rocks to look for snakes forever. I was surprised at his reaction; but as I told you before, he never wanted to talk much about those days. I guess he just wanted to forget."

Juno finished making some notes. Then, as if verbally summarizing the facts he had just learned would help to interpret their significance, he said, "Avram Goldstein and Morris Golding were brothers. Both were in Dachau at the same time, and both survived. Both were killed by a Luger, likely the *same* Luger, on the same evening, and probably by the same assailant, who, it appears, both brothers knew and hated—your uncle, too, had that same look of fear and hatred on his face. Each had a scar on his left side that can't be explained by highly qualified police pathologists."

Golding stared at him. "My God! What the hell's going on?"

"I'm not sure I know." The tone of Juno's voice emphasized the frustration he felt.

Renée broke the uncomfortable silence. "I'm afraid I can't shed any more light on that situation than Lieutenant Juno has, Mr. Golding; but I'd like to ask you a few more questions." She, too, referred to her notebook. "Does the name Asher Ben Levi mean anything to you? Do you recall your father ever mentioning it?"

"No. Who is he?"

"An Israeli physician who was also killed by a Luger at Kennedy Airport on Tuesday evening."

"Are you implying there's a connection between . . . ?"

"We don't know," Juno cut him off abruptly. "He was a Jew, and he was killed by a bullet from a Luger on the same night as your father and your uncle. That's all we know for the moment." Juno frowned. "Let's get back to your uncle, if you don't mind. Tell us everything you know about him. And then we'd like to talk to your mother."

The snow had stopped by the time they headed back toward New York City. Their questioning had led to one dead end after another. Neither of them spoke until they were sitting in the line of cars at the entrance to the Lincoln Tunnel.

"Shit!" Juno hit the steering wheel with his fists.

"Are you commenting on the traffic or the day in general?"

"It's not the day *or* the traffic; it's this damn investigation. Nothing makes sense. There are three dead men in the morgue, each killed with a Luger on the same evening; two are related. If it were only those two, we'd have something to go on; and I'd at least know where to start. It's Ben Levi who *really* has me stumped. He's much younger than the others and has neither the scar on his left side nor the numbers on his left forearm; and just to complicate things, he had no obvious ties with the diamond trade like Golding and Goldstein. Where the hell does *he* fit into all of this?"

"If he does."

"What do you mean?"

"We don't know yet if the bullets match."

"You've got to be kidding! You mean to tell me you still doubt it? Jesus Christ! They were all killed by a Luger—"

"—and they were all Jews. I'm well aware of that, but we've had no final word from Ballistics."

"Well, use that damned thing and find out." Juno pointed toward the radio beneath the dashboard.

The ballistics report confirmed his assumption: the bullets removed from all of the murder victims matched perfectly; one gun had been used.

"Both Golding and Goldstein were diamond merchants. The New York diamond district does about four hundred million dollars in business a day. Considering it's dominated by Orthodox Jews and the murder weapon was a Luger, we ought to consider the possibility that the Nazis are trying to wrest control of the diamond market from the Jews. But that still leaves Ben Levi."

Renée glanced at him. "Remember the Balabin and Tal case a few years ago?"

Juno thought for a moment. "They were the two Israeli diamond cutters who murdered a diamond broker. What about them?"

"Maybe it's not the Nazis but some militant Israeli group that's behind all this, using the Nazis as a cover."

"You *are* a cynical bitch. Maybe Ben Levi was killed simply because he was a witness to Goldstein's murder; that seems more likely than Jews killing Jewish diamond merchants and tossing in an Israeli doctor just to confuse the issue. You're really reaching this time."

"Not necessarily. Remember, Balabin and Tal killed a *Jewish* diamond broker. Besides, as much as you have a soft spot for the Jews, sometimes they *do* get carried away."

"It's worth looking into. We should go back over the files on all the crimes committed in the diamond district in the past few years."

"I'm with you." Renée settled back as Juno maneuvered into the tunnel. "Where to now?"

"I told Davis we'd check in with him when we got back."

"It's after six; he's probably gone by now."

"He said he'd wait; he wanted to be brought up-to-date before he went home."

The two Israelis sat by the window, their eyes on the main door of police headquarters and the entrance to the garage beneath it.

Shem, a small dark-skinned man, spoke with little overt emotion. "There will be a lot of questions asked about Asher, you know."

"I've already sent a wire. Absolutely *no* information will be given out about him." Grossman, a younger man with fair features, checked his watch and scanned the street in front of the restaurant. "No sign of Juno." He held up his hand. "Hold it. That man in the light blue sedan . . . the one at the stoplight. Isn't that Rolfe Penzel?"

Shem shaded his eyes with his hand and squinted. "It is!"

"What the hell is he doing *here?*"

"He was reported in the New York area about a month ago, but last week he suddenly dropped out of sight . . . a few days before Asher was killed."

"Damn! That son of a bitch could be just the man we're looking for—he's a Nazi hit man!"

"He's turning into the garage!"

Grossman was already heading for the door. "Keep an eye on the garage! I'll get the car and pick you up at the entrance!"

The reception room was dark, but the wedge of light from the office door and the angry voices from within left no doubt that Commissioner Davis was there. Renée cleared her throat to announce their presence.

"Come right in." Davis seemed relieved at the interruption.

Nodding to Davis, she collapsed into the chair next to Joseph Mann seated rigidly in front of the desk. Despite their conversation the previous evening, Juno felt his stomach muscles tighten at the sight of the pathologist.

"Sit down and relax." The commissioner nodded to the empty chair next to Renée. "Dr. Mann and I were just discussing the Golding case. We were talking about the scar; I thought we could benefit from Mann's professional opinion as to whether it had any bearing on our investigation." It was obvious that Davis was trying to impress them with his ability to keep well informed about individual cases despite his administrative chores. "But tell us what you two have come up with."

Acutely aware of Juno's change in mood, Renée ignored the fact that the commissioner had directed his question to her partner; she began to deliver a detailed report of their progress.

Juno was grateful for the few moments' reprieve; he found himself concentrating his attention more on the pathologist than on what Renée was saying. There was something cold and distant about Mann; in fact, as long as Juno had known him, the only expression that he seemed to permit himself was a sterile, humorless smile. Juno had once said that certain people's faces developed characteristics peculiar to their professions—in Mann's case, it was a mask of death. At the time, it had been a facetious statement.

Annoyed with himself for allowing the pathologist to upset him, Juno tried to view the situation more objectively. Saul had taught him that there was some good to be found in the worst of men; the problem was to find it in Mann. But no matter how hard he tried, it was impossible to overlook the pathologist's short temper, his abuse and intolerance of those who worked with him, and his obsessive-compulsive personality. Mann's solicitous attitude toward him during their recent encounter had been totally out of character, and it troubled Juno. . . .

"What do you think, Pete?" Davis's words startled him.

"Sorry, sir. I wasn't paying attention." Juno bit his lip, he rarely got caught at such a disadvantage.

"We were just saying that the Golding murder appears to be evolving into a case of major proportions," Renée said quickly. "The commissioner has suggested that I follow up on Ben Levi while you concentrate on Golding and Goldstein."

"That sounds reasonable." Juno didn't care if it was or not; this was one time he agreed with his partner's philosophy that a strategic retreat was sometimes wiser than a poorly formulated attack. "We're used to dividing up the work without losing track of one another."

"Fine." Davis stood up. "I want a daily report of your progress, in person if possible; if not, by phone." He looked hard at the two detectives. "Something about this case stinks. I don't like it." He turned to Mann. "I want you in on all future discussions. I'm convinced that scar is significant. Keep at it. If you come up with anything, call Lieutenant Juno or Sergeant Tracy immediately."

"Of course. I have already told Lieutenant Juno I will help in any way I can. In fact, I suggested to him that Mr. Golding's religion—he was a Jew, you know—may be more important than his profession, especially since the murder weapon was a Luger."

Davis thought for a moment. "Follow up on that, Pete."

Juno merely nodded.

The telephone rang. Visibly annoyed by the interruption, Davis answered, frowned, and handed the phone to Juno.

The detective was surprised to hear Joshua Fields's voice.

"Where have you been? I've been trying to reach you for hours!" Fields did not wait for a response. "I have to see you, Peter. As soon as possible."

Juno could not remember the last time his brother had called him "Peter." There was something ominous in the sound of his own name. "Want to meet someplace, or shall I come to your apartment?"

"No. Meet me at the Presbyterian Emergency Room. Know where it is?"

"Sure. I'll be right there."

"Good." Fields hesitated. "Be careful."

Frowning, Rolfe Penzel slid down farther on the seat. Despite the lateness of the hour—it was just past seven—the garage beneath the administrative offices of the New York City Police Department was not deserted as he had anticipated. Although the number of people had dwindled since 6:30, one was enough to prevent him from accomplishing his mission; he knew no excuses would be tolerated by Reichmann.

Suddenly aware of the silence, he sat up halfway and peered over the dashboard. The garage was empty. Still, his uneasiness persisted. Ordinarily he was confident when embarking on an assignment; but that was because he had formulated, studied, revised, and polished his plan of action until no doubt remained that he could carry it out successfully. Reichmann had made it clear to him that this task was urgent. There had been no time for his usual cautious and detailed planning.

The sound of footsteps on the concrete walkway startled him. Reaching for the Luger lying next to him on the seat, he checked the clip to be certain it was full, rechecked the silencer, and released the safety. Without moving, he surveyed the garage, paying special attention to possible routes of escape. Adjusting the rearview mirror, he could see a figure running toward him. Reichmann's description of the Greek detective had been exceedingly accurate. Penzel smiled as he weighed the gun in his hand and let the trigger rest lightly against the pulp of his index finger. He would not aim and fire until Juno had passed him.

Pressing himself down and back into the seat, he listened as the steps sped by. He sat up cautiously and scanned the garage one more time; except for the rows of parked cars, it still appeared empty. Steadying his wrist on the door, he framed the back of the raincoated man on the top of the sight.

He hesitated. A car had driven down the ramp; he could hear it slowly approaching. Despite the exigency of this mission, Penzel knew that success was rarely achieved by rushing headlong into a situation where the odds were stacked against him: a gun battle in the police department garage would be foolhardy.

He pulled out and headed toward the exit. As he passed the oncoming car, he noted its occupants. "Israelis!" He spat out the word and gritted his teeth; he had seen the two men someplace before.

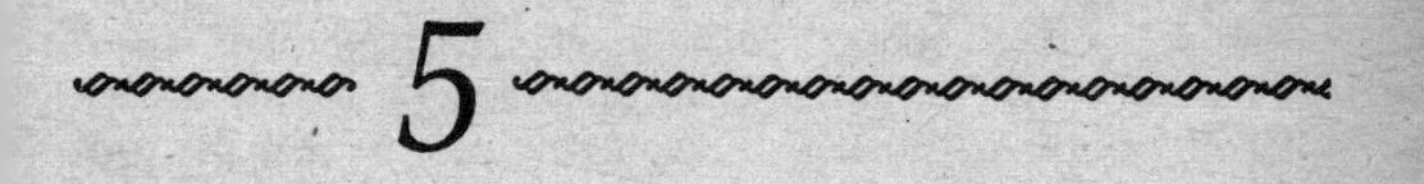

5

Juno identified himself to the guard at the Emergency Room entrance and was directed to the receptionist, who smiled at his approach and informed him that Dr. Fields would be with him shortly.

The crowded waiting room was filled with a mélange of languages and the stale smell of tobacco, liquor, and unwashed bodies. An intern knelt on the floor to examine the torn eyelid of a wailing infant held uncertainly on the lap of a pale, frightened girl who looked too young to be its mother; a nurse in a green scrub dress stood in one corner to apply an Ace bandage to the limp wrist of a lanky, smiling black man; a derelict wrapped in a worn overcoat took sips from a bottle concealed in a wrinkled brown paper bag despite uncontrollable paroxysms of wet cough. It was a depressing scene, and Juno was relieved to see his brother walking quickly toward him down the stretcher-lined corridor; but his concern mounted at the sight of him.

Peter Juno knew his brother well. Joshua Fields was a man of habit. He found a routine that suited him, and he kept to it compulsively unless an emergency forced him to depart from it. Whatever had prompted him to alter his structured existence this evening was grave; that was apparent from the look on his face.

Fields led Juno by the arm into a small room and closed the door. Scrutinizing his brother closely, Juno waited for him to speak. Fields appeared exhausted: his eyes were hollow, his face drawn, and his movements rigid as he settled himself onto the cot on one side of the room and motioned Juno toward the shabby armchair opposite him.

"Intern's on-call room," Fields apologized. "Nothing fancy, but we can talk here without being disturbed."

"You look tired. What's so damned important that the professor is playing intern?"

"You remember my German cleaning lady—the one you asked about last night?"

"Sure." Juno laughed. "You didn't call me all the way down here to tell me she's got another free day, did you?" The anguish in his brother's eyes made him regret the remark before he had finished it.

"She's dead, Peter."

It was a combination of the statement and that damned "Peter" again. "Sorry, Josh. Really I am." He *was* sorry, but he wasn't there to offer sympathy. He knew it and Josh knew it. It was time for the rest of the story, but Josh would have to tell it in his own way.

"I think there are some things you ought to know about Mrs. Schonberg's death," Josh said, "especially since you seemed so concerned over that phone call last night."

"Mrs. Schonberg?"

"My cleaning lady," Fields said. "I got to know Eva Schonberg fairly well in the year or so she was my housekeeper. On the days she worked, she'd come in about noon and stay till seven or eight. She was a lonesome soul, and I think she purposely worked those hours so she'd be there when I got home and have someone to talk to and fuss over for a few minutes. She always made sure that I had enough to eat and that my shirts were clean. I liked the attention. She was a typical Jewish mother—"

"Jewish? I thought you said she was German."

"She was. A German Jew. Nothing so surprising about that; there used to be a lot of them. Her husband had been a jeweler—one of the biggest diamond merchants in Germany—until the Nazis came into power. Although he lost everything, he was enough of a figure in the Jewish community to be useful as a puppet administrator in some sort of council that helped manage

Jewish affairs—relocations and things like that. The Nazis had one in every big city and town; they were called Judenräte. So he was able to keep himself and his wife relatively safe until 1943, when he raised too much of a fuss about what was happening to the Jews he was relocating. As a result, the Schonbergs were sent to a concentration camp where Mr. Schonberg was exterminated a few months before the war ended. Fortunately, she survived."

"Which concentration camp?"

Fields thought for a moment. "Dachau."

Juno barely nodded. "Go on."

"Like most women her age, she had some medical problems; but she rarely talked about them, and I never asked—it was really none of my business. About a month ago, though, she mentioned that she wasn't feeling well; but she continued working, and I didn't think any more about it—until tonight.

"I was on my way out when the Emergency Room paged me. Mrs. Schonberg was there asking for me. When I got there, she was in pretty bad shape."

"What do you mean?"

"I mean she was *damned sick!* What the hell did you think I meant?" Fields closed his eyes and rubbed his temples with his fingertips. "Sorry, but I've got a lousy headache."

Juno reached into his pocket and threw a small tin of aspirin to him. "Take two." He got up and poured his brother a cup of water from a cooler in the corner and then sat down again. "What I meant was *how* was she sick? I take it she wasn't shot or stabbed or beaten, or you'd have told me."

"I can describe her signs and symptoms to you, I can tell you the mechanism of her death, but I can't put all of the pieces together."

"Is that so unusual? After all, you weren't her regular doctor. You arranged for an autopsy, didn't you?"

"Of course! And please don't misunderstand me. I'm not alarmed because I'm stumped and my ego is bruised. All of us, no matter how good, miss diagnoses, make mistakes, and sometimes even kill a patient because of an error in judgment."

"Then what specificially is bothering you about Mrs. Schonberg?"

"We have the pieces; they don't fit. A white woman. Sixty-seven. Past history of being in Dachau. In generally good health since coming to the United States in 1948. For the past month she has had rapidly increasing fatigue; headaches; lapses of memory; intermittent loss of vision, speech, and bladder and bowel control; muscular weakness; loss of sensation; and inability to perform a variety of relatively complicated neurologic functions such as calculations, fine movements of the hands and fingers, and maintenance of balance. Then suddenly one evening it *all* goes; she ends up with what amounts to *no* nervous system. She just loses one neurologic function after another faster than we can compensate for the loss; and finally she's lost more than we can replace with machines or drugs, and she's dead."

"Wait a minute." Juno held up both hands. "I get part of what you're saying, but not all of it. Mrs. Schonberg had some sort of problem with her nervous system, and whatever it was killed her rather quickly. Right?"

"Right."

"I gather diseases of the nervous system don't usually act as rapidly as hers did." It was in part a statement, in part a question.

"Some do." Fields enumerated the possibilities. "Acute viral encephalitis, an unusually acute form of multiple sclerosis, an overwhelming intracerebral bleed or lack of blood, the end stages of certain infiltrating tumors, and damage resulting from excessive exposure to certain poisons and drugs."

"Well, couldn't she have had one of those?"

"She could have—but she didn't. Besides, even the entities I mentioned don't involve *so much* of the nervous system."

"When you say 'she didn't,' I take it you have proof."

"Presumptive evidence, not absolute proof. By history, physical examination, the laboratory tests we could get, and from the gross autopsy findings, she did *not* have any disease I know of that could have caused the clinical picture I saw. We have blood and tissue put aside for more complete analysis and viral studies."

"You've already done the post-mortem examination?"

"Just the gross exam. I thought it was important. It'll take a couple of days to get the final microscopic evaluation."

"Did you clear it with the medical examiner's office?"

"Of course! We know the rules when a patient dies so quickly. Besides, we have a pretty good pathology department." Fields smiled. "Probably a lot better than yours."

"No argument. So what did your eminent pathologist find?"

"Nothing. Absolutely nothing. But that's not so uncommon; diseases of the nervous system may result in no gross structural changes, yet there may be significant microscopic alterations. Besides, all we did was examine the surface of the brain, spinal cord, and representative nerves. A more detailed inspection will be done after fixation in formaldehyde. I'm afraid we'll have to wait for the answer—if there is one."

"Let me get this straight. You're worried because of the *way* in which Mrs. Schonberg died and the fact that there appears to be no readily available explanation for her illness and her death."

Fields nodded. "But that's not why I called you. As much as I value your expert opinion on many subjects, medicine isn't one of them."

"Then why?"

"Because a couple of things besides Mrs. Schonberg's death seem too coincidental. And above all—and don't laugh or accuse me of playing detective—because I think that something terrible is happening."

Juno stared at his brother. There was no levity in Fields's voice, no smile on his face; the fear in his eyes conveyed his feelings unmistakably.

"I'm listening."

"First, the disease is atypical in that it is overwhelming and diffuse and does not fit any of the possibilities I mentioned to you. Second, Mrs. Schonberg was a Jew in a concentration camp during the Hitler regime. I'm not sure whether or not there's a relationship between her and that man you were so upset about, but you must admit there are similarities in their backgrounds. What I consider to be most significant, however, is something she told me—something that scared the hell out of me." Fields hesitated. "*Mr.* Schonberg had the same symptoms in *1945* that she had for the past month. In fact, she was certain he was sent to the gas chamber because he was so sick that he was incapable of working."

"That was over *thirty years* ago!"

"That's just my point . . . and I questioned her carefully. Despite the fact that she was so sick, I took the most detailed history possible. I wanted whatever she had hidden in her memory about her husband's illness that might help me treat the disease that was killing her. She wouldn't change her story; she was adamant about it until the very end: she and her husband had the same illness over *thirty years* apart!"

"But it's not possible. . . . Is it?"

"I've been wondering about it for hours. No disease we know of has an incubation period that long. Serum hepatitis, rabies, and monkey B encephalitis may have an incubation period exceeding six months—but *not* thirty years! There are some diseases that may relapse later. Brill's disease, also called recrudescent typhus, can recur forty or fifty years after the initial episode; but Mrs. Schonberg never had typhus—I asked her—and the illness that killed her didn't look anything like typhus. Some diseases, like syphilis, occur in stages; but once again, none of them fit." He paused. "There are a few slow . . . But that's impossible; their existence wasn't even known then. I suppose it's possible that she died *coincidentally* of a disease that her husband had over thirty years ago, but you must admit the odds against that happening would be astronomical."

Even as a layman, Juno could understand the magnitude of the medical riddle Mrs. Schonberg presented; and as a policeman, he could not deny that there were several factors that linked Morris Golding and Avram Goldstein to Eva Schonberg. But to extrapolate these to a prophecy of an impending disaster and to attempt to relate an event that had occurred in a Nazi concentration camp over thirty years ago to those that had taken place in the past forty-eight hours was almost inconceivable. There was one component, however, that superseded all the rest and made it all seem plausible: Joshua Fields. Juno had the utmost respect for his brother's knowledge, insight, and ability to put things into their proper perspective. Fields was not an alarmist; he was able to separate the important from the unimportant and to deal with both accordingly; he always had a good reason for what he did. What it might be now alarmed the detective.

"Why did you bring me down here? Couldn't we have talked at your apartment?"

"I want to show you something." Fields got up and started out of the room.

Juno followed.

Away from the Emergency Room, the hospital appeared peaceful. The two men walked in silence down long, dimly lit corridors to a set of windowless swinging doors that squeaked discordantly on large brass hinges. Juno barely caught a glimpse of the fading words in worn black paint: NECROPSY—AUTHORIZED PERSONNEL ONLY.

The room was immaculately clean and excessively bright; the floor and the walls were covered with light tan tile, and the ceiling was made up of recessed lighting panels. Behind a desk in one corner, an elderly man, cigarette dangling from his lip, looked up from his newspaper as they entered.

"Evenin', Dr. Fields." He punctuated his greeting with a deep cough.

"Good evening, Lloyd. This is Detective Juno." Fields nodded toward his brother. "Thanks for waiting. We'll only be a few minutes."

"Take as much time as you need. I'll just open up for you." Picking up a small ring of keys, he hobbled to a wooden door in the center of the far wall and unlocked it. "Don't bother signin' in. I'll do it for you." He held the door open for his two visitors and stepped aside to let them enter.

The morgue was cool and silent and smelled of formaldehyde. It was long and narrow, perhaps one hundred by fifty feet; but it appeared smaller in the dim light provided by two fluorescent fixtures hanging from the ceiling. The concrete floor, painted battleship gray, sloped from all sides toward a central open drain and distorted the echo of their footsteps. Each side wall consisted of rows of large stainless steel locker doors. Against the far wall hung a single stainless steel sink above which were a soap receptacle and a paper towel dispenser. Two stretchers on wheels rested side by side at one end of the room.

Glancing at the name tags on the front of each locker he passed, Fields stopped in front of the one he wanted. He pressed the handle and pulled in one smooth effort. The metal slab rumbled out of its vault on two extension tracks that hardly seemed strong enough to hold it or the sheet-covered body that lay upon it. He looked at Juno's face.

"You okay?"
"I've been in morgues and seen bodies before. What do you want to show me?"
Fields undid the tie and fought with the sheet until the top half of the body was exposed.
Juno grimaced, felt himself pale, and took a step toward the wall to support himself. It was not the sight of death that upset him—he had seen it in all of its ugly forms—it was the face, a face unknown to him, yet strangely familiar because he had imagined what Eva Schonberg would look like. She must have been an attractive woman, but her features were now altered by rigor mortis. Her skin appeared waxy and yellow, with a dull sheen that reflected the dim light. The forehead was wrinkled and asymmetrical where it had been pulled forward to expose the skull to the dissector's rotary saw. The pathologist had done a lousy job of replacing the scalp, Juno thought with disgust as he looked at the ill-fitting whitish hair matted with dried blood. She was obese; and her pendulous breasts, large brown puckered nipples partially hidden in the skin folds, hung to each side over her upper arms. A long Y-shaped incision, the hallmark of the post-mortem examination, extended from her mid-chest downward and disappeared beneath the sheet; it had been closed too tightly with black cord, and a part of the bloodless edges of the skin and the thick layer of globular fat beneath it was exposed. Without knowing why, Juno reached for her hand. It was cold, dry, and inelastic; and he recoiled at the touch.
"Give me a lift with this, will you?"
Reacting automatically, Juno rolled the corpse from side to side as Fields pulled the cover to the knees. The skin of the abdomen was flaccid and wrinkled. The pathologist's incision continued in the midline, skirted the navel, and ended abruptly above the remnants of a triangular collection of wiry gray pubic hair. The thighs were heavy with a corkscrew pattern of ropy varicosities barely visible under the pallid skin.
"Well?" Juno looked across the naked form at Fields, who responded by reaching forward, grasping the body beneath the left shoulder and buttocks, and pulling it toward him.
Cold fear spread throughout Juno's body. His mouth felt dry,

and his racing pulse echoed in the back of his throat.

A clean, well-healed, slightly raised scar extended in a fine line from beneath the left rib cage in front to the middle of the left flank and stopped abruptly before reaching the back. As Fields pulled the body onto its side, Juno could see tiny suture marks—each about a centimeter from the one next to it—in parallel rows above and below the scar.

"At first glance, it appears to be a common surgical scar," Fields spoke as if he were standing at a podium in the front of a lecture hall, "except that there is no reason for its presence. There is no indication of surgery beneath it. The kidney and the spleen are intact and in their normal anatomic relationships to the surrounding structures. There is a small dimple on the surface of the spleen beneath the scar, but that is either a small splenic infarct or . . ."

Juno did not hear the end of the sentence. A series of seemingly related and unrelated events and circumstances rushed through his mind.

"Did you hear what I said?"

Fields's voice sobered him. Juno shook his head. "No. Sorry, Josh; I was just thinking about the scar. Let's get out of here; then we can talk." He helped Fields replace the shroud and slide the body back into the wall. Without speaking, they washed their hands at the sink.

"Cafeteria's probably open. How about a sandwich and a cold drink?"

"I'll settle for something to drink; I'm not really hungry."

They took the elevator up to the cafeteria. Fields was apparently unwilling to allow the events of the evening to spoil his appetite. He chose two cheese and bologna sandwiches, a piece of chocolate cake, and two cartons of low-fat milk. Juno placed only a diet cola on his own tray.

Fields talked between bites. "I didn't mean to upset you, but I wanted you to see that scar. Ludwick, the pathologist who did the autopsy, has never seen one like it before; and he's an experienced guy. It's not the scar that's so remarkable, but the lack of any reason for it—no sign of internal surgery or trauma to explain it. Ludwick took multiple specimens from the area; maybe the microscopic exam will give us some answers." He finished the sandwiches and started on his cake. "Your man from the concentration camp—the one who was murdered the other night—he had the same scar, didn't he?"

"But how did *you* know that?" Juno was not as surprised by the question as he appeared to be; he had learned long ago to expect the unexpected from his brother.

"Logic, and because I'm basically a cynical person who believes that evil is an intrinsic part of the world and that it will be discovered only if one suspects and expects its presence. It's like an unusual disease—if you don't think of it, you won't make the diagnosis. Besides, I heard bits and pieces of your conversation with Dr. Joy and gathered that something out of the ordinary had been found. When I tried to make some sense out of Mrs. Schonberg's story, it was evident that certain similarities existed between her and your man, and I began to wonder about the scar—did your man have it, too? Was *that* the peculiar finding at *his* autopsy? Only one way to find out—so here we are. Whatever the scar represents, it certainly adds a great deal of credence to the possibility that there is more than just religion and a history of internment in a concentration camp that binds these two people together."

"Three," Juno interrupted.

"Three?"

Trying neither to omit nor to overdramatize, Juno informed his brother of the death of Avram Goldstein, the little he had been able to learn about him, and all that he now knew about Morris Golding.

Fields listened intently. "I don't like this whole thing." He took off his glasses and wiped the lenses with the corner of his white coat. "At first I thought my concern might be unfounded, but I couldn't get rid of the feeling that something was very wrong. Now I'm convinced of it. The *three* people involved have too much in common for it to be coincidence. If Mrs. Schonberg had been murdered, it might be simpler. Then we could say that there was some sort of plot involving diamonds. But I don't think diamonds are involved at all. Mrs. Schonberg was *not* murdered; she died of some strange neurological disorder, the cause of which we have yet to discover. Therefore, we have to ask ourselves a very important question: Is there a tie-in between the murders and the disease? I think there is. Almost every other significant element suggests a connection between these people. Why not their deaths? Maybe Golding and Goldstein were killed because they were the key to Eva Schonberg. In some way those two men might have given us the information we need to explain what happened to her."

"But there has to be more to it than that," Juno said. "Nobody would commit two murders to hide something about an old German-Jewish cleaning woman."

"Not unless it was damned important, or"—Fields's voice became softer—"she was a small cog in a big machine, and it's the *machine* that really matters. In other words, how many other deaths have occurred, or will occur . . . and why?"

Juno frowned. "There's something else I think you should know. There has been one other death. An Israeli physician named Asher Ben Levi was shot with the same Luger on the same night as Golding and Goldstein."

The color drained from Fields's face, and his voice was barely audible. "My God!"

"You knew him?" Juno could not suppress his astonishment.

Fields nodded and looked away. "I knew Asher Ben Levi quite well. He was one of my residents when I first became an attending physician at the Mass. General. He was a little older, a little more mature than the rest; he stood out because he had limitless energy when it came to the study and practice of medicine. I wanted him to stay on for a fellowship, but he was anxious to return home to Israel. We became good friends while he was here. He thought that I knew everything there was to know about medicine and that all he had to do was stick to me and learn it." He laughed weakly. "I must admit, though, I encouraged it; he was a great boost to the ego of a fledgling professor."

Watching his brother struggle to maintain control, Juno felt a wave of sympathy; yet he knew there was no time for it. "I need your help, Josh. Ben Levi had almost no identification on him when he was found. We'd like to notify his next of kin. Can you give me an address?"

"Only a P.O. box number in Jerusalem. The mail was evidently forwarded from there to the kibbutz where he lived."

"Isn't that a bit unusual? Doesn't a kibbutz have some sort of postal service?"

"I don't really know. Ben Levi talked very little about his home, and I didn't see any reason to press him about it."

"Did he have any family?"

"I don't think so. He told me once that his parents had been killed during the Six-Day War. I don't remember him ever speaking about brothers and sisters."

Juno shook his head. "This man was supposedly a friend of yours, and you know almost nothing about him."

"You don't need to know a lot about a person to be a friend."

"But weren't you curious?"

"Not really. I guess it depends upon your point of view: I didn't ask any questions because I respected his right to privacy; you would have, because your job conditions you to do so." Josh reached across the table and squeezed his brother's hand. "Facts *are* important, Pete. Here are two for you to think about: first, Asher Ben Levi's parents had both been in Dachau—that much I do know; second, several days ago I received a telegram from him telling me that he was coming to New York to seek my help in, and I quote, 'a matter of the gravest urgency.'"

"But you don't know what he was referring to?"

"No."

"You really believe it's all tied in together—that the four deaths are somehow related to something that happened at Dachau over thirty years ago?"

"Right! And you wouldn't keep asking if you were so damned sure I'm wrong. Let's make an assumption: identical symptoms indicate the same disease. It's not always true, but often enough to make it valid for our purposes. If that's the case, Mr. and Mrs. Schonberg suffered from the same illness—but thirty years apart! Whether or not that's possible is unimportant; but it does establish a link between five dead people, not four, and between the present and the past. Therefore, I believe we have the right to extrapolate even further and say that if these five persons are somehow related by statistically significant similarities, there are likely others involved, too. I also think we can say that the problem did not begin yesterday or the day before, but more than thirty years ago—which gives us our first clue to that scar."

Juno drained the cup in front of him. The ache in the back of his neck had returned, along with an anxiety that seemed to be nurtured by each of Fields's statements.

"You lost me with that last one. I don't see how anything you've said so far tells us a damned thing about the scar."

"I'll tell you how. Like all of the German concentration camps, Dachau had its medical block where SS doctors disgraced their profession by performing experiments that stagger the imagination. I've read about some of them, and I don't want to go into detail. Those scars were souvenirs from Dachau. Mrs. Schonberg—and probably Golding and Goldstein—were guinea pigs for those bastards."

Juno winced. "How do you know that?"

"Mrs. Schonberg told me. When I examined her, I saw the scar and asked her about it. Unfortunately, she had lost most of her speech by then; she just about got out the two words 'Dachau' and 'doctor.' Believe me, at Dachau they didn't do surgery on Jews for legitimate reasons."

"Why didn't you tell me that before?"

"Because it wouldn't have made any difference. It's not where or how they got the scar that's important, but why."

"Well?"

"That I don't know."

"Let me get this straight. Are you trying to tell me that the Nazis did something to those three people with a specific plan in mind to attain some predetermined goal more than thirty years later? I can't believe it! If *Mr.* Schonberg had had a scar, I could understand the possible relationship between *it* and his death. But the others? Be realistic! Your theory that their deaths may be interrelated—even interdependent—makes sense. I can even buy your assumption that we may yet see more deaths. But that the scars—especially if they were the result of something that happened in Dachau—are a major clue is hard to believe."

"Then please explain Mrs. Schonberg's death and the fact that she and her husband probably died from the same cause."

"I can't, and I don't have to. As I said before, many things go unexplained." Juno wasn't certain if he believed his own argument. "Look," he went on, "part of what you said is pretty convincing, and I admit that I share a good deal of your concern.

I'm just not sure what you want me to do about it. In the cases of Golding and Goldstein, at least we have a crime. But Mrs. Schonberg died of natural causes, although I'll agree they're peculiar. If something comes up during my investigation, I'll let you know immediately; then I'll do whatever needs to be done."

"That may be too late."

Juno thought for a moment. "Is there a phone I can use?"

"Right over there." Fields pointed to a telephone on the wall.

"If your assumption that this is more than an isolated cluster of deaths is correct, the medical examiner's office should have some record of others who have died from a similar disease; they should also know if any of them had that damned scar. Would you agree?"

"If it were a medical examiner's case, yes; if not, there's no reason why his office would have been informed."

"Very sharp. But in New York, I think it's likely at least one or two would be processed through that office."

Josh nodded.

"Okay, then, I'm going to call and find out."

It took Juno less than five minutes to obtain the information he was seeking from Pathology. Returning to the table, he slumped into the chair and rubbed the back of his neck.

"I think the whole world is mad! There have been two other deaths from a diffuse degenerative disease of the nervous system of unknown cause in the past week; both were elderly Jews, concentration camp survivors, both with unexplained scars on their left sides." Juno leaned across the table. "Look, Josh, level with me. No bullshit, no statistics, no medical jargon. What do *you* think is going on?"

Fields pushed his chair back from the table. "I think that a number of Jews who were in Dachau during the war are being—or will be—killed by something that attacks the nervous system and is in some way related to that scar. I'm at a complete loss to explain it further, but I'm convinced that Golding and Goldstein—and perhaps Asher Ben Levi—were killed because somehow they could have shed light on this situation. Does that satisfy you?"

"For the moment. It certainly gives me something to go on."

Juno took out his notebook and began to write as he spoke. "I'll arrange for you and a pathologist—Ludwick, if you like—to have access to the records and the bodies of Golding and Goldstein. You've got to get as much as possible out of those scars—and quickly! They may represent the only concrete lead we have. You know what to look for from a medical point of view, but I want additional information as well. Can you tell how old the scar is and what kind of instrument was used to make it? Is there anything characteristic about it that might tell you what kind of doctor performed the surgery and how good a technician he was? Make those damned scars talk! If you need more help, I'll get one of our forensic pathologists to lend you a hand."

"Do you mind if I consult a friend of mine?"

"Who?"

"A fellow by the name of Ari Sokolov; he's an Israeli sociologist based in New York. For years he's been interested in diseases that seem to have a predilection for Jews."

"I didn't realize there were any others beside Tay-Sachs."

"Believe it or not, close to a dozen."

"I think the number may just have increased to thirteen. Sure, talk to this Ari. Learn as much as you can about those Jewish diseases. Then you can explain it all to me." He rubbed his eyes. "We've got to find out, however, if this is affecting *only* Jews—there were non-Jews at Dachau, too—and if there are other outbreaks of the disease. If so, where and in whom. Maybe there are just isolated pockets whose locations may help us. Meanwhile, I'll check to see if there's been an increase in the number of seemingly motiveless murders."

Fields stood up. "When do we start?"

"Right now! As you would say, 'Stat!'"

"Now just a minute . . ." Fields stopped short and listened to a voice paging him from the loudspeaker. "That's for me. Can you wait at least until I see what it is?"

"Sure. Only don't be too long; we've got a lot to do." As he watched his brother make his way between the tables toward the phone, Juno felt better. The pain in the back of his neck had eased, and his fatigue had subsided. Stimulated by the challenge, he was anxious to embark on the investigation.

Fields was not finished with his call. He'd give him another minute or two before saying good-bye. He wanted to see Renée and fill her in on what had happened.

Fields now had his back to him, his forehead against the wall. His legs were apart, his right hand pressed the phone to his ear, and he gestured with his left arm and hand as if he were angry or concerned. Suddenly Fields turned to Juno. His face was white—almost the same color as the coat that hung limply on his slender frame. The phone dropped from his trembling hand; he took one step forward and then staggered back against the wall and slid slowly downward.

Juno reached him as he hit the floor. Fields sat motionless, his eyes wide and deep within their sockets. With pale, quivering lips, he kept repeating, "Dad's dead . . ."

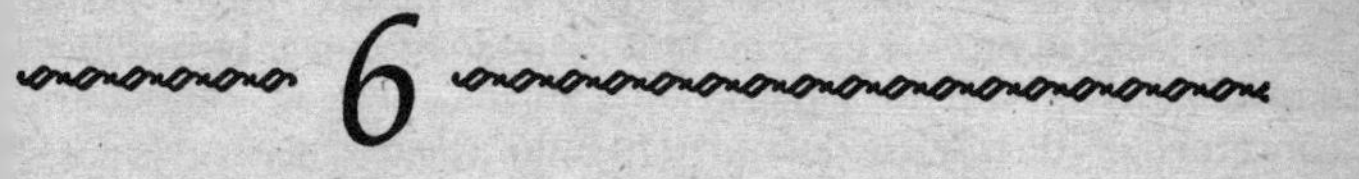

6

Fighting to control his rage, Thaddeus Reichmann listened to Rolfe Penzel's voice on the phone. The fact that Israeli agents had thwarted Penzel's attempt to kill Juno made Reichmann acutely aware that such tasks could not be accomplished with the same facility with which they had been achieved over thirty years ago—he was dealing with a new, aggressive breed of Jew. It also appeared that things were moving faster than he had anticipated. He would have to be even more careful and cunning.

He slammed down the phone and walked back through the living room, where he removed a heavy parchment folder from the wall safe. At his desk he wiped away the dust that had accumulated on the outside of the folder, undid the ties, and gently emptied the contents: three laboratory notebooks, each with a brown leather cover labeled in finely written German script along the worn binding. As he opened the first, his lips quivered uncontrollably; the words and numbers written in his own hand so many years before stared back at him from pages crisp with age.

It was not hard for his memory to traverse time. The faces, the bodies, and the cries of anguish still evoked no emotion; but the purpose they had served and what they now represented sent a wave of excitement through him. Licking his lips, he scanned the pages, stopping here and there to read a passage in detail or to remember the circumstances resulting in a specific notation. The observations recorded there substantiated his interpretation of the events of the past week. He pounded his fist on the desk. They were wrong when they said there could never be another Holocaust. *He had made it happen again!*

Exhilarated, he replaced the notebooks in the folder and locked it in his desk. He poured himself some wine and began to relax. Glancing at his reflection in the surface of the goblet, he knew there was one other who also had to be eliminated. The corners of his mouth curled into a sneer at the thought of Joseph Mann.

Slamming the door to her office in frustration, Renée Tracy threw her coat on the chair in the corner, leafed through the message slips on her desk, and collapsed into the worn swivel chair.

It was just past ten o'clock, and the only thing she had accomplished since starting out early that morning was to come to the conclusion that no one knew anything about Asher Ben Levi; or if they did, they were keeping it a secret. Turning to the appropriate pages in her notebook, she reviewed the little she had been able to learn about the Israeli physician.

The Massachusetts General Hospital in Boston verified that Asher Ben Levi had been a resident in internal medicine there; but after that, they had no knowledge of his whereabouts or his professional activities and no forwarding address. The American Board of Internal Medicine in Philadelphia had a record of his having passed their examination at the end of his senior residency year; but they, too, had no further information about him. The National Medical Library in Bethesda, Maryland; the Library of Congress in Washington, D.C.; and the World Health Organization Library at the United Nations complex in New York—all of which maintained comprehensive lists of medical and paramedical personnel on a worldwide basis—did not list him as a member of any professional organization in Israel. The Israeli embassy in Washington was uncooperative. She was still waiting for replies from the Israeli Ministry of Health and from the Minister of Communications in Jerusalem, the latter in the hope that his office could trace the post-office box through which Josh had communicated with Ben Levi.

In truth, however, Asher Ben Levi—who he was, where he lived, and why he had come to New York—was hardly uppermost in her mind. Her thoughts were with Peter Juno. She wished she could have gone with him, but he had insisted that she continue working on her part of the investigation. Never before had separation been so painful, especially since she felt strongly that he needed her; but she knew that the only way to keep him was to let him go.

Halfheartedly she turned back to the notebook to see what else he had asked her to do.

"Together. That's what brothers *should* be." It was one of his father's favorite expressions. Juno could almost hear Saul saying the words as he looked at Josh sitting beside him.

It had been snowing since they arrived in Chelsea, and the limousine skidded and swayed as it headed slowly up Washington Avenue, turned left on County Road, and then onto Everett Avenue toward the cemetery. They rode in silence except for the clicking noise of the wipers hitting the outer edges of the windshield. They were grateful that the medical examiner of Suffolk County had no interest in Saul's death so that the burial would not be delayed beyond the limits set by the Jewish religion. The arrangements for the funeral had been accomplished smoothly. The only major conflict thus far had been Josh's encounter with Henry Lipschitz, the doctor who had cared for Saul.

Juno had tried to dissuade him from going, but Josh had insisted. "I just want to *talk* to him. When he called to tell me about Dad's death, he described some of the symptoms of the disease that killed him—they were similar to those of Mrs. Schonberg. I want to satisfy myself that there's no connection."

"How could there be? Dad was never anywhere near Dachau," Juno had countered. "He couldn't have had the same disease."

Juno had no objection to a rational discussion between his brother and Lipschitz, the man who had been the family's physician ever since he could remember. What disturbed him was that his brother was basically a stubborn, inflexible, overbearing snob regarding the practice of medicine. He could not and would not tolerate sloppiness or mediocrity; he excelled, and he expected others to do likewise. For him there was only one kind of doctor—a *good* one. Although he was mild-mannered and kind—perhaps even meek—in every other aspect of his life, he was ruthless in his intolerance of bad medicine.

Lipschitz had agreed to meet the two men in the doctor's lounge at Chelsea Memorial Hospital at 3:15 the previous afternoon but had not arrived until four o'clock, a minor discourtesy, Juno had thought, but one that had infuriated Fields's sense of punctuality. Nevertheless, the conversation had started innocently enough: a reasonable question had stimulated a reasonable answer, and the discussion had progressed in such a way that even Juno had understood it. Saul had not been feeling well for two or three weeks; there had been increasing fatigue and short periods of difficulty with memory and speech . . .

Juno had listened carefully to Lipschitz for more information; Fields, for a flaw in the older physician's story. Fields found one.

"I don't understand why you didn't put him on a respirator." Fields started his assault benignly.

"What for?"

"To breathe for him, dammit! With his diaphragm and intercostal muscles paralyzed, he couldn't move his chest. If a patient can't move his thorax, Henry, he can't develop negative pressure in the thoracic cavity; and the lungs won't inflate. That's what respirators are for; they mechanically blow air and oxygen into the lungs in a predetermined cycle that simulates normal respiration."

"I know that. I meant for what purpose? Your father had almost no nervous system. What was I saving—a couple of lungs just so I could blow air in and out of them with a fancy machine?"

"How did you know he had no nervous system? Are you a neurologist? Did you get an electroencephalogram or an electromyogram? Did you do a lumbar puncture or a brain scan or any other test to prove it? Did you have a qualified neurologist substantiate your impression?"

"No. When a man is dead, tests don't prove it or bring him back to life. My eyes and ears and what I learned in medical school and over and over again in years of practice told me so. I did my best."

Lipschitz had dropped his guard and delivered his chin.

"Your 'best' wasn't and isn't good enough—for my father or for anyone else for that matter! I don't know exactly what killed my father. He probably would have died anyway; but he deserved a chance, Henry—a *better* chance than *you* gave him!"

Juno had wanted to say something, but the elderly doctor had picked up his black bag and left without another word.

Reichmann's voice was firm. "I will tolerate no more failures," he told Penzel over the phone. "I'm giving you another chance because I have faith in you. Don't fail this time! If you expect to share in what I am about to achieve, you must prove yourself worthy. Now where are you?"

Reichmann nodded at the response to the question. "Good. You know what to do. These men must be eliminated; they know too much. Meanwhile, I'll carry on here. Don't call me again. Just come back to New York when you've accomplished your mission." He hung up.

His ability to act quickly to neutralize any threat would determine his ultimate success. Even those whose peripheral involvement could be viewed as a potential danger would have to be killed. Turning to his newly drafted list of antagonists, he began to formulate his plans to deal with Joseph Mann.

Because of the biting wind and the snow, the rabbi had cut the funeral service short; only a few friends of the family remained to pay their respects.

Not since that night in Athens as a child had Juno felt so alone. Saul's death had robbed him of a father a second time, but now he was a man and could fully understand the enormity of the loss. Only Josh's arm linked in his prevented him from sinking into a state of total despondency.

"Peter, I've got to talk to you!" Henry Lipschitz's voice above the wind interrupted Juno's grieving.

Juno turned and gave the elderly physician a reserved smile.

He was pleased to see him; whether or not Josh had been right about the man's medical qualifications, he was glad the argument hadn't kept their old friend away.

"I've been trying to reach you. Can we talk someplace?"

"We've been in and out a lot trying to tie up loose ends; we'd like to leave tomorrow. Josh and I are driving back to the house in a few minutes. Why don't you come by when all of this is over?"

"No! I have to talk to you alone! Now!" Lipschitz took him by the arm and started to lead him away from the small group of mourners. "Tell Josh I'll drive you home."

After speaking to his brother, Juno joined Lipschitz on the snow-covered path leading to the main gate of the cemetery. "Okay, Henry, what can I do for you?"

"Can we talk in my car? It's parked near the chapel. It's warmer there, and I can have a cigarette."

"Sure." Juno followed the physician along the narrow walkway and was amazed at the older man's speed and agility. Heads bent against the wind, neither of them noticed the car parked at the opposite end of the circular driveway or its driver, who had slipped down out of sight as they approached.

As Juno brushed the snow from his hair and coat, Lipschitz turned on the motor and the heater and then reached into his pocket for a cigarette. He lit it and inhaled deeply. Suddenly he turned toward Juno. "I want you to speak to Josh for me."

"Look, Henry, Josh is like that. He gets carried away with his idealistic approach to the practice of medicine. He didn't mean anything; he was just upset by Dad's death. Let him cool off. I'm sure he'll call you or write to you to apologize after he's had time to think things over."

"He was probably right—at least in content. Maybe his method was a little crude, but like you said, that's Josh." He took several puffs on his cigarette. "But that's not what I wanted to talk to you about. That's unimportant. What *is* important, perhaps unbelievable, is what I'm about to tell you. You *must* tell Josh about it."

"Why not tell him yourself?" Juno looked at his watch. "He'll be back at the house soon."

"Josh wouldn't listen to me; even if he did, he wouldn't believe me!" Lipschitz's eyes were filled with fear, and his lower lip trembled. "I can talk to you, Peter; I can't seem to talk to Josh—we haven't been able to communicate since the day he started medical school. Please listen to what I have to say."

Lipschitz seemed to choke on the cigarette smoke and on his own words. "Earlier this week they buried an old patient of mine, a Mr. Mendelsohn, a man I've taken care of for many years. *Mr. Mendelsohn died of exactly the same disease as your father.* Not a *similar* disease—*the same one!* Now I may be a lousy doctor in many ways, but I've had *some* experience. I've never read about, heard about, or seen a disease like this before; and I haven't the slightest idea what it is. I don't know anything about statistics, but I do know that two people just don't die from the *same* crazy neurologic disease in a couple of days without a reason! Something is terribly wrong here, but I don't even know how or where to start looking into it. Talk to Josh . . . tell him . . . convince him! He'll know what to do." He stubbed out the cigarette and reached for another.

Juno looked away. Knowing so much more than Lipschitz, he understood the implications of the man's words all too well. He felt a wave of nausea spread over him and swore silently at himself and then at Josh. The lack of any relationship between Saul and Dachau had caused them to drop the consideration that Saul's symptoms, although similar to those of Eva Schonberg, might be the result of the same disease. And Josh's attack on Lipschitz had prevented them from probing further into what now appeared to be an incontrovertible link between the two deaths.

Juno turned back to Lipschitz. "I want some quick answers, Henry. Don't ask any questions; just tell me what I want to know. There may be a lot more to this than you realize. How many deaths have you seen like that of my father and this other patient of yours?"

"Only the two."

"Never before—at any time?"

"Never."

"Was Mendelsohn ever in Dachau?"

"Why?"

"No questions, Henry."

"Yes. He was there during the last year or so of the war. A French family hid him until then, but they were caught."

"Now think carefully. Did your patient have a scar on his left flank?"

"How did *you* know?"

"Never mind. Did Saul have the same scar?"

"No."

"Do you know how Mendelsohn got the scar?"

"He said it was the result of some sort of medical experiment in Dachau. That's all he would say about it."

The chill that spread over Juno was not due to the cold. It appeared that the Holocaust had never really ended but had lain dormant like a sleeping monster waiting to be awakened. But how? And by whom?

"What is it?"

Lipschitz's words startled him. "Nothing, Henry." Juno collected his thoughts. "Did my father know Mendelsohn, and if so, how well?"

"They were good friends. . . . They had a couple of business deals together . . ." He stopped abruptly. "Wait a minute. About a month ago, your father stayed with Mendelsohn for a few days. Mendelsohn's wife, Bertha, was in the hospital; he was very upset about it, and Saul didn't want him to be alone. But it was for a very short time, not more than five or six days."

"What was wrong with Mendelsohn's wife?"

"She had some vague neurologic symptoms . . ."

"What were they?"

Lipschitz didn't answer.

Juno repeated the question. "What were the symptoms, Henry? Did she have the *same* symptoms? *Saul's* symptoms? *Did they all have the same symptoms?*"

"Yes!"

"Was Mrs. Mendelsohn ever at Dachau?"

"No."

"Where is she now?"

"At home. I wouldn't let her come to the funeral. . . . Oh, my God! I have to go, Peter. I'll drop you at home on the way. Please talk to Josh and get back to me. I'll be with Mrs. Mendelsohn;

I've got to see what I can do for her." He gunned the motor and reached for the shift lever.

Suddenly there was a loud crack. Instinctively Juno brought his arm up to cover his face. He turned to yell a warning to Lipschitz, but it was too late. The physician grabbed his forehead; blood erupted through his fingers and spilled onto the steering wheel.

Juno rolled to his right, opened the door, reached inside his coat, and hit the ground in a kneeling position behind the protection of the door. "Shit!" He spat out the word with disgust at the realization that his hand was empty. It had been nothing more than a reflex action.

He never went anywhere without his service revolver. On duty or off, he always carried it with him; he had been trained to be prepared for any contingency—except this one. The gun was in New York, safely locked in the roll-top desk in his apartment; there had been no need to take it with him to his father's funeral. With mounting frustration he watched a light blue sedan pull away, skid, and disappear into the snow. Cursing, he smashed his fist against the side of the car, stood up, and walked around to the driver's side.

Lipschitz was dead. Juno bent over and covered the body with his coat. As he rushed into the chapel to look for a telephone, one thought haunted him: if Lipschitz had been murdered because of his relationship with Saul and the Mendelsohns, then certainly the names Fields, Juno, and Tracy were high on the killer's list.

There was no answer at the house. He raced for the car.

His hand on the doorknob, Juno glanced over his shoulder, first to the right, then to the left, and then down Gardner Street toward Carey Square. There was no light blue sedan—only the snow and the darkness. With the annoying realization that looking over his shoulder was now a routine but necessary fact of life, he pushed open the door.

The bright light in the hall caused him to blink, but it gave him a feeling of security. "Josh! We're leaving. I'll explain on the way." He shouted loudly enough so that his voice carried throughout the house. Walking into the empty kitchen and then into the living room, bare except for an aging sofa they hadn't been able to sell, he checked to be certain they hadn't forgotten anything. He was into the dining room before it hit him. Stopping short, he cocked his head and listened. The silence was oppressive; there had been no answer, only an echo. His muscles tightened. Without moving, he shouted again; still no response. Josh must have returned and gone out again. The thought annoyed him because he wanted to get started for New York immediately and worried him because Josh might be anywhere, totally unaware of potential danger. Walking back into the hall, he stood at the foot of the stairs; called again; and when he received no answer, decided to get on with the preparations for leaving.

Almost everything had been put away on the first floor; only the hall closet and the upstairs remained to be checked. Casually he slid open the closet door. It was empty except for his brother's overcoat. The overcoat! It was the only one Josh had brought with him. Panicked, he flew up the stairs in giant leaps, pulling himself forward and upward by the banister. The guest room was empty; so were the two smaller bedrooms.

He found his brother in the master bedroom, their parents' room. His scream caused the walls to vibrate.

Joshua Fields lay face down on the floor. The back of his blood-soaked jacket was torn apart by three gaping holes where the bullets had exited, scattering fragments of bone and bits of flesh throughout the room.

Juno forced himself back to reality. With small, awkward steps he approached the body, knelt beside it, and ran the back of his hand across the bloodstained cheek. He seemed to feel the last remnants of warmth fade beneath his touch. Removing his brother's glasses from beneath his forehead, he turned them over between his fingers—the frames were intact, but the lenses were smashed; he held them to his breast and wept until his whole body shook.

He vowed he would find a way out of this nightmarish maze and destroy those responsible for it. He knew he was a good cop, yet that was not enough. He needed help—not only from Renée but also from those who would give it freely and without reservation because their lives, too, were at stake: the Israelis. He would find a way to get to them.

Knowing he should touch nothing, he nevertheless could not leave his brother lying in a pool of blood. He carefully rolled the body on its back.

He shuddered, blinked in a futile attempt to make the scene disappear, and screamed again with anguish and hatred beyond the limits of human comprehension. Pinned to a ragged edge of Josh's jacket near the wound that had torn open his left chest was a Star of David cut from a piece of heavy yellow construction paper. The word *"Jude"* was scrawled across it in blood.

7

Josh's funeral left Juno empty. Mechanically he went through the motions of what had to be done, and then he drove back to New York.

Keeping to his decision to stay away from his own apartment, he called Renée from a phone booth at the corner of Eighth Avenue and Forty-seventh Street. She had moved temporarily to the apartment of a friend who was in Europe, as he had instructed her to do, and he arranged to meet her there. It was safer to make the next call from a different booth. He found one on the corner of Forty-eighth Street and Broadway, placed his call, and waited.

"I have your party, sir," the operator said.

"Mr. Cohen?" Juno covered his left ear to block out the sounds of traffic and pressed the phone closer to his right.

"Yes?"

"This is Peter Juno. You said to call if I needed anything."

"What can I do for you, Mr. Juno?"

"I need ten thousand dollars."

As executor of Saul's estate, Cohen had informed Juno that there would be close to half a million dollars when Saul's business was sold. Although Juno had intended to donate the entire sum to Columbia Medical School, he was becoming more aware that wars—private and public—cost a great deal of money;

he would spend it all, if necessary, to get those responsible for Josh's death.

"No problem. Give me the name of your bank, and I'll have the funds forwarded immediately. It'll take overnight for the draft to clear. Anything else?"

"No. That's all for now. Please send the money to the Manufacturers Hanover Trust; the account's in my name."

"Certainly. Look, Mr. Juno . . ." Cohen hesitated. "I know you don't know me well, but your father and I were good friends; I'm aware of how he felt about you. With Josh gone, you're Saul's only heir. Although the will has to be probated, I can advance you whatever you need within reason; Saul made provisions for that."

"Thanks, Mr. Cohen." As Juno hung up, there was a burning sensation in his throat; and tears filled his eyes. Saul was still looking out for him.

Stepping out into the cold air, he headed for a phone booth across the street.

The ballistics division of the Chelsea Police Department told him nothing he hadn't already suspected: the bullets that had killed both Lipschitz and Fields had been fired from a Luger. He arranged to have the slugs sent to New York for comparison with those that had been recovered from the bodies of Golding, Goldstein, and Ben Levi.

The pathologist at Chelsea Memorial Hospital who had performed the autopsies for the medical examiner of Suffolk County agreed to forward his reports to him when completed.

There was nothing more he could do for the moment, so he hailed a cab.

Renée kissed him warmly, gently drew him into the entrance hall, and held him tightly as he buried his face in her shoulder. "Take off your coat and sit down. I've made us a drink." She swallowed hard and bit her lip to keep it from trembling. His face was drawn, and the lines that usually gave it a chiseled appearance now only accentuated the look of fatigue; there was a hollow grayness to the skin below his eyes, and the lids were heavy with sorrow.

She helped him off with his coat and jacket, loosened his tie, brought him his drink, and settled herself on the floor in front of him. "Feel up to telling me what happened?"

In a monotone Juno related the events that had occurred from the time he met Josh at the Presbyterian Emergency Room until he returned to New York City late that morning. ". . . the connection between the neurologic illness of my father and Mrs. Mendelsohn—neither of whom had been in Dachau and neither of whom had the scar—and that of the others appears to be the fact that *both* of them were *exposed* to *Mr.* Mendelsohn; *he* had been in Dachau, and *he* had the scar!"

"Wait a minute," Renée interrupted. "Are you trying to tell me this disease is contagious?"

"I don't know. I've also considered the possibility that it might be inherited; but I just don't know enough about that kind of thing."

She shook her head in disbelief. "My God! *A fatal disease that is passed from Jew to Jew!*" She shuddered. "And Dachau? The scars?"

Juno summarized the conversation he had had with Joshua Fields after seeing Eva Schonberg's body, then turned to the present. "Anything on Ben Levi yet?"

"No. I'm almost ready to believe he never existed."

"He existed all right. There's a body in the morgue to prove it. I'd give a month's salary to know what he wanted from Josh."

"I'll keep working on it, but I think you should take some time off."

"No. I want to get back to work. Have you spoken to Davis?"

"Just once. He wants us to devote our time exclusively to the Golding, Goldstein, and Ben Levi cases." She hesitated. "He wanted me to give you a message. . . ."

Juno sat up and looked at her suspiciously.

"He extends his sympathy but stresses that there are to be no vendettas. He'd like you to call him."

"Later."

"Come on, Pete. I think he's trying to be reasonable. Why antagonize him?"

"Because right now I don't trust *anyone*—except you, that is. And I won't until I know what's going on."

"But he's the police commissioner."

"Which means he knows exactly what you and I do, and when. From now on, we're going to make certain *no one* does. Has anyone else been asking questions?"

"Only Dr. Mann."

"What the hell did *he* want?" There was an element of hatred in Juno's voice.

"To check our progress."

"What'd you tell him?"

"There wasn't anything to tell."

"Fine. Let's keep it that way."

She shrugged. "Someday you're going to have to talk to someone about whatever's between you and Mann. Why not tell me? I care."

Juno rubbed the bridge of his nose and felt the tightness in his throat and the moistness in the corners of his eyes. He knew she was right.

Without looking at her, he told her about the night in the town outside of Athens: the pounding on the door, his father's cries for help as the men in the black uniforms dragged him out, threw him down the stairs, and hurled him against the wall across the alley. As Juno spoke, he could still hear his mother's screams as she ran after them. He clenched his fists. There were two volleys from SS pistols: the first cut his father down; the second tore into his mother's back as she raced to him. He shivered, and tears ran freely down his cheeks and into the corners of his mouth. He wanted to scream, but he did not; he bit his lip until it bled. Instinctively he put his hands over his ears to blot out the sound of the gunfire and of the vicious laugh of the man who stood over his parents. And in the dim light of the alley, he saw it: the twisted cross of black stark against the white disk on a scarlet arm band—and he never forgot.

He licked at the tears and with the back of his hand wiped away the blood from his mouth. For years he had suppressed the painful memory beneath the love Deborah and Saul and Josh had given him. Now they were gone—all of them; but it was the manner in which Josh had died that had stripped away the last remnants of his self-control.

As she listened, Renée began to understand. It was not Mann, the individual, whom Peter Juno despised; but Mann, the German. A German finger had pulled the trigger that had killed his parents; and the small boy who had watched it happen was incapable of anything but an all-consuming, undiminishing hatred. The intensity of the pain had been assuaged by time and love; but Josh's murder had reopened the wound and left it raw, perhaps beyond repair.

She ran her hand lightly over his cheek, turned his tear-stained face to hers, and kissed him gently. "I'm glad you told me," she said.

Tsve Shem and Mordecai Grossman stood in the shadows of the doorway and watched the light go out in the window on the fourth floor. They were still smarting from the reprimand they had received from their superiors earlier in the day. Both knew that the criticism was justified.

Despite the fact that the Israeli government had a price on Penzel's head, they had been specifically directed to avoid overt actions. Not only had Penzel escaped from them; but if he had recognized them, their entire operation might be in jeopardy. Furthermore, in their eagerness to find Asher Ben Levi's killer, they had been lax in their surveillance of Joshua Fields. Their mission now had but one objective—to watch Peter Juno and to report in detail the progress of his investigation. Neither Shem nor Grossman knew why the Golding and Goldstein murders were relevant, but neither had dared to ask.

Both men discarded their cigarettes and stepped farther back into the shadows as a man in a trench coat emerged from the stairwell directly across the street. They watched him cautiously . . . and waited.

Juno found the world unbearable. Time did not seem to pass, for every second was filled with identical pain; and this phenomenon made him restless and angry and occasionally manifested itself in irrational outbursts that caused him to question his ability to go on. Despite his relationship with Renée, the predominant sensations that persisted through it all were an overwhelming feeling of loneliness and a sense of loss. Nevertheless, he finally forced himself to attend to Josh's personal effects in New York.

* * *

"Sorry about your brother." The uniformed man held the door for Juno. "Dr. Fields was a real gentleman. Don't see too many of them these days."

"I guess not." Juno turned away. He had been dreading this visit to Josh's apartment, and the conversation wasn't making it any easier for him.

"Think you'll move in? Your brother always told me he wanted you to come live with him." The man accompanied him toward the elevator.

"No, I don't think so. I've already got a place."

"Want to sublease Dr. Fields's apartment? I have someone who might be interested."

"Not yet. I'll just leave it the way it is for now. . . . How'd you hear about my brother?"

"Funny thing. Just a few minutes ago, a fellow who was going to visit some people on the seventeenth floor—Apartment 1733, I think he said—told me he had heard about Dr. Fields's death. Wanted to know if his apartment was for rent."

"Specifically my brother's apartment?" Juno fought to maintain his composure; this was a time for caution, not folly.

"Yup."

"What'd this guy look like?"

The doorman paused to think. "He was a big man. Nothing else about him made him stick in my mind."

"Thanks." Juno was grateful for the elevator's arrival. He waited for the double doors to close, put his hand inside his coat, and checked for his gun. This time he was prepared.

When the elevator reached Josh's floor, Juno removed the revolver from its holster and released the safety. He felt a surge of strength with it in his hand, and he began to function as he had been trained to do. He looked in both directions, found the hallway empty, and walked slowly toward Joshua Fields's apartment, his back firmly against the wall, his footsteps muffled by the rug. As he approached the side of the door, he reached out, covered the peephole with his hand, and pressed his ear against the cold wood beneath it; there was no sound from within. Using the side of his shoe, he flattened the carpeting in front of the threshold; no light emerged from the narrow space between it and the bottom of the door.

No longer making any attempt to be quiet, he unlocked the door, turned the knob, felt it give, and stepped back against the wall. It was an old trick. If there were an assailant, he would take his position for the attack—behind the door—only after he heard it start to open in a normal fashion; to do so prematurely exposed him to the risk of having it smashed in his face. By delaying, Juno hoped to entice the intruder—if indeed someone were waiting for him—to become impatient. He would now be at the peephole to see what had happened to the person who had unlocked the door.

Juno counted slowly to thirty and then, with a sudden burst of force, kicked the door open and rushed into the foyer. There was a loud crack as the knob hit the wall, and then silence. Feet apart, knees bent, weapon ready, he turned in all directions. No one came at him through the darkness. Sweat pouring from his forehead and down his spine, he continued to wait, ready to kill, wanting to kill, hoping to kill the man he was certain had taken his brother's life. His breath came in gasps; his heart drummed in his chest; the hair on the back of his neck bristled. But there was no one.

He began a systematic search of the apartment. Everything appeared untouched and in its normal place, and he chided himself for overreacting to what might well have been an innocent inquiry. Setting the safety on his revolver, he replaced it in its holster and walked back into the kitchen. Dreading the task ahead, he took his time poking around the cabinets and drawers; finding a few cans of beer in the refrigerator, he drained one, opened another, set it on the dining-room table, and began the unpleasant job of taking inventory. He started with the foyer closet.

The man came at him from behind the wall of clothes as he opened the door. It was a well-timed, vicious attack that caught him totally unprepared. The man was fast and agile; before Juno had a chance to recover, he found himself immobilized. In a matter of seconds his attacker had forced him to his knees and now stood behind him with his forearm around his neck and his knee against his back. Juno cursed himself for his carelessness. He made one last attempt to wrench the arm from his neck, but his effort only caused his opponent to tighten his hold until Juno was certain his Adam's apple was being pushed up into his throat and that his spine was on the verge of snapping. A wave of lightheadedness spread upward, but one thought kept him from surrendering to oblivion: if his assailant had meant to kill him, why hadn't he fired at him from the closet?

"Who are you and what the hell are you doing here?" It was a coarse, angry whisper, spoken with an unfathomable accent; but the man obviously meant Juno to answer, for he released his grip sufficiently for his vocal cords to move again.

"Fuck you, you bastard!" There was almost no sound from his bruised larynx. Before he had time to utter another syllable, he felt himself being flung to the floor. His forehead burned as the force of the thrust ground his face into the carpet. Picking himself up, he tried to shake off the effects of the fall.

"Turn around . . . slowly! Butt on the floor, knees up, hands folded around them. Wiggle your little finger the wrong way, and I'll blow it off!"

Juno swore silently as he felt the absence of weight beneath his left armpit. Under other circumstances he might have admired the man's ability to throw him and remove the revolver from its shoulder holster in one motion—this person was as slick a pro as he had ever encountered. He did as he was told and had his first unobstructed view of his asssailant. He was tall and well-built, perhaps six-foot-two, two hundred pounds; there was not an ounce of fat or excess weight on the muscular frame that was clearly evident through his coat. Ruggedly good-looking, he appeared to be in his mid- to late thirties. He had short auburn hair; darker eyebrows; brown, somber eyes; a broad but not excessively large nose; thin lips that reflected determination and purpose; and a prominent chin. His large hands with their well-manicured fingernails suggested that he was not someone who usually did his own dirty work.

Juno found the fact that he was threatened by his own weapon rather than the expected Luger evoked a certain boldness in him. "Who are you?"

"Since I have the gun, I'll ask the questions first. Who are *you?* And why are you searching Dr. Fields's apartment?"

"I'm Dr. Fields's brother."

"Your name?"

"Juno. Peter Juno." He tensed slightly as he realized how incongruous his answer must have sounded. "I've got some identification in my pocket if you'd care to see it."

"No need for that. I recognize the name. Josh spoke of you often." The man smiled, held out his hand as if to help him get up, and laughed as he saw Juno eyeing the revolver. "Sorry." He reversed the position of the weapon and offered it to Juno handle first.

Juno hesitated, took the gun, and stood up without bothering to grasp the outstretched hand. "You obviously knew my brother. Who are you? And how the hell did you get in here?"

"Ari Sokolov. Three years in an Israeli commando unit and five in Israeli Intelligence teaches you a lot about opening locks." He grinned.

Juno thought for a moment. "Sokolov! Josh mentioned you; he was going to get in touch with you. You're the man who's interested in diseases that affect Jews."

"Josh did get in touch with me. He called from Chelsea just before your father's funeral."

"Did he tell you about his theory that there might be some connection between this neurologic disease and the Nazi concentration camps?"

"Yes. He seemed convinced that there was a direct relationship. I've been looking into it."

"And?"

"It seems he was right. But I'm getting ahead of myself. Let me start from the beginning." Sitting back, Sokolov lit a cigarette. "For some time now, my major interest has been learning more about diseases that are seen predominantly in Jews. In fact, I wrote my master's thesis on the subject. About five years ago, I came to New York and set up a small organization, the International Society for the Study of Genetic Diseases in Jews. It is mostly supported by private donations. We've got seven people working at our office. For administrative purposes, the home office is in Jerusalem; but ours is really the center of the operation.

"After Josh called, I contacted our offices throughout Europe. There's data to support your brother's hypothesis. I was supposed to meet with him when he got back to New York; but when I heard he'd been killed, I came here to see if he'd left any notes that might help."

"How did you know he was dead?"

"The two agents who had been assigned to watch him notified Jerusalem he had been killed. I was told shortly thereafter."

"Do they know who killed him?" Juno felt his muscles tighten.

"No, but they're checking; they have sources your police force doesn't."

"I want to know of any leads they turn up."

"I'll see what I can do. Anything else before I go on?" Sokolov crushed out his cigarette in the ashtray.

"No. But I'll probably have questions later."

"What we have so far is what appears to be an atypical type of acute degenerative disease of the central nervous system that seems to be affecting only Jews. I agree with your brother that the murders of those two men . . ."

"Golding and Goldstein?" Juno tensed. Why had Sokolov not mentioned Asher Ben Levi? It was unlikely that Josh had neglected to tell him about the physician's murder.

"Yes . . . Golding and Goldstein. They were probably shot to stop them from revealing some clue."

"And Josh? Why was he killed?"

"To keep him from finding out what the disease is."

Juno frowned. "You haven't told me anything I didn't know."

"Then let me fill you in on the most recent statistics. The disease has now been recognized worldwide. It seems to have a very characteristic clinical course. Over a thousand people have died from it—all Jews. Seventeen percent had been in Dachau; sixty-three percent of those had the scar on their left side. It appears that the disease is increasing in frequency; it must, therefore, be quickly identified and stopped."

Juno got up and poured two beers. "Tell me something about Jewish genetic diseases."

Sokolov took the beer and sipped it slowly. "In order to understand, you've got to know something about the Jews. Their early pedigree was characterized by intramarriage and incest; between 1350 and 800 B.C., a common gene pool probably existed among them. However, the purity of their genetic foundation began to decline during several key periods. First the Assyrians, then the Babylonians, and finally the Greeks and Romans conquered them and took them into captivity, so that by A.D. 70 they were scattered throughout the Roman Empire. In 1492, at the height of the Spanish Inquisition, they were expelled and migrated to North Africa, to other parts of Europe, and back to Palestine. In the last three centuries, persecution sent waves of Jews to North America. Some did move east, however, and settled in Palestine. You know the modern history, of course.

"The dispersion, assimilation, and intermarriage of the Jews," Sokolov continued, "have made them relatively heterogeneous from a genetic point of view. Nevertheless, there are still certain diseases of genetic origin that are more common in Jews. Tay-Sachs disease, a fatal inherited metabolic disorder, is probably the best known; but about a dozen have been identified."

"Amazing, isn't it?" Juno drained the last of the beer. "The conviction that Jews should marry only Jews has always been one of the predominant means of ensuring their survival."

"Exactly." Sokolov lit another cigarette. "It is a striking paradox: the very strength of the Jews has created a startling weakness in them."

"Could someone—a very sophisticated geneticist, for example—take advantage of a specific weakness in the genetic makeup of the Jews to create the disease?"

"It's conceivable."

"Could such a thing have been done in the 1940's . . . at Dachau?"

Sokolov did not answer immediately. "No, I don't think so," he said. "The science of genetics was hardly developed at that time."

"Then how do you tie in Dachau and that scar?"

"I can't. Maybe the disease is a quirk of nature or a medical experiment gone wild."

"In other words, what we're seeing may not be a *deliberate* plot against the Jews."

"Yes, that's right. But that doesn't explain the murders." Sokolov rubbed his chin and looked away as if searching for the answer in the tiers of smoke rising slowly toward the ceiling.

"I have one more question," Juno said.

"Yes?"

"A while back you mentioned the deaths of two men, Golding and Goldstein. There was a third . . ."

"I know: Asher Ben Levi. Killed by the same Luger on the same evening as Golding and Goldstein."

"Why didn't you mention him?"

"I'm not permitted to say too much about him. Evidently he encountered the disease on his kibbutz and suspected what was happening; because he trusted your brother, it seems he decided to seek his help."

"Without telling anyone?"

"We're not sure. He spent a day in Jerusalem and two in Tel Aviv before he left, but no official sources were notified of his concern or his trip."

"Then you think he was killed because he knew of the disease?"

"I'm not permitted . . ."

"Why not? What the hell is going on?"

"The question of Asher Ben Levi is totally out of my hands."

"Well, it's not out of mine! He was killed at Kennedy Airport, and it's the New York City Police Department's responsibility to investigate his death. I'm going to find out who he was, why he was killed, and how his murder is related to the other deaths—one of which, if you will remember, happened to be that of my brother."

"I understand. Give me a day or two. Perhaps I can get authorization to tell you more."

"From whom?"

"From the prime minister of Israel."

Juno sat back, stunned. "Then what do we do now?"

"We try to find a way to identify and stop this disease before it progresses much further. Can you get a few days off?"

"No. But I don't have to report in, so if you need me . . ."

"Good. You're going to Switzerland."

"But why?"

"Because we need help, and I want you to meet the people who are going to give it to us. That's all you have to know for the moment." Sokolov picked up a pad of paper and a pen and began to write. "Take this flight out of Kennedy. Stay at the Dolder Grand in Zurich. Travel under a false name; I'll arrange it.

You'll be contacted once you get there." He started to put on his coat. "Whatever you do, *be careful!* Tell as few people as possible about your trip, and *no one* the specific details. And for God's sake, don't mention our conversation to anyone. It's imperative that no word gets out about the disease."

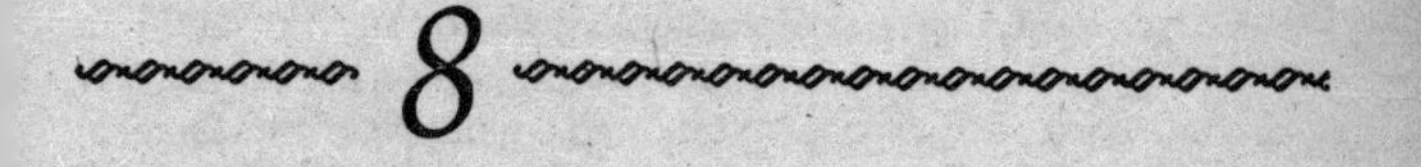

8

Reichmann slammed the clip into the Luger, placed the gun in his center desk drawer, and glared at Penzel seated in front of him. "Juno is still alive," he said, "and the Israelis are breathing down our necks—"

"I told you: it was snowing, and the car windows were fogged up. How did I know the old man and not Juno was in the driver's seat?" Penzel had turned away from Reichmann. Now he looked at him boldly.

"You are *supposed* to know!"

Penzel felt himself redden. He leaned forward so that one hand rested firmly on the edge of the desk. "I've never failed before, but that's because *I* was allowed to make the plans. If anyone's to blame, it's *you!* You give the orders and expect them to be carried out instantaneously. But you can't point your finger at a New York City police lieutenant and say, 'Kill him,' and expect it to happen just like that." Penzel snapped his fingers. "These days it's just not that simple. You want something done? Fine. Tell me what and give me the time to do it properly. And please—keep your Luger! The police aren't amateurs; let *us* not act like amateurs. Fool them, confuse them, send them on a wild goose chase . . ."

Reichmann sighed. "Why is it that fools can never admit failure? They can only give reasons why they did not succeed."

Penzel glared angrily at the man behind the desk. "I told you—"

Reichmann held up his hand. "You've said enough! Now shut up and listen! You shoot two helpless doctors, and you want an Iron Cross. I could have sent a schoolboy to do *that*. But send you out to eliminate a man with a little cunning, and what do you do? You come back with excuses. You catch a glimpse of two Israelis, and you run." He paused and pyramided his hands in front of him. "Unfortunately, I have to make do with what's available; there's too much for one man to do alone."

Penzel forced himself to remain calm. "Despite my angry words, Herr Reichmann, I wish to be of service to you and the Party."

"And you shall." Reichmann reached into his desk.

Pleased by his reprieve, Penzel sat back in his chair and reached for a glass of wine. The first bullet hit him in the neck, the second in the chest just above the left nipple.

Juno made the dinner reservation at Barbetta's for six o'clock. Fettucini, rack of lamb, and fresh strawberries left them satisfied; and they drank their coffee silently, content just to be together, until the waiter brought the check.

Smiling sadly, Renée pushed her chair back. "I'll drive you to the airport."

"No. Please don't. I'll feel better if I know you're safe at the apartment." He caught her gently by the wrist. "Please sit down for a moment. We've got time."

She looked at him questioningly.

"I just wanted to say thanks."

"For what?"

"It's been a bad time for me; Saul and Josh were all the family I had. I don't think I would have made it through all of this if it hadn't been for you. . . ."

"That's what friends are for."

"You're more than a friend."

She placed her hand over his. "I'd like to be."

"You are. When this is over—"

She put her finger against his lips. "When it is, then we'll talk. I'll be here."

* * *

"Flight 101 departs from Gate 33 at 10:05; it will start boarding at 9:30." The girl behind the Swissair counter handed Juno his boarding pass.

Sokolov had given him a passport in the name of Robert Sears, and he cleared security without incident. In the boarding area, he scanned the faces of the passengers; there seemed to be no one concerned about him. He was especially cautious because he was again traveling without his service revolver, but this time it was not by choice but rather to maintain his cover—airport security would accept no reason for Robert Sears to be armed. Sokolov had assured him that he would be provided with a weapon in Zurich.

He glanced at his watch; there was enough time to try Ballistics before boarding. What Roger Baldini had to tell him was no surprise: the bullets that had killed his brother and Henry Lipschitz matched those recovered from Golding, Goldstein, and Ben Levi.

"I suspected as much. Anything else?"

"I have an urgent message for you to call Dr. Joy at home."

"What the hell does he want?"

"I don't know. Do you want his number or not?"

"Might as well give it to me." He noted the pathologist's number on the back of his boarding envelope.

"I haven't had a chance to tell you how sorry I am about your dad and your brother. If there's anything I can do . . ."

"Thanks, Roger." Juno hung up and dialed again. The line was busy. He swore silently and tried one more time unsuccessfully and decided that whatever Dr. Joy had to tell him could wait until his return.

For the first time in days, as events began to move more rapidly, Juno felt stimulated. He had two drinks after the plane reached cruising altitude and ate the late supper with gusto.

At first, the man in the aisle seat beside him, a young chemist from an industrial plant in Winterthur, near Zurich, worried him. The man's blond hair, gray-blue eyes, and sharp features were a bit too Aryan; but his pleasant smile and the warmth of his broken English mixed with Swiss-Deutsch allayed most of Juno's fears. They exchanged small talk until the lights were dimmed for the movie.

Juno loosened his tie, removed his shoes, and settled himself on the pillow propped against the window. Excited by the prospect of his meeting in Zurich, he found sleep difficult; and as he shifted restlessly, he was unaware of the scrutinizing glances of the man next to him.

The Zurich-Kloten Airport was crowded, and Juno had trouble following the signs. Still concerned about his safety, he examined the faces around him as he waited. He stiffened suddenly and spun around as he felt someone grab his arm from behind.

"Sorry. I did not mean to startle you. I saw that you were having some problem with the signs, and I thought I might help." It was the man who had sat next to him on the plane.

"Thank you." Juno scolded himself for overreacting; his survival depended on his newly assumed identity, and there was no reason for Mr. Sears to be nervous. "I guess my German isn't as good as I thought."

The man laughed. "I will translate for you. In fact, I have a car here at the airport; perhaps you will allow me to give you a lift. Where are you staying?"

Juno felt the muscles in the back of his neck tighten. "Someone is supposed to meet me."

"Fine. But if no one appears, I will be glad to drive you."

They cleared passport control and retrieved their luggage. Juno reassured his newly acquired companion that he was now quite capable of fending for himself and bid him good-bye. He stopped in the men's room, waited awhile, and then went to find transportation.

At first he paid no attention to the small gathering of people in front of the currency exchange window, but the high-pitched screech of a police whistle and the sight of two uniformed men approaching at a run from the far end of the terminal caused him to stop. Trying to appear no more than a curious onlooker, he edged his way toward the group now distinctly forming a circle around something in their midst and peered in. The sight made him recoil. The Swiss chemist was stretched out grotesquely on the floor, blood pouring from his forehead. He had been shot once; the marksman was a professional.

Badly shaken, Juno turned and walked quickly toward the exit. With growing apprehension he identified himself to the uniformed driver standing beside the limousine with the crest of the Dolder Grand Hotel on its side, got in, and slid down into the seat. It was obvious that the chemist was not who he said he was. But who was he? And who had killed him . . . and why? The boldness of carrying out the execution in a crowded airport had demonstrated to Juno that his adversaries could strike swiftly and unexpectedly at any time. He would have to be careful. He shuddered as the car pulled away from the curb and into the traffic heading toward Zurich.

The Dolder Grand, easily one of Zurich's most deluxe, typified the outstanding hotels of Switzerland. Unaccustomed to the graciousness displayed by everyone from the driver to the desk clerk, Juno felt somewhat uncomfortable and out-of-place and almost signed the register in his own name rather than that of Robert Sears. There were no messages waiting for him. He went directly to his room.

Like the rest of the hotel, the bedroom and its adjoining sitting area were tastefully furnished. A glass door led to a small balcony that overlooked a gravel path leading into snow-covered woods; he checked to be certain that it was inaccessible from the ground and that the door could be securely locked, and then called room service.

A pleasant waiter brought his lunch and set it out on the coffee table. He ate leisurely, then showered and shaved, and stretched out on the bed for a nap.

When he awoke, the room was dark; it took him a moment to get his bearings. Through the windows he could see heavy snow falling, illuminated by spotlights scattered throughout the grounds of the hotel. Stretching lazily, he gathered the comforter around him to enjoy its warmth, but sat up suddenly and reached for the phone. The concierge informed him that it was just past seven P.M. and that there had been no calls or messages for him. With mounting concern that something had gone wrong, he nevertheless concluded that he had no choice but to be patient; so he went downstairs to dinner.

The dining room exceeded his expectations. He enjoyed the meal and lingered over coffee and dessert until jet lag overtook him. On the way back to his room, he stopped at the concierge's desk to check for messages; there were still none. Faced with no plans for the next day and knowing he could not tolerate another prolonged period of inactivity, he weighed his alternatives.

"Your first time in Switzerland, Herr Sears?"

The question startled him. "Yes."

Laughing, the concierge answered Juno's unasked question. "It is part of my job to remember the names of our guests."

"It's a beautiful country."

"You will see just how beautiful on your tour tomorrow."

"I will?" Juno looked at him with guarded curiosity.

"Of course! The Rhine Falls is one of the most outstanding attractions in our area." Noting his guest's surprise, the concierge excused himself momentarily, checked a page in a looseleaf appointment book, and returned. "The car will pick you up at nine A.M. in front of the hotel to take you there, with a return trip via Schaffhausen. It is a private tour; they are the best. Although the weather is cold, you should enjoy yourself. Just dress warmly."

"I'm sure I'll find it most interesting." There were a dozen questions he wanted to ask, but he restrained himself.

"Would you like a wake-up call?"

"Yes. Seven thirty." Juno headed back to his room. Apprehensive but excited, he was anxious for morning to come now that contact had been made.

His exhilaration ended abruptly at the door to his room. A piece of transparent tape he had placed across the bottom of the door had been torn. Cautiously he unlocked the door and entered. He saw the made-up bed with its turned covers, folded comforter, and a piece of Swiss chocolate lying on his pillow next to a menu for ordering breakfast, and laughed aloud. The maid! Still, remembering his encounter with Sokolov, he began to search the room. As he felt beneath the pillow, his fingers touched cold steel. He hit the floor face down. Nothing happened. After a few moments he sat up and carefully removed the pillow. The weapon was a .38 revolver similar to his own. Next to it was a box of shells and a handwritten note: "Have a good trip. Ari."

Not knowing whether to swear or laugh, Juno replaced the gun under the pillow, hung up his jacket, loosened his tie, took off his shoes, and lay down to relax until it was time to call Renée.

At two A.M. he placed the long-distance call, but there was no answer; he smiled at the thought of Renée working late. After two more unsuccessful attempts, however, his amusement changed to concern; but he chided himself for his emotionalism. It was for just this reason that they had agreed to limit their involvement with one another. Right now it was essential that each concentrate on the job; there would be time when he returned to reassess their arrangement.

Fatigue overtook him. He would call her tomorrow.

The Peugeot headed away from the city toward the German border. Bright sunlight and the smell of cold air stimulated Juno and gave him a feeling of limitless energy. The driver, a dark-haired, dark-skinned Italian named Pietro, speaking English with a heavy accent, pointed out the landmarks.

The trip to the Rhine Falls took about an hour; it was just past ten o'clock when they pulled into a large parking lot abutting a small souvenir and concession stand. Pietro led Juno up a narrow cobblestone street into a small building that doubled as a ticket office and gift shop, then down stone steps to a small overlook. Juno marveled at the view above him, where the river picked up speed and then crashed downward almost sixty feet over a precipitous shelf and onto rugged reefs of rock. For a fleeting moment he forgot why he was there until Pietro prodded him forward and pointed to another observation deck on top of one of the large rocky formations in the middle of the falls.

"We'll take the boat." Pietro indicated a small craft rolling in the current toward a concrete landing platform at the base of the rocks. "Your friends will meet you at the top."

Sitting on opposite sides of the boat on the two parallel benches behind the captain, the two men barely spoke although they were alone. The trip was rough; they bounced through the current, made a short stop on the far shore, and then headed into the turbulence at the bottom of the falls to the landing at the base of the rocks.

The steps leading to the observation point were steep and wet, with occasional patches of ice. Clinging to the handrail, Juno was amazed at Pietro's dexterity and stamina. Breathless, they reached the top and rested against the rail. A burly man in a fleece-lined jacket was the only other occupant of the rock platform; he appeared to be interested in nothing but the adjustments on his camera. Juno pulled up his collar as he watched the small boat make its way back through the torrents of water below them. There was no one waiting for it on either side of the river.

The roar of the water made it almost impossible to hear. Juno found himself becoming increasingly impatient as the cold wind mixed with the icy spray began to numb him. Turning to the driver, Juno started to shout, but stopped abruptly as the man's body suddenly shuddered. Pietro grabbed the side of his head, staggered, and fell against Juno, knocking him backward against the rail. As they slid to the ground, the image of the man in the fleece-lined jacket, a smoking revolver in his hand, flooded Juno's vision. A lancinating pain crossed his right cheek as a bullet smashed into the railing beside him. Reacting automatically, with total disregard of the searing pain in his left shoulder as the man's third shot tore into him, Juno ripped his right glove off with his teeth, pushed himself away from the awkward weight of Pietro's body, reached for his gun, rolled over once, and came up with his finger squeezing the trigger. His first bullet hit his assailant in the neck and hurled him backward against the guardrail; the second tore open the center of his jacket above the left breast and scattered fleece over the stream of blood. With uncontrolled hate he fired again and again and watched fascinated as the man's body leaped with the impact of each bullet. Only the click of the hammer caused him to stop. Without moving, the revolver still held tightly in his outstretched hand, he stared at the motionless corpse draped over the railing. Rising to one knee, he grabbed his left arm; the movement sent a wave of pain through his shoulder and neck. A trickle of blood spread over his fingers and spilled onto the ice at his feet. He stuffed his handkerchief into his sleeve to stop the bleeding, then reloaded his gun, put it in his pocket, and bent down to Pietro.

"Thank you, my friend." Pietro reached up and squeezed Juno's hand.

"You okay?"

"It's just a flesh wound. The wind must have spoiled his aim. And you?"

"Same. Who the hell was he?" Juno nodded toward the man he had just killed.

"I don't know, but he knew we were going to be here. The others must have found out there was a security leak, but too late to warn us."

"I thought you people were supposed to be pros."

"We are." Holding his head with one hand, Pietro got up on one knee. "But so are they."

After ministering to each other as best they could, they searched the dead man for identification, found none, and together pushed his body over the railing into the waters below.

His left arm hanging loosely in a makeshift sling, Juno followed Pietro down the stairs to wait for the boat.

The surgeon was extremely capable, a carefully chosen friend of Pietro. He unquestioningly agreed to inform no one of their wounds. It was almost five P.M. before they left the clinic.

As they drove toward the airport, Pietro told Juno what he was to do. "You can't go back to the hotel; I'll have your luggage delivered to you. You have a flight to Paris at seven: Swissair flight 708. I've already made the reservation. Clean yourself up before you get on the plane; you're a bloody mess."

"But why Paris?" Juno asked.

"The people you were supposed to meet are there. There *was* a security leak; that's why they didn't come to Zurich. We must all be extremely cautious these days."

At the entrance to the main terminal of the Zurich-Kloten Airport, Juno shook hands with the man and thanked him.

"Shalom, my Greek friend," Pietro said.

Juno watched the Peugeot until it disappeared around a bend.

"Shalom, Pietro." Juno found his eyes blurred by tears. A certain closeness developed between men who had faced death together. "Shalom." He repeated the word silently to himself and headed for the men's room.

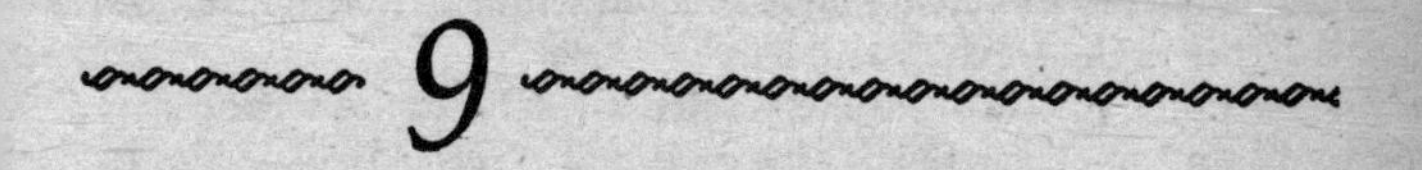

9

Situated on the left bank of the Seine on the quai de Grenelle, the Hotel Nikko de Paris was in every way the antithesis of the Dolder Grand. Its starkly modern design was enhanced by bright colors, geometric shapes, and an extensive use of marble, glass, and chrome.

Ignoring the curious stares at his injured arm, Juno checked in and immediately went to his room. Undressing for bed was more of a chore than he had anticipated since his shoulder, now cleanly sutured and tightly bandaged, was almost immobile; but a sedative and two drinks were enough to put him to sleep.

At exactly eleven A.M. the telephone rang. A man with a harsh voice and a heavy Israeli accent verified Juno's identity by asking him his place of birth, the name of his brother, and his father's surname when Juno first met him; recited a series of cryptic orders; and then hung up.

Following the directions he had been given, Juno took a taxi from the hotel to the Place de la Concorde, waited five minutes, hailed another cab to take him to the front of the Hotel Grand, and then a third to drop him in the center of Montmartre. With little difficulty he found the café he was seeking, proceeded to the second floor, and knocked briskly on the door of the last room on the left.

The door was opened cautiously by a tall, well-built, sandy-haired man who introduced himself as Gerald Yashon, shook Juno's hand, led him into a sparsely furnished sitting room, and took his coat. Another man and a woman Juno estimated to be in her early thirties sat at a table covered with a simple white cloth.

"This is Dr. Davide, and . . ."

Stepping forward, Juno extended his hand to the second man.

"I am Mikal Har-Even," the man said. "*This* is Dr. Davide. Dr. *Lori* Davide." He gestured toward the woman beside him.

"It's a pleasure to meet you, Mr. Juno." She smiled good-naturedly. "I've heard that Greek men are male chauvinists; now I'm convinced." She took his hand. "I knew your brother. He was not only a fine physician but also an exceptional human being; we shall all miss him." Sitting down, she motioned to Juno to sit beside her.

Mikal poured each of them a glass of wine, and Juno was given a brief introduction into their backgrounds. It was obvious that they already knew a great deal about him.

A sabra born in Tel Aviv, Mikal was an Israeli agent, a member of the Mossad, that branch of the Israeli intelligence service responsible for gathering and analyzing intelligence data abroad and for handling special assignments in any area of the world that affected Israel; he would say no more about that. Mikal had black curly hair that fell almost in ringlets over his deeply tanned forehead. Bushy eyebrows above dark brown eyes, a large nose, and a wide mouth reminded Juno somewhat of Saul—that was in the Israeli's favor. He was not excessively large—about five-foot-nine—but had well-developed arms and shoulders, a broad chest, and a narrow waist and hips. His manner was friendly, but his bearing left no doubt that, if one's enemy, he could be a lethal foe.

Like Mikal, Gerald was both a sabra and a Mossad agent; but he, too, would not discuss the details of his credentials. At twenty-nine, he was a political-science major and needed only two more years of part-time schooling to fulfill the requirements for his doctorate—but that would have to come later. His job: to protect Dr. Davide at all costs.

The most interesting of the group to Juno was Lori Davide. Now a full professor at Hebrew University Medical School in Jerusalem and the head of the Division of Genetic Research and

Clinical Genetics at both the school and at Hadassah Hospital, she had graduated from Smith College and Yale Medical School, finished her internship and residency in internal medicine at the Massachusetts General Hospital, and completed a three-year fellowship in genetics at Johns Hopkins. Then she had returned to Jerusalem to accept her present position. At thirty-six, she was the youngest professor at the school and had already published over forty papers in a variety of scientific journals both in Israel and in the United States. Her field of expertise: the diagnosis and treatment of Jewish genetic diseases.

Juno watched her closely as she started to speak; the tone of her voice was intense.

"I'll summarize our findings in as simple terms as possible," she told him. "A disease characterized by acute degeneration of the central nervous system is afflicting Jews the world over. To the best of our knowledge, close to two thousand Jews have already died from it. We cannot yet accurately categorize the disease or determine its exact cause.

"We don't fully understand why the disease seems to affect only Jews, but our investigations suggest that Jews have a genetic defect—probably on the thirteenth chromosome—that makes them susceptible to the disease itself or to whatever causes it. There's some evidence that the gene involved controls the synthesis of a single protein, an enzyme, that's involved with nerve cell membrane permeability. In other words, some Jews—I say 'some' because we're not certain just what percentage have the genetic defect—have a gene that under normal circumstances produces a substance necessary for central nervous system integrity and viability; it is *this* gene that is susceptible to *this* disease and when affected, functions improperly. The result: destruction of the nervous system."

Juno eyed her critically. Lori Davide looked every bit as much a woman as she sounded like a professor. The best of the Semitic features—long dark hair, large brown eyes, high cheekbones, a strong nose, and full lips—complemented a well-developed body. She used little makeup and was neatly dressed in a loose blue wool sweater that accentuated her breasts and a matching tweed skirt that was just a little too tight over her buttocks; she appeared stylish yet unpretentious in the clothes of the contemporary career woman. Juno thought longingly of Renée. He would try to call her again as soon as the meeting was over.

"We still have to determine the depth of transmission of the gene from one generation to the next," Dr. Davide was saying. "In other words, how much Jewish blood a person must have to possess the genetic defect."

"Is there *any* known occurrence of the disease in non-Jews?" Juno asked.

"Not so far."

"Do you think there's a connection between the disease and the scar that some of the victims had on their left sides?"

Lori Davide frowned. "I'm not sure. The scar was probably the result of some sort of medical experiment performed at Dachau. At the time this procedure was carried out—sometime between 1942 and 1945—there was no radiology equipment that could accurately demonstrate the precise location of internal organs. I think the scar simply represents a surgical incision made to expose the surface of the spleen so that something could be injected into it. In every autopsy performed on a victim of the disease who had the scar, a dimple was observed on the lateral surface of the spleen. The histology—the microscopic anatomy—of the dimpled area and the region immediately beneath it revealed a linear collection of fibrous or scar tissue. Our best guess is that the dimple represents a puncture wound probably made by a needle of moderate size; the area below it, the tract of the needle and whatever was injected through it."

"Then you do think the disease started in Dachau over thirty years ago!"

"I didn't say that."

"But you implied it."

"No. I simply gave you a reasonable explanation for the scar."

"Please don't be coy. I think we've all come to the conclusion that there's a link between Dachau, the scar, and the disease. You've just told me that you found evidence—presumptive evidence, if you will—that something was injected into the spleens of those with the scar. Do you mean to tell me that you don't think the injection is directly related to the disease?"

"I am not trying to be coy; I'm trying to make sure that we're not guessing. Of course we're considering such a relationship, but we must prove it."

"For the sake of our present discussion, let's assume it's so. What about those people who have the disease but who don't have the scar?"

"That strongly suggests that the disease is caused by a communicable infectious agent. We've yet to learn if this is direct transmission or if there is an intermediate host such as an animal or a vector such as an insect."

"An infectious agent hanging around for *over thirty years?*"

"Unlikely, granted, but possible; right now there's just no other logical explanation."

"Did you find anything else?"

"The reaction in the spleen was rather unusual. . . ."

"In what way?"

"The splenic defense mechanisms seemed to have failed in some way. You see, anytime the body is invaded by something foreign to it—a microorganism or any strange protein, for that matter—certain reactions occur to expel the invading substance or to contain it. An important part of this response occurs in the spleen; in this case, almost none occurred. That may explain the persisting nature of whatever was injected—"

"Which was . . . ?" Juno interrupted.

"That, my friend, is what you would call the 'sixty-four-thousand-dollar question.'"

"Can you find the answer?"

"I'm not sure, but we'll certainly try."

"But what if you can't?"

She hesitated. "If we can identify the invading agent—for the sake of discussion, let's say it's a microorganism—and can cure or prevent the disease it causes, there's no problem; however, if we can't isolate it or even if we can but there's no prophylaxis or cure, we're left with one alternative: to change the affected gene."

"Can you do that?" Juno looked at her with astonishment.

"It won't be a matter of *if* we can. We'll *have* to!"

For a moment, no one spoke.

Juno broke the silence. "From what you've said, I take it you're convinced this is not a *natural* disease."

"All available evidence indicates that it isn't."

"And there's no doubt in our minds that the Nazis developed it at Dachau," Mikal added. "Even if Lori wants further proof, I don't. We even think we know the name of the doctor responsible for the medical blocks at Dachau."

"What?" Juno felt his heart pounding. "Who?"

"His name was Thaddeus Reichmann. We're still trying to uncover the identity he assumed when he escaped the Allied forces in 1945, but—"

"Then he's the man we want!"

"For the moment, presuming he's alive, he's our number one suspect. But there were several doctors at Dachau. Although Reichmann was in charge, we don't know if he actually performed the experiments."

"How will you be sure?"

"We'll turn the world upside down if we have to, but we'll find Reichmann. Then we'll know!"

Juno pondered Mikal's words. The Israelis had a firm conviction about success; it permeated their past, it was a part of their present, and they anticipated it for the future. However, he detected a hint of uncertainty in Mikal's voice. Despite the amazing speed with which the Israelis had mobilized their scientific talent and set in motion their highly efficient and effective intelligence machine, they were obviously afraid. Previously, every danger had come from without and had been overcome; but this new menace came from within and was terrifying because it was genetically linked to their being Jews. Their only hope was to find out what it was and to attempt to alter *it* rather than themselves. They had every right to be afraid.

"Anything else, Mr. Juno?" Gerald interrupted his thoughts.

"Yes. . . . You're aware of the Golding and Goldstein murders?"

Mikal and Gerald nodded. Juno told them of Josh's and Sokolov's theories. "The question now is *who* killed them?"

"We think Reichmann killed Golding and Goldstein for just the reasons your brother and Ari hypothesized."

"Do you know about the Swiss chemist who was shot at the Zurich Airport?"

"Yes," Gerald said, "but he was neither a Swiss nor a chemist."

"Then who the hell was he?"

"Mordecai Grossman, a Mossad agent."

Juno winced. "Why did he take such an interest in *me?* And why was he killed?"

"He'd been assigned to make sure you got to us safely. We think his assassin was a Nazi agent. If so, it certainly supports our theories that Reichmann *is* our man and that's he's still alive. You must be getting close to him."

"Why would Reichmann think that I'm closing in?"

"Reichmann's clever. If he killed Golding and Goldstein, he knows that you're in charge of the investigation. Whether you're a significant threat to him or not, he won't take chances."

"Then that would explain the attempt to kill me in Switzerland."

"Exactly. We've learned that the man you shot at the Rhine Falls was Eric Creider, one of their best. We're quite certain he was the man who killed Grossman. You must be very good."

"Thanks." Juno managed a smile. "But this whole thing still doesn't make sense. Who killed my brother . . . and the others . . . and why?"

"We think it was Reichmann—or one of his men—for the same reason he's after you: to eliminate *any* threat to himself, no matter how remote."

"When you find Reichmann, he's mine! I want him!" Juno shouted. He could feel his calm cracking.

"Hold on. We know how much Dr. Fields meant to you, but this is no one's *personal* war. We'll find Reichmann, but we want him alive. Meanwhile, we pool our resources and whatever information any of us uncovers."

"All of it?"

"*All* of it."

"Fine. Then let's change the subject for a minute. Who was Asher Ben Levi?"

The three Israelis exchanged glances. Gerald spoke. "Sorry, but that's an internal matter."

"To hell with that!" Juno snapped. "This is 'no one's personal war,' remember?"

"Ben Levi's dead. He can't help us find Reichmann. What difference does it make who he was?" Gerald remained calm. "This disease is an even greater threat to the Jews than Hitler was; unchecked, it could mean the end of our people. We will not let that happen!"

"And because I'm not Jewish, my interest in all of this is less than yours. Is that it?"

"I didn't say that."

"No. But you implied it." Juno's eyes narrowed. "Well, let me tell you all something: I may have been born into the Greek Orthodox faith, but most of my life was molded by Jews. The father, the mother, and the brother who took me into their home and cared for me until the day they died were Jews. But you're right. I'm not here *just* to save the Jews; I'm here because two men I loved were killed by and because of this damned disease, and I want to see their deaths avenged!" He paused, fighting to regain his composure.

Lori Davide spoke softly. "We're partners, Mr. Juno. We're glad you're here; we want and need your help. Get to know us; we'll try to get to know you."

Juno hesitated. He knew he had no choice: it was unlikely that he could find Reichmann without them. But he'd be on his guard. He turned to Gerald. "What do you want me to do?"

"You and Mikal will return to New York City to search for Reichmann. Dr. Davide and I will go back to Israel."

"What makes you think Reichmann's in New York?"

"Because the first murders were committed there."

"And who knows New York City better than a cop?"

"Exactly. And besides"—Gerald smiled—"we know you're extremely good; and we want the best we can find." The Israeli paused. "For your own safety, and ours," Gerald went on, "I suggest you tell no one—not even your superiors—the true nature of the situation. It's vital that we keep the number of persons who know to an absolute minimum, because . . ."

Suddenly Gerald stopped and held up his hand.

There was a soft knock on the door, followed by silence, and then a second knock. At a signal from Gerald, Mikal went to the door, opened it, and stepped outside.

In less than a minute he returned, bolted the door behind him, and collapsed into a chair. His face was pale.

"What is it?" Gerald demanded.

"Tsve Shem was found dead early this morning. He had been brutally tortured. . . ."

"Who was Tsve Shem?" Juno asked.

"A Mossad agent who was working with us." It was Lori who answered.

"Your driver in Zurich," Gerald added coldly. "He was supposed to meet us here. The Nazis must have been following him and . . ."

A cold sweat erupted on Juno's forehead. "If the Nazis know we're in Paris, why the hell are we just sitting here?" He pushed back his chair.

"Mikal!" Gerald barked after glancing at Juno indignantly. "You and Mr. Juno take the car. Drive to that small airfield near Versailles. Rent a plane and fly back to Zurich—they won't expect you there. Then take the first available flight to New York. I'll be touch with you in a few days. For God's sake, *find Reichmann!*"

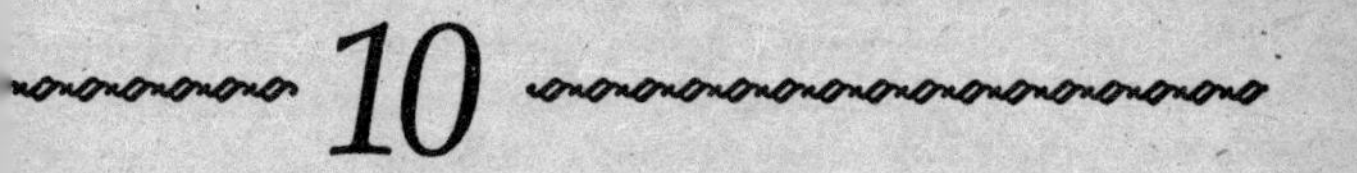

10

Juno nodded impatiently as the official returned his passport. Half-walking, half-running, he made his way through the crowd in the baggage claim area, snatched his bag, and headed toward the shortest line waiting for clearance through customs. Mikal joined him in a few minutes, and together they rushed for a cab.

Juno hardly spoke during the ride into Manhattan. He had been unable to reach Renée, and that worried him. Although he was confident that she could take care of herself in almost any situation, he knew she was sometimes reckless in her disregard for danger. And Reichmann had to be dealt with cautiously. The Nazi did not hesitate to kill anyone he viewed as a threat, and Renée was . . . Suddenly he was numb with fear; he knew he would break if she were . . .

He was out the door before the cab had come to a complete stop. With total disregard for Mikal as he struggled to pay the driver, Juno flew into the building and up the stairs, skidding to a halt in front of the door to the apartment. He hit the bell once and then pounded on the door.

"Come on, Renée. Come on!" he shouted softly as he hit the door again with his fist.

There was no answer. He tried the door. Locked! He kept his finger on the bell, swore, and checked his watch. She should have been home by now! Without further hesitation he stepped back, kicked in the door, and burst into the apartment. At the door to the bedroom he stopped. Without moving or uttering a sound, he stood there and stared at her.

Her nude body, sprawled across the bed, was distorted with rigor mortis; her skin, once almost flawless, was a sickening yellowish-purple color that deepened into irregular blotches of blues and reds where the blood had settled to clot in vessels no longer bearing life. Rivulets of dried, caking blood ran from her nose and the corners of her mouth. Three gaping bullet holes marred the surface of her left breast. All of this in itself might have shattered the sanity of even the strongest man, but there was more: carved deeply into her right breast was a crude Star of David.

For every man there is a breaking point beyond which pain and anguish overcome the complex system of interrelated checks and balances that inhibits irrational thought and action. For Peter Juno this might have been it. But Saul had taught him well; from somewhere in his subconscious, Saul's words reached forth to pull him back from the edge of madness: "If you allow hate or anger to destroy you, you surrender the opportunity and the ability to right the wrong that has provoked it; if you can overcome it and convert it into determination and energy, you will be able to do what must be done."

He walked slowly to the bed, closed her panic-stricken eyes, covered the body with the sheet, and turned to face Mikal, who now stood in the doorway to the bedroom. The Israeli started to speak, but Juno interrupted him. "Please don't say anything; I know what you're feeling, and I appreciate it." His voice was frighteningly calm; he spoke with no overt emotion. "In a very short time I have lost my father, my brother, and a woman I loved. These bastards have set the rules; now I, too, will play by those rules." He held up his hand. "I want no lectures. Either you are with me, or please go back to Israel. You can't stop me. I won't let anybody stop me!"

Juno reported Renée's murder and arranged for a team from Commissioner Davis's special task force to take over. Then he and Mikal checked into the Park Lane Hotel. Even with sedatives and half a bottle of Scotch, it took Mikal several hours to get him to sleep.

Yet the rest did no good. It was with despair only that Juno pushed open the door to the police commissioner's waiting room.

"Good morning—" The secretary started to deliver her usual sterile welcome, but Juno cut her short with an icy glare and walked unannounced into Davis's office.

Davis was alone. He looked worn and tired. "I'm sorry about Sergeant Tracy," he said. There was no change in his facial expression. "Dr. Mann, Dr. Joy, and Roger Baldini are dead, too. Each was shot with a Luger—the same one that killed your brother and the others." The commissioner watched Juno as his words echoed through the uneasy silence that pervaded the room.

Juno forced himself to remain calm. "When I spoke to Baldini from the airport before I left, he gave me an urgent message to call Dr. Joy. I tried, but the line was busy."

"He probably wanted to tell you about Mann's death; he did the autopsy."

"Mann was the first?"

"Yes. Then Joy and Baldini."

"Anything significant about their autopsies?"

"According to the report, Mann had that scar on his left side and concentration-camp numbers on his left forearm. Nothing special on Joy and Baldini, but you can check for yourself."

"I'll do that." Juno made a mental note to check the Oriental pathologist's original notes on Mann's autopsy and the autopsy reports on Joy and Baldini. Davis was an administrator, not a cop; minor details frequently led to solutions of major crimes. The image of Josh's corpse and of Renée's ravaged body exploded over and over again before his eyes; he vowed to himself that he would not rest until . . .

"What are your plans now?" The commissioner's words startled him.

"I'll concentrate on the Golding and Goldstein murders. Maybe something will turn up about Ben Levi, too. Anything else I should know?"

"There's been one other Luger killing, but this one doesn't make sense at all."

"What do you mean?"

Davis opened a folder on his desk. Slipping a photograph from beneath a paper clip, he handed it to Juno.

"Rolfe Penzel." Juno frowned. "He's a professional hit man. What the hell does he have to do with all of this?" He passed the picture back to Davis. "Same Luger?"

"Slugs match perfectly."

"I'll see what I can come up with." Without another word, Juno turned and left.

Juno watched while the two men in yellow ponchos and rain hats finished filling the grave. Only he and Mikal, along with a handful of friends, had attended Renée's funeral. Her parents were dead, and he had requested that there be no formal police burial. Her death was a personal loss, and he wanted to mourn in private; he had asked Mikal to come because he felt the Israeli understood and because he dreaded being totally alone.

It was cold and wet and silent except for the wind and the sound of shovels against the dirt. The cold drizzle settled on his hair and his eyebrows and dripped down over his cheeks to mix with his tears.

When the funeral was over, Juno went back to work. He began with Penzel. It was rumored that Penzel had leanings toward the neo-Nazi movement; Juno had seen it mentioned in Penzel's file when his name had turned up on a list of suspects about a year ago. He called Mikal and asked him to check with Israeli Intelligence while he reviewed the police reports.

Penzel's body had been found in his car parked a block from the apartment where Juno and Renée had been staying. The coroner's report noted that evidence of recently ingested wine had been detected in the stomach and upper small intestine, along with partially digested remnants of oysters, veal, and a vegetable resembling broccoli, suggesting that the dead man had known his killer well enough to share dinner with him. From the descriptions of the two wounds, Juno concluded that either Penzel had been shot at close range or his killer had been an excellent marksman: one bullet had entered the front of the neck just to the right of the midline, severing the jugular vein and piercing the right carotid artery, the major vessel bringing blood to the brain; the other had penetrated the left chest just above the nipple and had torn a hole in the heart. The only other signs of trauma were several linear abrasions on the backs of both legs and on the left shoulder, indicating that Penzel had not been shot in the car but had been killed elsewhere and his body moved.

He returned the file to the clerk. "May I see whatever effects were found on the victim?" he asked.

"Sure, Lieutenant." The clerk hesitated. "Sorry about Sergeant Tracy. Damned good cop for a lady . . . I mean—"

"Thanks. I know what you mean." Juno swallowed hard. "Now that envelope . . . and I'd like to see his clothes, too."

In minutes Juno had confirmed his theory about the killing: the scrape marks on the backs of the heels of Penzel's shoes, the tear in one of the cuffs of his trousers, as well as the abrasions noted on the backs of his legs, were likely caused by the body being dragged; the abrasion on the left shoulder suggested that the killer had had some difficulty positioning the body in the car.

Juno deduced that Penzel had been caught completely off guard: the Beretta found in his pocket still had the safety on and had a full clip. A man like Penzel would have fought back if threatened; he had not even drawn his gun.

"I have that information you wanted on Penzel," Mikal said as he let Juno into their room at the Park Lane.

"Let's have it." Juno took out his notebook and sat down at the table in front of the window.

"Penzel was well-known to us. He was a diehard neo-Nazi. Although he made his living as a hired assassin for anyone who could pay the price, he donated his services to the Party; he had a reputation as one of their top hit men. It seems he was as good as they claimed—there's evidence that he'd killed more than a dozen of our agents."

"What had he been doing lately?"

"Don't know. He dropped out of sight about two weeks ago."

"Just about the time all of this began." Juno thought for a moment. "I'll bet he went to work for Reichmann."

"Then who killed him?"

"Reichmann. The bullets recovered from Penzel's body match those recovered from Reichmann's other victims."

"Why would Reichmann kill one of his own men?"

"To throw us off the track enough to buy him some time."

"So where do we go from here?"

"You said there were other doctors at Dachau. If it isn't Reichmann who's behind this, we're going to waste a lot of valuable time chasing the wrong man. We've got to establish a direct connection between Reichmann and the disease."

"How do you propose to do that?"

Juno turned to a page in his notebook. "Reichmann must have had a very specific reason for killing Golding and his brother. There are dozens of Jews in the New York area who were in Dachau. Why kill *those* two? Besides, if he waited long enough, the disease would probably have gotten rid of them for him. If he ran the risk of murdering them, they must have represented an unusual threat to him. There's something more to Morris Golding and Avram Goldstein than appears on the surface; I want to know what it is. Let's go!"

"Where?"

"To New Jersey to see Morris Golding's widow."

Sarah Golding managed a barely perceptible smile as Juno introduced Mikal as his new partner without revealing his true identity. The haggard look on her face disturbed him. He remembered her as an attractive woman with immense self-control. Now, as she led them through the foyer into the living room, she looked older and less sure of herself.

"What can I do for you, Lieutenant Juno? I've already told you everything I know." Her voice trembled, and she glanced downward as if examining the moist handkerchief she twisted nervously around her fingers.

Watching her rekindled Juno's emotions. The last time he had met the woman, Josh, Saul, and Renée were alive. He felt the pain in the back of his neck return and throb in concert with the ache in his left shoulder; but he told himself to ignore it.

"How is your son?" he asked.

Mrs. Golding looked at him and then at Mikal through tear-filled eyes. Her lips quivered uncontrollably; she seemed intent on tearing the handkerchief to shreds. "Stephen is dead."

Juno took a moment to recover. "How did he die?"

"The doctor isn't certain. Some sort of stroke or something."

"Had he been ill?"

"I don't really know. I think he tried to hide things from me; but Nancy—that's his wife—said he'd been having periods of weakness, loss of memory . . ." She stopped abruptly and dabbed at her eyes.

At first Juno was too surprised to think; then the full impact of Sarah Golding's words hit him. He tried to remain outwardly calm; but within, he was struggling to contain the turmoil of fears and doubts that threatened to overwhelm his last remnants of self-control. When he had been told that almost two thousand Jews had died from the disease, he had reacted with the same detached objectivity with which he viewed the statistics of crimes committed in Manhattan in any given year: he was intimately involved with a few of them; the rest were meaningless numbers. Until now, Saul's death and Josh's and Renée's murders had been the focal point of his interest and his efforts; but Stephen Golding's death from the disease suddenly brought the full scope of the problem into focus. He was more certain than ever that the key to that disease lay in the murders of Morris Golding and Avram Goldstein. He had to find it!

"I'm sorry about your son. I didn't know." Juno paused. "If you feel up to it, I'd like to ask you some questions."

"More questions?" Sarah Golding stood up and paced nervously about the living room. "I've told you everything I know."

Juno eyed her carefully. There *was* something different about her. When he had first met her, she had been patient and cooperative; now even the mere mention of further interrogation unnerved her.

"I just want to double-check a few things. I'll try to make it as short as possible."

"I understand." She stopped and stared into the fireplace with her back to her two visitors.

"Your son told me that Mr. Golding had that scar on his left side when you married him. Is that so?"

"Yes."

"Any idea what it was from?"

"No. Morris never told me, and I never asked."

"We think the scar was the result of medical experiments performed at Dachau. Did your husband ever talk about them?"

Sarah Golding did not respond.

"Mrs. Golding?"

"He never said a word about any experiments."

Juno tensed. "And he never told you about an SS doctor at Dachau, a Dr. Reichmann, who performed those experiments on him, his brother, and dozens of other Jews?"

"I told you, Lieutenant, I don't know anything about the scars he and Avram had. I don't know. I never asked. I don't care. All I know is that my husband is dead." She turned suddenly to face Juno and Mikal. Tears rolled down her cheeks, and her face was ashen and hollow. She stood stiffly, arms straight by her sides, fists tightly clenched. Her body heaved as she sobbed. "What do you want from me? What are you trying to do? My husband was a good man. He only did . . ." She gasped and brought her hand to her mouth, her fist still clenched; she turned back to the fireplace and wept softly.

Whatever Sarah Golding knew about the scars and Dachau and Reichmann, it somehow implicated Morris Golding; and she was not about to destroy his memory merely to complete the case records of his death. But Juno had to know. He had to get her to reveal her knowledge of what had happened to her husband at Dachau and why it might have cost him his life more than thirty years later.

He put his arm around her shoulder and led her back to the sofa. "We both know you're trying to hide something, Mrs. Golding. Whatever it is might be important in helping us to find the man who shot your husband."

Sarah Golding did not answer.

"I know you've been through a lot, but I must know. Please tell me."

She closed her eyes and rubbed her temples with her fingertips. "I've told you everything."

"No, you haven't. You've been avoiding direct answers to almost every question I've asked you."

"Are you accusing me of lying?" She glared at Juno.

"No. Not lying, just circumventing the truth. But why? What did your husband do at Dachau that was so terrible that you can't face it even now?"

"Who do you think you are—"

"Look, Mrs. Golding," Juno interrupted. "I know you asked your husband about that scar; Stephen told me that. Did *he* lie?"

As if suddenly oblivious to the presence of the two men, she stared at the ceiling while tears flowed down her cheeks. She bit her lower lip to keep it from trembling.

Juno continued. "I never mentioned Mr. Goldstein's scar; you did. How did you know he had it? I never implied that your husband did anything wrong; you did. All I did was ask you some simple, straightforward questions; how you answered them was your own doing." Juno softened his tone. "Your son died of a disease that has something to do with your husband's murder, and both are linked to something that took place in Dachau over thirty years ago. I want you to tell me what that was. Not for any police record but to try to keep a lot more Jews from dying from the same disease. I won't leave here until you tell me." He paused, watching her closely.

Sarah Golding removed an envelope from a pocket in her skirt, turned it over and over again in her hands, and finally placed it on the coffee table in front of her. "This is from my husband's safe-deposit box. I didn't know he had one, but I found the key when I was cleaning out some of his personal effects. This envelope was the only thing in it." She pushed it toward Juno.

He read the handwritten words on the front: "To be opened only at the time of my death," and could not help but think to himself that it was a rather unoriginal statement. He wondered if the contents were indeed as significant as he was anticipating. He unfolded the letter and began to read.

Dearest Sarah,

You will not be reading this until I am dead and at last free of the guilt I have lived with for all these years. No matter how I tried, I could not bring myself to tell you for fear of losing your love and your respect.

Although there is no defense for what I did, I beg you who were not there to try to understand what it was like in

Dachau in 1942 and early 1943 when it seemed to us behind the barbed wire fences that Germany would rule the world forever. When awakening every morning precipitates overwhelming anger that you did not die during the night, when you fear that you will live more than you fear that you will die, when your only hope is that the end will come quickly with a minimum of pain and suffering, you lose the ability to reason.

Then suddenly one day you see a guard split open the head of a twelve-year-old boy with a pickax, you watch an SS bastard mutilate the face of a friend with a riding crop, you listen to the unending screams of the man who sleeps next to you provide entertainment for a sadistic group of officers who torture him under the guise of punishing him for a minor infraction of the rules. Although you have seen many similar incidents, this time, for some unknown reason, something snaps inside of you. You suddenly realize you do not really want to die. Somewhere in your subconscious beneath all the terror and all the agony, there is still the desire to survive. It smolders within you until the spark ignites and becomes a blast furnace that consumes the last remnants of rational thought that have allowed you to differentiate between right and wrong. Then you are willing to do anything, say anything, believe anything, think anything so long as it will keep you alive. That is what happened to Avram and me. We had become animals with only one goal in mind—to survive. And that is why we did what we did.

In late 1942, we learned through the camp grapevine that a new doctor had come to Dachau. His name was Thaddeus Reichmann, and he had been sent by Himmler to perform secret medical experiments on some of the inmates. These experiments were different from others at the camp, because in the beginning it seemed that all the subjects survived and because the inmates who were used neither suffered nor knew what had really happened.

Avram and I were chosen about a month after the experiments began. It was not what I had expected. Reichmann himself or an assistant met each subject individually.

In my case it was Reichmann. He explained that he was evaluating a new type of ether. All that would happen to me was that I would be put to sleep, an incision would be made in my left side to test the ether's anesthetic value, I would be kept in the hospital until the wound healed, and then I would be reassigned to my usual work. Afterward I was to come to the camp infirmary once each week to be checked. At first I was suspicious, but then I remembered that the others *had* survived as he promised. I really had no choice anyway.

Reichmann seemed kind enough, especially when he told me supposedly in confidence that he did not like the whole business any more than I did and that he hoped the war would end soon so he could go back to his usual practice of medicine. I must admit I was taken in, but then again, I *wanted* to believe him.

After a while some of the prisoners who had been used in the studies became ill and died. Word spread throughout the camp that Reichmann was not really testing an anesthetic, but rather some sort of disease-producing germ that caused a horrible type of brain destruction. Things became more difficult for the doctor. Inmates tried to escape or committed suicide rather than be used as experimental subjects. Others contrived the most ingenious ways of sabotaging his work, despite the constant scrutiny of the guards.

Like all at Dachau who considered the camp their private empire and the prisoners their personal slaves, Reichmann began to construct a system of spies and informers to ensure the continuity of his regime. Like the others, he, too, used Jew against Jew by threatening or bribing the few who agreed to serve him. By this time, we were more enticed by his promise of a cure if we became ill than by his threats. Neither Avram nor I could decline the offer.

Once again I must emphasize that survival was uppermost in our minds, and it superseded any feelings we had for our fellow prisoners or any conception of what was right or wrong. We did what Reichmann ordered us to do because our world now consisted of no one and nothing but ourselves. All we cared about was that we would live. We watched and we listened and we reported what we saw and what we heard to Reichmann himself. And he did make us well when we got sick.

In the two years Avram and I worked for the doctor, we learned a great deal about the man. In truth he was an evil, egomaniacal, sadistic murderer who littered his self-defined path to success with the bodies of untold numbers of unwilling victims and the souls of those who were forced to serve him in his endeavor. Even if we had wanted to stop, we could not. We were trapped—by him, by our fellow inmates, and by ourselves. He could have had us killed. If *he* did not, he knew the other prisoners would have if they discovered our treason against them. But most of all, nothing could force us to reject living, especially considering the price we had already paid.

In April of 1945, when word reached the camp that the Allies were approaching, we knew Reichmann would have no choice but to kill us. We knew too much about him and what he had done. We were the witnesses who could hang him. So we began to devise a means of escape. Under normal circumstances no one escaped from Dachau. But with the Allies barely twenty miles away, there was a chance we could reach their lines before we were caught. For our plan to succeed, we needed a diversion. Again you must remember that Avram and I were now numb, almost inhuman creatures bent only upon ensuring our own existence. We cared little—if at all—if others suffered for our actions. We escaped while the few guards who still remained at the camp massacred a barracks of prisoners. We had informed the Germans that those poor, unknowing, miserable wretches who were no more than shadows of humanity were planning an uprising. The sounds of machine-gun fire from the camp were still audible when we met an Allied combat group scouting the area.

We had survived. But how many had died so that we could live? We were free of Dachau at last, but we would never be free of guilt.

Avram must make his peace with himself and with God in

his own way. I can only ask your forgiveness and pray you will understand. Whatever I did, it was worth it to have lived to share my life with you.

I love you,
Morris

Juno stared at the pages in silence. Finally he shook his head and looked up. "May I?" He started to pass the letter to Mikal.

"Of course." Sarah Golding's whisper was barely audible.

No one spoke until Mikal had finished reading. "Thank you." He folded the letter and gave it back to her. "If it's any consolation, that letter is of great value to us."

Both men watched with compassion as Sarah Golding buried her face in her hands and sobbed.

"Your husband was right, you know." It was Mikal who spoke. "We were not there; we do not know what it was like. I, as an individual Jew, cannot and will not sit in judgment—and neither should you."

Juno put his hand on her arm. "Your husband loved you and your son dearly. Love the *man*. What he was or what he did over thirty years ago must not change that."

Sarah Golding looked up and smiled wanly. "Thank you."

Juno and Mikal got up to leave. They had what they had come for: the link between Reichmann and the disease. And they had unexpectedly learned something of even greater value: *Reichmann knew the cure!*

11

They parked the car in the garage next to the hotel and ate at a delicatessen on Seventh Avenue. Recognizing that Mikal was troubled by Golding's letter and what it portended for the Jewish race, Juno persuaded the Israeli to take a walk to alleviate the tension. As they headed downtown, Mikal noticed a discount store and stopped to look at the window full of radios, television sets, and stereo equipment. Neither paid particular attention to the two powerfully built men who had joined the small group of window shoppers in front of the display.

"There are even better stores farther down the avenue. If you'd like, we can stop in a couple and compare prices." Juno led Mikal by the arm through the crowd to the curb. "Then we can go to Rockefeller Center and the NBC television studios. I think they have evening . . ." Juno stopped abruptly as he felt the muzzle of a gun jammed into his ribs. Despite the cold wind, he felt the beads of sweat erupt on his forehead and in the small of his back. He glanced at Mikal on his right; the Israeli had also been caught unawares.

"Just keep your hands at your sides and keep moving. Walk toward Fiftieth Street at a normal pace." The man's voice was cold and unwavering.

Juno needed time to think; he slowed his gait. Each time they walked past a large window, he studied the reflection of the two men who held them prisoner. The one behind him was about his size; Mikal's captor was several inches taller than the Israeli.

Juno flinched as the muzzle dug into his side.

"Keep walking. Don't slow down again. It makes no difference to us whether we kill you two now or later; but if it's here, somebody else might get hurt. It's up to you. Now move!"

Juno swore under his breath. He had been in similar spots before, but each time it had been with a partner with whom he had worked out and rehearsed a method of escape from such situations. He was about to find out how well he and Mikal functioned spontaneously as a team.

Following orders, they turned into Fiftieth Street, where Juno let himself be shoved to the right and stumbled into Mikal. "Next corner . . ." Juno's whisper was amputated as he was hurled against the building. His head and shoulders crashed into it, his knees buckled, and he felt his breath cut short. A dull throbbing ache spread through his left shoulder. Before he could regain his balance, his assailant was on him. His fist smashed into Juno's jaw; his forearm rammed into his throat, pinning him against the wall. Pain shot through Juno's neck; his larynx felt as if it were about to give. He gasped for breath; when he tried to cry out, there was no sound. With his free hand the man removed Juno's gun from his holster; then suddenly he let go. As Juno slid to the ground, he caught a glimpse of Mikal. Feet apart, hands against the building, he, too, was being relieved of his gun. For a moment Juno forgot his pain—Mikal had been carrying a Luger!

"Get up!"

Looking up, Juno had his first good look at his attacker. Blue eyes. Blond hair. Sharp features. A face devoid of feeling. Picking himself up, Juno brushed himself off and rubbed his jaw and his throat. The predominant emotion he experienced was hatred—the man in front of him personified everything he despised.

"Get going," the man barked. "We have a car down the street."

Juno walked more slowly and waited for the gun in his back again. At the instant he felt it, he dropped to the sidewalk and rolled to his left. He hooked his right foot behind the ankle of the man standing over him and slammed his left foot into the man's shin, causing him to topple backward before he could fire. As Juno dove for his adversary's throat, he saw that Mikal had followed his cue.

With unbridled hate and anger, Juno smashed the man's hand against the concrete; the gun flew into the gutter. With the threat of the weapon eliminated, Juno attacked relentlessly despite the pain in his left shoulder. He pounded his fist into the man's face. Blood and teeth flew everywhere; one blow broke his nose; another opened a wide gash above his left eye.

"Rotten, lousy, fucking Nazi!" Juno hit him again. "Pig! Bastard!" His arm and hand ached, but he started to swing again. Somehow he heard Mikal's scream above his own.

Juno turned and leaped for the second man who had managed to free himself from Mikal's grip and was now taking careful aim at the Israeli who had fallen backward into a cluster of trash barrels at the curb. Juno hit the Nazi just as he pulled the trigger. As they tumbled to the sidewalk, Juno heard Mikal's sickening groan.

Pulling the man up with him, Juno swung savagely, caught him squarely in the abdomen, and then brought his knee up. The man's head snapped back; he looked at Juno blankly and then collapsed. As he rushed to the Israeli, Juno heard a car screech to a stop. Bullets ricocheted off the barrels around them. Dragging Mikal into the gutter, Juno shielded him with his body and searched desperately for one of the weapons that had been lost in the fight. Finding one, he fired repeatedly as the two men who had emerged from the car dragged their companions into it and then sped off.

Sitting up, Juno saw several frightened onlookers come out of the doorways in which they had taken refuge. A policeman was making his way toward him through the crowd.

"I suggest you get us out of here with as few questions as possible," Mikal mumbled—and then collapsed.

It had taken some doing, but they had gotten back to the hotel in less than two hours. Juno's story that he had been shopping on Fifth Avenue and had come to the aid of a holdup victim who preferred to remain anonymous satisfied the desk sergeant, who was willing to set aside the usual report in return for a "good word" to the police commissioner who was about to make additional appointments to his special task force. Fortunately the bullet had passed through the fleshy part of Mikal's side; his wound was tended by a police surgeon who owed Juno a number of favors and was more than happy to forget the incident for a case of Crown Royal and two tickets to the Rangers-Bruins hockey game the following week.

Mikal swallowed the Scotch in one gulp, coughed, and laughed. "It seems one of us is always feeding the other liquor." He reached out and took Juno's hand. "I don't know what to say, my friend. You saved my life. I am grateful."

"You would have done the same for me." It was as much a question as a statement.

The Israeli smiled. "Of course I would. Not as handily, though. You *are* good. You're quick. . . . But we can't waste time with compliments. You saw my Luger?"

Juno nodded.

Several minutes passed before Mikal broke the uncomfortable silence. "I think you're entitled to an explanation. Although I may lose my head for it, I'm going to tell you about Asher Ben Levi and the Luger. You have a right to know if you're going to risk your life. The Nazis will be back. We must be able to depend on one another without question." Mikal hesitated.

Juno looked unflinchingly into his eyes. "Of course."

"Asher Ben Levi was a physician on a small kibbutz in northern Israel. That fact is no secret. What's not known is the nature of that kibbutz and its inhabitants. To be a member, one must be a survivor of a Nazi concentration camp or a direct descendant thereof. The kibbutz is called Yad Yanush—in memory of one of the heroes of the Holocaust. Many of the Jews who live there are not just survivors; they are men and women who either were key witnesses against the Nazis in the war-crimes trials at Nuremberg and in Israel or whose testimony could incriminate Nazis not yet caught. Many, including Asher Ben Levi's parents, had been in Dachau.

"After the first trials, several people who had testified and two or three of those who were being kept in protective custody for future testimony were murdered by assassins supported and directed by Nazi organizations. To protect the survivors, the government of Israel established the kibbutz for them; Israeli law clearly defines the few who may know the essence of the kibbutz and the identities of its inhabitants, unless the prime minister himself orders otherwise.

"Shortly after its formation, a group of those living there banded together in an organization for self-protection as well as retribution. It's called the Dom—'*dom*' is the Hebrew word for 'blood.' Its purpose: the elimination of all Nazi war criminals still at large."

"Then they're killers!"

Mikal smiled. "When you found Renée—didn't you want to kill?"

Juno looked away; he did not answer. After a moment he turned back to Mikal. "What about Asher Ben Levi?"

"He was"—Mikal cleared his throat—"the leader of the Dom."

"No wonder we couldn't find out a damned thing about him!" Juno shook his head. "A physician—a man supposedly dedicated to saving lives—was the leader of a secret Israeli vigilante group. My God!"

"Don't prejudge him, Pete. Asher was a fine physician and a feeling, caring man. But he hated the Nazis with a passion that equaled his love for his own people." Mikal's voice trembled with emotion as he spoke. "The Jews have endured five thousand years of persecution. We know nothing can undo what's been done; all we can hope to do is to prevent it from happening again."

The events of that night outside of Athens suddenly flooded Juno's mind. Hatred obscured the fine line between right and wrong. He thought of how he felt when he had found Josh and Renée, and he shuddered. "Why did Ben Levi come to the United States?"

"After six people on his kibbutz died of the same strange neurologic disease, he became suspicious and began to look for a common denominator among them. You know what he found: they had all been in Dachau, and they all had that scar. He knew he needed help; he came to New York to seek that help from your brother."

"But why Josh?"

"Asher had a special feeling for your brother. He wanted help from someone he could trust."

Juno leaned forward. "A little while back, you used the word 'we.' Was that colloquial or did you mean 'we'?"

"I meant 'we.' I, too, am a member of the Dom." Mikal's tone offered no apology.

"And the others? Gerald . . . Dr. Davide . . ."

Mikal nodded.

Juno shook his head. "But you and Gerald are Mossad agents!"

"There's no conflict of interest. The Mossad is dedicated to the preservation of the state of Israel; so is the Dom."

"And Sokolov?" Juno asked.

"He's a Mossad agent, but he's too much of a conservative to belong to the Dom. You probably won't be dealing with him again anyway."

Juno thought for a moment. "That fellow killed at the Zurich Airport—what was his name?"

"Mordecai Grossman. He was also a member of the Dom. Tsve Shem, too."

"Jesus Christ!"

"I don't blame you for being angry. We should have told you everything in Paris, but Gerald has a tendency to be overcautious—it's safer that way.

"Shem and Grossman had been ordered to keep an eye on Ben Levi. Unfortunately, they couldn't prevent his death or catch his killer. When we learned that you were assigned to investigate Asher's murder, we had them follow you in the hope that you would lead us to his murderer—almost surely Reichmann or one of his men."

"And that Luger you're carrying?"

"The Luger is the Dom's trademark. We think it adds a nice touch of irony."

"I see." Juno frowned.

"Shem and Grossman were also supposed to watch Dr. Fields until we could contact him, but they got too involved in looking for Asher's murderer," Mikal continued. "Once Dr. Fields was killed, there was all the more reason to follow you. Before that, finding the killer was just a part of your job; after your brother's death, it became your crusade."

"You sound as if you didn't want me to catch Reichmann."

"That's just the point. We didn't."

"But why?"
"Because *we* want Reichmann. We want him tried in Israel!" Mikal was shouting now. He paused, took a deep breath, and continued more calmly. "We manipulated Sokolov into sending you to Europe because we had to determine for ourselves exactly where you stood. The attack on your life at the Rhine Falls suggested that you were closer to Reichmann than we thought. Under the circumstances, we hoped you would work with us to find him; it could save valuable time."
"And if I refused?"
"We would have had you killed."
"What?" Juno glared at the Israeli.
"You wanted the truth. There it is. I suppose, considering what I've just told you, that it seems rather an odd way of trying to establish trust."
Juno hesitated. His instincts told him that Mikal was what he professed to be—a loyal ally; still, Juno wondered about the longevity of their alliance. "What were *your* orders?"
"A fair question. Nothing specific. I'm to use my best judgment. I'll tell you this, however";—the warmth had disappeared from Mikal's voice—right now we want Reichmann. And I'll kill you before I'll let you get to him without us."
Juno was silent. He poured himself more Scotch and sipped it slowly.
Mikal watched him. "I know what you're thinking," he said. "We've been together now for two days. If I'd been sent to kill you, you'd already be dead."
"Now I'll be honest with you." Juno was seething. "If push comes to shove—if one lousy Nazi or one crazy Israeli so much as looks cross-eyed at me—I'll blow his brains out! And that goes for *you*, too!"
The two men glowered at each other. Then Juno held out his hand. He felt an inexplicable closeness to the Israeli. Mikal grasped the hand firmly; it was a tenuous and uncomfortable gesture of truce.

12

Burying her face in her arms, Lori Davide tried to find solace in the darkness. She was tired, frustrated, frightened; and her head throbbed unmercifully. Her own hypotheses and the suggestions offered by the consultants with whom she had just met had not provided the answers she was seeking. Over and over again in her mind she reexamined her research.

She and her colleagues had reached the point where they could accurately define the infecting agent, its portal of entry, its mechanism of action, and the pathogenesis of the disease it produced. What Thaddeus Reichmann had used in Dachau was a strain of virus that caused an illness that scientists would only later label a *slow virus disease*. Although some of the inmates at Dachau who had been exposed to Reichmann's virus had died quickly because they had received an overwhelming dose of the microorganism, the majority responded slowly, with the final evolution of the infectious process manifesting itself many years later.

Actually, one form of slow virus disease, scrapie, a fatal progressive degenerative disorder of the central nervous system that occurred as a natural infection in sheep and goats, had been identified in the mid- to late 1930's. In the 1950's, 1960's, and 1970's, a number of other such diseases were recognized. Kuru, a disease found in the Eastern Highlands of Papua, New Guinea, was the first proven human slow virus disease to be studied and was shown to be associated with the ritual of cannibalism, during which participants contaminated themselves with the brains and viscera of their victims. The time between infection and the appearance of the symptoms of kuru ranged from four and a half years to more than thirty years. A variety of other diseases previously of unknown etiology, such as the presenile dementias, were also demonstrated to be slow virus diseases; and even multiple sclerosis, Parkinson's disease, Huntington's chorea, amyotrophic lateral sclerosis, focal epilepsy, and certain forms of schizophrenia are thought to be due to slow viruses.

A slow virus disease would explain what was now occurring in the Jews. A large number of index cases had been infected in Dachau. The recipients who survived emigrated the world over; and the virus continued its slow but relentless course asymptomatically, while its victims remained unaware of the killer parasites in their bodies. What made the disease even more dangerous was the remarkable increase in the numbers of the virus in those overtly ill and the ability of the microorganism to be passed *at that time* from infected to uninfected persons in a sufficiently large quantity to cause the rapid deaths of the recipients.

The infected Jews from Dachau had left the camp carrying not only the instrument of their own destruction but also that of their fellow Jews—they were biological time bombs set to go off over thirty years later.

Although the disease itself and its affinity for those of Jewish origin was terrible enough, the real catastrophe of what had occurred in Dachau went far beyond the injection of a slow virus. Not only was the virus transmissible from man to man and susceptibility to the disease it caused passed from generation to generation, but Lori had discovered that *the virus itself was passed from parent to offspring*—the ultimate demise of the Jewish race was an integral part of the biologic process of procreation! The members of one generation would play a role in the annihilation of the next, until the Nazi's dream of a Jew-free world came true.

What Lori still lacked was that vital piece of information that rendered all else useless by its absence: a means either of stopping or of curing the disease.

Nothing—theoretical or tested in the laboratory—seemed to work. Interferon, a substance produced by the body to defend against viral infection, was of no value. The drug rifampin, occasionally useful in some virus infections; arabinoside A, an antimetabolite effective against some *Herpes simplex* virus infections; and artificial nucleotides, substances that could disrupt the process of viral replication, had failed. Only the theoretical possibility of inducing a genetic alteration to render the susceptible gene resistant remained to be considered, but the concept itself raised certain disturbing and unanswerable philosophical and moral questions: if a gene marking Jewish origin—or any gene for that matter—was altered or removed, was a Jew still a Jew? Lori shrugged her shoulders. She was a scientist, not a philosopher; she dealt with physical phenomena, not spiritual ones. She would leave the challenge of that puzzle to the rabbis.

Sitting up, she rubbed her eyes in anger, frustration, and fatigue. She wanted to swear, to scream, to cry out to God to help her. . . .

A knock on the door provided relief from the overwhelming tension.

"Come in."

"How did it go?" Gerald smiled sympathetically and sat down beside her.

"As I expected." She gathered up the papers on the table in front of her. "A lot of good ideas that won't work."

"Here are the latest statistics; I picked them up in the computer center on the way down."

Lori analyzed the numbers and digested their meaning. The disease had caused almost three thousand deaths now; the Nazis had again instituted their Final Solution. An enemy that could be seen only with an electron microscope would ultimately accomplish what the Third Reich had been unable to do during its entire existence; and the culprit would do it accurately, efficiently, and completely.

She pushed her chair away from the table and handed Gerald the report describing her progress—the prime minister and the Cabinet were meeting that evening to hear it.

"I'm going for a walk," she said. "I need some air."

What she needed was to know that there was life around her.

She was tired of death. She did not want to hate; she wanted to love. The terrible realization that only she stood between her people and their destruction had suddenly struck her, and she was terrified.

Reichmann adjusted the fingers on his gloves, checked the time, and unlocked the door with one of the keys he had copied from the several on Joseph Mann's key ring. Head down, hands in his pockets, he slipped through the rear entrance of the city morgue, walked quickly to the elevator, pushed the call button, and waited for the doors to open. Nervously he glanced over his shoulder and down the empty corridor. No one. The elevator came, but he did not relax until the doors had closed behind him.

He got off on the fourth floor and looked carefully in all directions. Convinced that he was alone, he made his way between the desks and other furniture in the outer office illuminated only by a small night light. Halfway down the main corridor he stopped at the door marked "Records." He let himself in and waited for his eyes to accommodate to the darkness. The room had a musty odor and was overheated by the two radiators hissing steam at each end of the parallel rows of filing cabinets that filled the room.

He turned on his penlight, found the row he wanted, and began to check the yellow cards inserted into small brass frames on the front of each drawer. The top one in the second cabinet on his right was labeled "Lu–Me." He unlocked it and slid it open. With the light held in his left hand, he ran through the protruding row of tabs with his right until he came to the one marked "Mann, Joseph (Joy)."

Removing the folder, he opened it and began to read the several typewritten sheets. Satisfied, he slipped the papers into the inside pocket of his coat and replaced them with sheets he had brought with him.

As he made his way back through the outer office, he stopped suddenly. There were footsteps at the far end of the corridor. He checked his watch—the night watchman was ahead of schedule. He reached for his Luger but then decided against it. He still needed information from Dr. Joy's office. If the guard gave the alarm before he could kill him, he would still have time to escape; but security would be doubled thereafter. It would be wiser to return on another night, he thought, and headed for the back staircase.

"What did the prime minister have to say?" Lori did not look at Gerald; she knew her latest report to the Cabinet could only be seen as an admission that they had failed.

"Not much." Gerald could not hide his depression.

"Any word from Mikal?"

"He seems impressed with Juno since they uncovered that letter from Golding. He's convinced that they'll find Reichmann. That should take some of the pressure off you, since it appears the Nazi bastard has a cure for the disease."

"I hope so. I'm still going on with my work. We must have an alternative plan in case they don't find him in time—or not at all." Lori found her thoughts dwelling on Juno. She had liked him from the start. Although his looks would attract any woman, it was his dedication to the few he loved that appealed to her most. But he was not a Jew, and that mattered—especially now. She found herself torn between a slowly growing desire and a persistent sense of responsibility; she wavered between what she wanted and what she felt others wanted of her. She blushed.

Gerald looked at her and forced a grin. "It appears Mr. Juno has more than one admirer."

She tried to glare at him, but found her lips quivering into a smile.

"Be careful, Lori. There could be problems. If there are, you know what we'll have to do. Our number-one priority—"

"—is the cause."

"More than that this time. You know that."

"I do . . . but I don't like being deceitful with friends . . . and I'm tired of the hate. There must be a better way."

"Perhaps." He paused. "Now fill me in on Reichmann's accomplishments at Dachau."

"It appears that Reichmann was completely caught up in the fanaticism of the SS. In 1942 he was directed by Himmler to engage in a research project to investigate a method of cultivating viruses as possible biological warfare agents. Reichmann's work was channeled through the Ahnenerbe. The reason for this requires explanation.

"In 1933 Wendell Stanley, an American biochemist, demonstrated that viruses were protein-containing solid particles. At that time relatively little was known about growing viruses except that they could multiply only inside of living cells. Therefore, in the early years of virus work, animals, especially monkeys, were used for the propagation, recovery, and identification of these microorganisms. It was only later that fertile eggs and cell cultures came into widespread use.

"Reichmann recognized that the ideal animal in which to cultivate viruses to be used in human infection was man himself. Since Jews were cheap and readily available and since no one in the Nazi hierarchy was likely to censure him for losing a few, he was sent to Dachau for the express purpose of conducting medical experiments evaluating the human body as a culture medium for viruses. The Ahnenerbe was simply the administrative instrument through which he got his funds. Reichmann discovered that virus infection might alter the genetic composition of a cell; Himmler, convinced that such a mechanism had infinite possibilities, ordered the Ahnenerbe to give Reichmann carte blanche.

"From what I've put together thus far, our explanation for the scar is correct. A direct injection of virus-containing fluid was introduced into the spleen; because it is a highly cellular and vascular organ, Reichmann must have felt that it was ideally suited for viral growth. A quick incision was made, the spleen was exposed, and the virus was inoculated under direct observation. Apparently things did not go as he had anticipated. Some of the subjects developed splenic infection, others a slowly progressive viral illness characterized by fever, enlarged lymph nodes, and various blood changes. Of these, most ultimately died. He was probably utilizing a very crude virus solution that was contaminated with a variety of infectious bacteria and other viruses. But he obviously succeeded in some cases. We're seeing the results of that success now." She sighed. "That's the best I can do from the information available. I'm afraid only Reichmann can tell us the whole story."

"Then let's hope Mikal and Juno find him." Gerald paused. "Do you think Reichmann knew what he was doing? That he was *trying* to wipe out the Jews?"

"I don't know. You can ask him yourself when Juno and Mikal find him."

Gerald hesitated. "Do you think we'll survive?"

"I don't know that either." She stood up suddenly, turned and looked out the window behind her desk, and rubbed her temples with her fingertips. Her headache was back. She knew what it was now: this time it had started with numbness and tingling in her arms and legs and weakness in her left hand.

13

Returning to his office, Juno called Commissioner Davis. As long as he gave Davis the impression that he was being kept up-to-date on the investigation, he anticipated no interference from his boss. He picked up the several books and articles on the history and activities of the neo-Nazi Party in America that he had requested from the police library and then called Mikal at the hotel to let him know he was leaving for the morgue to review the autopsies on Mann, Joy, and Baldini.

As Juno slipped into his coat, the telephone rang.

"Lieutenant Juno? Dr. Ludwick here."

At first puzzled, Juno suddenly remembered that Ludwick was the pathologist at Columbia who had done the autopsy on Mrs. Schonberg. "Yes, of course. Dr. Ludwick. What can I do for you?"

"I've been trying to reach you for several days . . ."

"I've been away."

"Of course. I'm sorry about your father and Josh." There was a pause. "I'm calling because I have some information on those speciments Josh asked me to take on those two victims with the scars."

"You got them?"

"Yes. I thought you had arranged it."

"I told Josh I would, but then everything happened so quickly . . ."

"I hope I didn't do the wrong thing, then. Josh called me from Chelsea and asked me to go down to the city morgue and get them. He said you'd had it okayed but to use your name if there was any problem. A Dr. Joy was very cooperative—let me have anything I wanted. He didn't ask for any authorization; said if you wanted me to have some samples, that was fine with him."

Juno shut his eyes and swallowed hard. Josh was always ten steps ahead of him. He missed him terribly. Juno cleared his throat. "You did nothing wrong. I'm glad there wasn't any problem."

"None with Dr. Joy. But that Dr. Mann is rather a pompous ass, isn't he."

"I don't understand."

"As I was leaving with the specimens, that fellow Mann came in; Joy introduced us. Mann wanted to know what I was doing there. I made the mistake of telling him. My God, did he make a scene! He actually accused me of unethical conduct and tampering with evidence. Seems he thought I was impinging on his territory or questioning his judgment. Damned insecure fellow."

Juno smiled. "I take it you got out of there in one piece."

"Damned right I did. I wasn't about to take any nonsense from that officious bloke—besides, I owed Josh for a few times he'd saved my hide on difficult diagnoses."

"Good for you. Now what about that information?"

"Those two men with the scars, Golding and Goldstein, had early signs of nervous system degeneration identical to that in Mrs. Schonberg. Did Josh tell you about her?"

"Yes, he did." Juno swore under his breath. Why hadn't Joy seen it? He was the best pathologist in the medical examiner's office.

"The medical examiner didn't find it,"—Ludwick seemed to have anticipated Juno's thoughts—"because he wasn't looking for it. I found it in the microscopic exam only because I had the advantage of having seen the disease in its full-blown form in Mrs. Schonberg. In its early stage, it's very subtle; it wouldn't be recognized if a pathologist wasn't specifically searching for it."

"Anything on the scar?"

"Best I can come up with is that it was used to expose the spleen so that something could be injected into it. What, I don't know; but I *can* tell you the cause of the disease that killed Mrs. Schonberg."

"You can?" Juno had to force himself to remain calm. He gripped the receiver until his knuckles shone white.

"Yes, but I'm not sure I can explain it over the phone. It takes a bit of background to understand it. Do you think you could come up here for a bit?"

"Where are you now?"

"In my office."

Juno looked at his watch. It was almost noon. "When do you go for lunch?"

"I don't. I bring a thermos and sandwich from home and eat here."

"Good. I'll come right down. Where's your office?"

"Same building as Josh's old office, but two floors down."

"I know where it is. . . ."

Juno hurried across the small quadrangle sitting amidst the gray Gothic buildings of Columbia Medical School and headed toward Ludwick's office.

Ludwick, a tall, imposing man who looked like a sergeant major in an English war movie, put down his cup of tea, wiped his mustache, shook the crumbs from his laboratory coat, and came around his desk to greet Juno with a broad grin.

"Glad to see you. Josh often spoke of you. Can I offer you some tea?"

"No, thanks. Please finish your lunch."

"It can wait. Damn bottles don't keep tea warm anyway. Let's go into my lab. I've jotted down some charts and diagrams on the wall slate to illustrate some things for you."

Juno followed the lanky Englishman out of the door and down the corridor crowded with cartons, storage cabinets, and a variety of unused and discarded scientific equipment. Ludwick stopped at a door with a frosted glass pane marked "Private." "Damn," he muttered. "I told my tech never to leave it unlocked." He pushed the door open, stopped, and took one step backward. "Good God!"

Pushing Ludwick aside, Juno rushed into the laboratory. The room was a shambles. Broken glassware was strewn everywhere. Drawers and cupboards had been torn open and their contents emptied on the floor. Two microscopes, a scale, and a slide projector lay smashed in a corner.

"Goddammit!" Juno pounded his fist on top of one of the laboratory benches.

"I'll find out who did this! My tech and secretary will be back from lunch in a few minutes. Then we'll see who has been sneaking around here. Meanwhile"—Ludwick drew himself up and straightened his lab coat—"let me show you what I've found. I've set out the results on the board there." The pathologist nodded toward a blackboard on the back wall; it had been protected with a white sheet.

"Sure." Juno followed him through the broken glass that littered the floor.

"I think you'll find this fascinating. I know what I'm seeing, but I'm not sure I can put it all into perspective. I'd like to ask you some questions about Golding and Goldstein." Ludwick reached up to pull down the sheet that covered the blackboard. "I've tried to make it as simple as—"

"Shit!" Juno's exclamation filled the room.

The blackboard had been wiped clean. Nothing remained of what Ludwick had written. In its place, a single word had been scrawled in red chalk: *"Jude."*

"I don't understand. I simply don't . . ." Ludwick was trembling uncontrollably. His ruddy face was now stark white. He steadied himself against the wall. "Why did someone do that? What's going on, Lieutenant?"

Juno struggled to control himself. "It was done to frighten you."

"Well, the bloke certainly succeeded in doing that."

Juno helped the physician back to his office, poured him some tea, and drew up a chair in front of his desk. "When did your secretary and laboratory technician leave for lunch?"

The pathologist took a long swallow of tea. "They're supposed to leave at twelve-thirty, but they disappear around noon or a little after." He smiled. "You know how help is these days."

"When will they be back?"

"They're entitled to forty-five minutes, but they take an hour." He glanced at his watch. "They'll be back soon. Why?"

"I want to know if they saw anyone hanging around here this morning. Did you?"

"No, not that I can think of. . . ."

"Were you here all morning?"

"No. This is my day for lectures to the second-year medical class. I got back just after eleven-thirty."

"And you heard nothing?"

"No. Believe me, I'd have heard someone making that mess."

"I'll wait for your secretary and technician and ask them. Maybe they did."

"Damn! They weren't here either."

"How come?" Juno asked suspiciously.

"My tech was down in the cold room in the basement all morning; she had some work there. And my secretary went to a meeting at the dean's office. I couldn't make it, so I asked her to go and take notes—curriculum planning, that sort of thing."

It was clear to Juno that Reichmann had spent a great deal of time and effort keeping tabs on Ludwick. Reichmann was expanding his operation rapidly; his resources seemed inexhaustible. But if Ludwick had what he claimed to have, the Nazi was in for his first setback. Juno gritted his teeth. "If you feel up to it, I'd like to hear your thoughts about the cause of the disease that killed Mrs. Schonberg. I think I can handle the scientific part without a diagram if you don't mind my interrupting with questions here and there."

Ludwick did not respond.

"Dr. Ludwick?"

Juno leaped up. The pathologist sat stiffly in his chair. His eyes stared straight ahead. His pupils were constricted. A whitish foam oozed from the corner of his mouth. Juno tore open Ludwick's shirt to feel for a heartbeat. There was none. He hit him sharply over his left chest with the side of his fist. Still none. And then he saw it: a Star of David on a simple gold chain. Ludwick was a Jew!

Staring in disbelief, Juno staggered backward and tried to

think. Instinctively he pulled out his handkerchief and used it to pick up the cup of tea the pathologist had just drained. The odor of almonds was unmistakable.

From a phone booth on 168th Street, Juno reported Ludwick's death to the nearest precinct commander; by labeling it "Routine," he estimated he would have about seventy-two hours before the information reached the police commissioner's desk and he had to explain his role in the circumstances surrounding the pathologist's murder.

He sped downtown to the morgue, still puzzled by Joseph Mann's reaction to Ludwick. It was common practice for the medical examiner's office to seek consultation from and to give help to other pathology departments, especially those of the medical schools in New York City. From the beginning, Mann had taken an unusual interest in this case; he had even participated actively in Goldstein's and Ben Levi's post-mortem examinations. Did it have something to do with Mann's having been in a concentration camp and the scar on his left side? What had Mann known? What was he looking for? And why? Juno asked himself these questions over and over again, but he could not come up with satisfactory explanations.

Even after he had reviewed the reports on Joy and Baldini, Juno was still no closer to the answers.

"May I have the one on Dr. Mann?" He returned the two folders to the clerk at the morgue record room.

"Sure, Lieutenant. Dr. Joy did that one. It had been tied up in the district attorney's office until yesterday, but I remember putting it back in the file myself. If you'll wait just a minute, I'll get it for you."

"Thanks."

In a few moments the clerk returned and handed Juno the folder.

Walking to the end of the counter where he could examine the file undisturbed, Juno spread out the contents and began to read.

There was something wrong!

Juno knew it after reading only the first three pages of the official autopsy report. Turning to the last page, he checked to see who had dictated it. Joy's name was typed under a blank line for his signature; beneath it, his title: Senior Pathologist, Medical Examiner's Office, City of New York. But there was no signature; in its stead were a certification by a representative of the district attorney's office stating why the report was unsigned—it had been transcribed after Joy's death—and a sworn statement by the secretary who had typed it that it was a valid and complete representation of the tapes she had heard.

The medical examiner's report was, Juno knew, a vital piece of evidence in a murder investigation. It was imperative, therefore, that it be exact in every detail. Juno had serious doubts about the report he had just finished reading. Both its authenticity and whether it had been prepared from tapes Joy himself had dictated were questionable. Not only was it too short—Joy's had usually been wordy—but certain elements that the compulsive Oriental would never have omitted were accentuated by their absence. Identification had been made from personal effects found on the person of the dead man and from the appearance of the corpse. Since the bullets that had killed Mann had destroyed his facial features, any pathologist worth his salt would have gone further. The scar was described, and the numbers on the left forearm had been noted—noted, but not *listed.*

Quickly Juno gathered up the sheets, replaced them in the folder, and returned it to the clerk. Joy had done the autopsy—Davis had told him that. But the Oriental had not dictated the words he had just read—he would swear to it! He didn't doubt for one minute that Reichmann had. But Juno wasn't interested in that or how the material had been switched; all he wanted to know was what Joy had seen when he had performed Mann's autopsy that was such a threat to the Nazi.

There were two of them. Both young and handsome, both eager and ready to do their part. These young Aryans were the new blood of the Fourth Reich.

Reichmann eyed them critically. His decision to at last come forward to reveal himself to a chosen few had been a difficult one, but he knew a leader could not be just a signature on an order or a voice on the telephone. A man who asked others to die for him had to do it in person. And it was working. Max, the taller one sitting stiffly near the glass doors to the balcony, had already proven himself—Ludwick would tell no one now.

"I'm proud of you, Max. You distinguished yourself this afternoon. It's made up for your failure to kill Juno and the Israeli." Reichmann patted the young man's bruised cheek and smiled to himself. He had seen a photograph of Hitler doing that as he presented Iron Crosses to a group of young people who had single-handedly wiped out a Russian tank near the Brandenburg Gate near the end of the war.

Now, finally, *he* was their leader.

Reichmann turned on his heel to face the other man waiting anxiously for orders. "I expect you to follow Max's example. I need some papers and tapes at the city morgue and some material from the city crime laboratory. Can you do it?"

"Yes, Herr Reichmann!" The man jumped up, clicked his heels, and saluted smartly.

Reichmann shivered with pleasure and returned the salute.

For several minutes Juno had been sitting in his car in the alley behind the loading platform of the city morgue. At midnight the security guard opened the rear door, checked in all directions, and then went back inside. Juno decided to wait a little longer before making his move. Concerned that Reichmann already knew too much about his activities, he had chosen to search for the original notes on Joseph Mann's autopsy after usual working hours in order to avoid calling attention to himself and the reason he was there.

By 12:30, having seen no other signs of the guard, he took his service revolver from its shoulder holster and placed it in the pocket of his raincoat. He backed out of the alley and parked his car at the corner of the street so that he could not be hemmed in by another vehicle and then made his way back to the loading dock.

Trying the door, he found it locked; it took him less than thirty seconds to open it with a special tool he carried on his key ring. Once inside, he unbuttoned his coat, loosened his tie, and tousled his hair with his fingertips; if he were challenged, he wanted to appear as if he belonged there—a detective tired after a long day but with a long night's work still ahead in the record room of the medical examiner's officer. The ploy might have worked better if he had walked in the front door, but he preferred not to be seen by the guard in the lobby or to have his presence recorded by his signature in the register.

Nonchalantly he walked down the corridor to the bank of elevators that would take him to the medical examiner's office on the fourth floor and paced impatiently as he waited for one to come. He hit the call button a second and a third time and rubbed his nose to relieve the sting caused by the acrid odor of formaldehyde and phenol that permeated the air.

The sound of a door closing interrupted the silence, and he reached for his revolver and released the safety. He heard the sound of running footsteps echoing in the corridor behind him, but they ceased abruptly. Without moving, he listened while his hand tightened around the handle of the weapon. Gun drawn, he turned and searched each of the three corridors that led to the elevators, but found no one.

The rumbling of the elevator as it slowed and then stopped again broke the eerie silence. Replacing the safety, he returned the gun to his pocket, wiped away the beads of sweat from his forehead, and stepped back as the doors opened.

He glanced at his watch—it was 12:50; he should still have ample time to come and go before the guard made his next rounds at 1:30.

As the elevator continued its slow ascent, however, Juno found himself growing anxious. He had waited until the building would be dark and deserted to avoid calling attention to himself and his purpose; delaying his move had seemed a prudent action, but now he wondered if he had waited too long. What if Reichmann's men had gotten there before him?

He stepped off the elevator and glanced to the right and left before proceeding past the administrative offices where Joseph Mann had worked and headed toward Joy's old office.

No pathologist, no matter how retentive his memory, could remember the mass of information collected during an autopsy; therefore, careful handwritten or dictated records were always kept, from which the final autopsy report was prepared. It was these original notes on Joseph Mann's post-mortem examination, along with the tapes from which the final report was to have been transcribed, that Juno needed.

No light shone through the frosted glass window that filled the upper panel of the door, and there were no external signs of recent visitors. His relief was short-lived as he tried the handle and found it unlocked; no door was left unlocked when it was meant to bar access to valuable material stored inside. He moved quickly to one side as he suddenly realized that his silhouette was clearly visible to anyone who might be hiding in the darkness of the office. The unlocked door could be an oversight on the part of a careless security guard, but the unexplained footsteps he had heard precluded such an oversimplification. Drawing his revolver, he stepped back, kicked in the door with his foot, and rushed in. With speed born out of experience, he scanned his surroundings and dropped to the floor on one knee. It was an automatic, but unnecessary, reaction; he had seen what he wanted in the light from the corridor.

The office was in ruins. The drawers of the desk and the two file cabinets in one corner were open, their contents strewn on the floor; all of the shelves had been stripped of their contents. Even the framed diplomas had been torn from the walls and lay amidst fragments of glass on the desk top and the floor. Nothing had been left unsearched or untouched.

There was one more place he might find something: the typing pool on the sixth floor—the tapes might still be there. Perhaps Reichmann had not thought of it. Bolting from the room, he headed for the nearest stairway, making no attempt to muffle his footsteps. He bounded up the stairs, disregarding the pain in his left shoulder as he pulled himself upward by the railing.

Taking two and three steps at a time, he quickly reached the sixth-floor landing, pulled open the stairwell door, and skidded to a halt. Raw hate and a terrible anger replaced his fatigue and his pain.

An elderly black security guard, his back propped against the wall, stared at him emptily. The front of his starched blue shirt was soaked with blood that still ran in crimson rivulets across his arm and down his wrist to a limp hand. His revolver lay unused at his fingertips.

Juno moved to the opposite wall and inched silently toward

the double doors that marked the entrance to the large rectangular room that housed the typing pool. His back pressed against the wall, his right arm raised, his index finger ready to pull the trigger, he was prepared to turn in any direction or to drop to the floor and fire. His mouth was dry, his heart pounded in his chest, and the beat echoed in the back of his throat. He could feel sweat trickle down his spine and collect in the small of his back. Yet he felt calm.

He peered cautiously into the room. A wave of nausea engulfed him, and he covered his mouth to keep from screaming or vomiting. The room was brightly lit. Everything was neat except for the desk directly in front of him. Its top right drawer was open, and two glistening blue plastic belts, a type used in older dictating and transcribing machines, lay on the floor beneath it in the shadow of the woman slumped awkwardly backward in the swivel chair that had been pulled out into the center of the floor. Recognizing the victim from the remnants of her features made the grisly sight even more painful for Juno; she was an Israeli, a part-time typist who usually worked odd hours because she had small children. Her hands and ankles were bound behind her with a piece of telephone cord. Her pantyhose had been used as a gag but could not hide the bruised, swollen mouth or the teeth that protruded through her lower lip. Her bloodstained blouse and the remnants of a white nylon bra hung in shreds about her. Her face and upper chest were masses of large purplish welts punctuated by clusters of cigarette burns. A Star of David had been hacked deeply into the flesh of her right breast. Bits of flesh, globs of fat, and clots of blood were spattered everywhere, even on the wall halfway across the room. Three bullet holes in her left chest still oozed dark red blood.

Juno clenched his teeth and fought to repress the volcanic rage erupting within him. It was obvious that the killer had found what he had come for; except for the few dictating belts on the floor, nothing else had been disturbed. Juno swore aloud and smashed his hand against the side of the nearest desk.

He placed his raincoat over the body to cover the gruesome sight, replaced his revolver in its holster, and opened the window to rid the room of the smell of death that seemed to permeate it. The cold air sobered him, and he stood for a moment and savored it with deep breaths. The sound of footsteps on the asphalt below startled him. He saw the shadow of a man and then the man himself running toward the fence that separated the morgue from the back of the city crime laboratory next door. The rhythmic echo of the footsteps was the same as that he had heard while waiting for the elevator just a short time ago. The man paused momentarily at the fence, scaled it effortlessly, ran toward the laboratory, and disappeared into the building.

"Baldini's office . . ." Juno spoke aloud.

He rushed from the room, raced down the stairs, through the deserted corridors, out the door, and across the loading area of the morgue. Ignoring the throbbing in his shoulder, he climbed the fence, dropped to the other side, and headed for the rear entrance of the crime laboratory—Roger Baldini's office was on the first floor toward the front of the building. In it was housed whatever information the ballistics expert had unearthed about the murder weapon that ultimately had killed him, too.

Aware that he was vulnerable in the open parking lot, he put his head down and dashed for the building, expecting at any moment to feel the thud of a bullet. He felt safe only when he had reached the protection of the wall next to the door leading to the rear of the first floor. Once inside, however, he would be exposed again for almost ten feet before there would be a doorway or another corridor that would provide cover for him; but he had no choice.

Drawing his gun, he lunged for the heavy steel fire door; pulling it open, he slipped inside and charged forward, stopping only when he was crouched safely behind the water fountain at the intersection of the two main corridors.

There was no sign of the man. Juno listened for any sound that might establish his whereabouts. There was none. Like the morgue, everything seemed quiet; but the silence and the emptiness were menacing. Advancing cautiously toward the front of the building, he made a cursory search of several places that might provide cover; there was no sign of anyone in hiding.

Although Roger Baldini's office, too, was empty, Juno knew that someone had been there before him: the door was ajar, the lights were on, and an open folder lay on top of the unlocked file cabinet in one corner of the room. On the floor beside it were several manila envelopes, their seals broken, their flaps partially torn. The folder labeled "Luger Killings" in Baldini's scrawl contained copies of the ballistics reports on each of the bullets that had been recovered from the bodies of Morris Golding, Avram Goldstein, Asher Ben Levi, and the others, identical copies of which he had in his own file on the case. What he did not have was whatever else had been there: the ragged corners of colored papers beneath two staples that had bound them to the folder showed where the sheets had been hastily removed. The envelopes were empty; the index slugs of the murder bullets were gone.

Angry and frustrated, Juno slumpled into the swivel chair behind the desk and tried to collect his thoughts. It was not difficult to theorize as to the motives underlying the murders of Mann, Joy, and Baldini; as with Josh, Renée, and the others, Reichmann had merely killed those persons capable of putting together any of the pieces of evidence he had left behind. Once again the German had demonstrated his propensity for thoroughness: even the most remote threat was eliminated before it could grow.

Juno found himself more concerned than angry. Someone was scrutinizing his every move! And the fact that his moves were predictable left him vulnerable. Reichmann had to be as familiar with his method of investigating a crime as he was. But how had the Nazi learned *that* much about him? That Reichmann might have infiltrated the NYPD and developed a working knowledge of the overall operation of Commissioner Davis's special task force was a frightening but realistic consideration. It would be necessary for him to be even more cautious and to alter his usual activities sufficiently to confuse and to conceal . . .

Suddenly he spun around in the chair, lunged for the light switch, and slid the door to the office shut with his foot, his revolver already in his hand. Someone was coming down the corridor.

Eagerly, he listened. The footsteps stopped just before the office. A barely perceptible shadow fell across the frosted pane that filled the upper half of the door. The man who had killed Josh and Renée could be on the other side of the wall! He smiled grimly, and his finger curled around the trigger; the sweat from his palm moistened the corrugated handle of the gun. He was ready. He had blotted everything else from his mind. He concentrated only on the gun in his hand as he waited for the next sound outside the door and the appearance of a silhouette against a background of light.

The world seemed to stop for an eternity. His adversary was either assessing the situation carefully before making his next move, or, by delaying, was hoping to get Juno to commit himself first.

Still Juno waited.

Without warning, the light in the hall went out. The door burst open. A figure rushed by him without touching him. There was a crash as the swivel chair toppled over, and another as it was hurled across the room.

But Juno was prepared. Without wavering, he estimated the man's position in the darkness, aimed, and pressed the switch.

In the sudden blinding light, he saw only two things: Mikal's face and the Luger pointed at his head.

14

Lori waited until the headache and the numbness had passed and her vision had cleared. She had gone through the usual stages traversed by the human psyche when faced with a fatal illness: denial, anger, frustration, grief, and finally an inner peace that would allow her to make the most of the time that remained.

Despite what she had been told about Golding's letter, she was skeptical about Reichmann having a cure for the disease; she was convinced that the Jews' only hope was to alter or remove the susceptible gene. She had reduced the problem to its simplest terms: time, money, and facilities. The basic scientific techniques were available; but applying them successfully in this situation required time—more, perhaps, than she had left. Hers was the only laboratory in Israel engaged in serious genetic research, and it was a fledgling operation compared to that in the United States that had been run by Joshua Fields. Fields had been on the threshold of developing methods for the rapid treatment and prevention of a number of genetic diseases. Now that Fields was dead, the problem was Lori's; to solve it, she needed far more than she presently had.

Her work involved basic human genetics.

Man is a mass of chemical and physical reactions working

together to control the complex systems that comprise his structural and physiologic framework. Although many of these reactions are similar or identical in all humans, those that are not determine individual differences. Each chemical reaction is governed by an enzyme, a protein that catalyzes it without being consumed by it. Each enzyme is synthesized in a specific and predetermined way according to a blueprint controlled by deoxyribonucleic acid—DNA—the building blocks of genes. Genes are arranged in long chains called chromosomes that are in every living cell. In the human cell, there are forty-six chromosomes, twenty-three pairs, each bearing thousands of genes. What each individual gene does is a vastly complicated puzzle; only recently have a few pieces been put into their proper places. On the thirteenth chromosome was the gene that marked Jewish origin; this gene was the target of Reichmann's virus—to the best of Lori's knowledge, these two properties resided in the same DNA fragment.

What she proposed to do was remove this fragment or gene by the use of a restriction enzyme that would chemically sever the appropriate strands of DNA that made up this "Jewish gene." If she was successful, the enzyme would precisely cut DNA at specific locations along the length of the molecule. She hoped to cut out the abnormal DNA and insert normal DNA at the previous locus of the abnormal gene. In other words, she planned to remove a specific link from a specific chain, replace it with a new and different link, and put the chain back together again. She had had some success using this technique in experimental animals and in bacteria to produce certain desirable characteristics. But this time she would be attempting the genetic manipulation in humans, and the slightest error could lead to mutation or death.

To accomplish the alteration, she required a source of a restriction enzyme that would cut the gene out neatly and cleanly from the surrounding genetic material and a supply of normal DNA. She planned to get both from a pool of non-Jewish human donors. However, she had no idea what would result from combining the two cut fragments of DNA with a new and different piece wedged between them. It might not work at all: would the complex physiochemical machinery of one person obey signals coming from the genes of another? It might kill the recipient. It could produce a monster. There was no way to know until it was done. But she had no choice.

She had started the experiment seven days ago. . . .

Lori inserted her progress report into a plain white envelope, sealed it, and placed it in the safe until Gerald arrived. He was adamant that the genetic alteration would not be needed, because Reichmann had the key to stopping the disease.

"If he created it," Gerald had argued, "he knows how to stop it. When we find him, we'll get it out of him."

"*If* you find him. And if you do, what if he can't—or won't—tell us how to stop it?"

Gerald had not answered.

Lori smiled. Gerald was an optimist. "If only science were so simple that one could always stop what one had started," she muttered to herself as she turned back to her plans for the second step of the genetic manipulation.

She looked up as Gerald entered and threw himself into a chair in front of her desk. "Things not going well?"

"More deaths. I don't know how long we're going to be able to keep this thing from the press."

"It's amazing we've been successful this long."

"The disease must be kept an absolute secret—at least until we find Reichmann and he tells us how to stop it!"

Lori did not answer. It was foolish to engage in that argument again.

"How are things with the Cabinet?"

"They're doing their best to run the country with some semblance of order. What else can they do? Life must go on. There's some talk of a military buildup, but that's just the hawks flexing their muscles. Some people have to have a war in their future or they can't be happy." Gerald paused. "And how is *your* work progressing?"

"Pretty well. I've completed phase one successfully."

"What about the rest of it?"

"I can't go any further without money and facilities. Phase one cost over a hundred and fifty thousand pounds, about thirty thousand over my allotted budget."

"As the Americans would say, 'This is no time to count nickels and dimes.' We're fighting for survival! Tell me what you need. I'll speak to the prime minister myself!"

"Gerald, the eternal optimist."

"The survival of the Jews is at stake! If by some chance you're right—Reichmann doesn't know the cure . . . or if we can't find him in time—then only your work can save us. The prime minister can't refuse what you ask." Gerald thought for a moment. "Of course, he'll have to give it to you *sub rosa*. There's no time for him to wait for Parliament to approve an allocation of funds; even if there were, we couldn't allow it, because then it would become a matter of public record."

"It's not only money I need. I must also have a very sophisticated laboratory facility."

"Then the prime minister will arrange to send you somewhere that has such a laboratory."

"Since when are you on such close terms with the prime minister?" Lori looked at him suspiciously.

"In times like these, he depends heavily on the Mossad. Shall we leave it at that?"

"Do I have any choice?" She didn't wait for his reply. "I'll tell you exactly what I need."

Gerald took a notebook and pencil from his jacket pocket.

"I need Joshua Fields."

Gerald looked up. "Don't be ridiculous! You know he's dead."

"Fields was on the verge of a breakthrough in the treatment of genetic diseases. I know enough about his work to make sense of his notes. Get me his research notebooks and arrange for me to work in his laboratory."

"How can I do that?"

"Just have your friend the prime minister make a phone call to the White House."

"Dammit, Lori. You know that's out of the question. Tell the White House we're in trouble, and you might as well take out an ad in *The New York Times*. Now, *you* be realistic . . ." Gerald stopped abruptly. "This Juno fellow . . . isn't he Fields's brother?"

"Yes."

"*He* can get you the notebooks."

For a moment, neither spoke.

Suddenly Lori wrote two lines on a pad in front of her, tore off the sheet, and handed it across the desk to Gerald. "Give this to the prime minister. Tell him that's what it will take to save our bloody necks!"

Gerald's eyebrows rose as he read. "A plane ticket to New York City and *ten million dollars?*"

"Take it or leave it. You think the Americans give things away? Let our government send it as a gift in honor of Joshua Fields and to further the work he started. That way it won't arouse suspicion. The Americans probably dropped Fields's program as soon as he died—to save the money. If we make the gift contingent upon restarting it, they'll do it. They never turn down money."

"You are a cynic." Gerald smiled. "You'll get what you need. . . . Start packing!"

"To the new Reich!" Reichmann lifted his glass and toasted the men seated around his dining room table. There were not two now, but eighteen. Their glasses were raised, their arms steady and their eyes fixed on him. The new generation of Nazis was flocking to him; he had known they would.

The disease was spreading, and with it, death for the Jews. Soon the demise of prominent Jews would create vacuums in government, in business, and in the arts—vacuums he and those he chose would fill.

He turned to the man immediately to his left. "You have the papers and the tapes?"

"Yes, Herr Reichmann." The man, a blond giant with icy eyes, reached beneath the table, withdrew the attaché case, unlocked it, and emptied the contents into a large earthenware bowl in the center of the table.

"Excellent!" Reichmann leaned forward, emptied his glass of wine into the bowl, struck a match, and lit an edge of the top paper. The flickering flames filled the room with an eerie glow. It was a torch Reichmann had seen before—at Nuremberg, in the camps . . . He watched the fire with fascination as it flared and then went out, leaving only ashes and a pall of smoke that rose toward the ceiling.

"And now to work. . . ."

He was ready to turn them loose. He had already chosen their targets.

15

Still shaken by the previous evening's near-fatal encounter with Mikal, Juno had informed the Israeli that he would be at Joseph Mann's office and had extracted a promise from him that he, too, would not act unilaterally.

Juno swore as he surveyed the empty room. It had been stripped of anything that might have provided a clue to the connection between the pathologist's background and his death. All that remained were the empty desk and bookcases; the walls, too, were bare except for several naked hooks where the physician's diplomas and awards had hung.

"Lieutenant Juno?" A stocky gray-haired man in a neat business suit extended his hand as he came through the door. "Mike Clayton, senior custodian of the building. My secretary said you were pretty upset. How can I help you?"

Juno waved his hand to indicate the empty office. "Who the hell cleaned out this place?"

Clayton shrugged. "I don't know, but we must have had a work order for it. My people don't do anything without one."

"Do you think you might find out for me?"

"Sure." Clayton dialed a number on the phone. "Marilyn? Look, find out who was responsible for cleaning up Dr. Mann's office, will you. Thanks." Putting his hand over the mouthpiece, he winked at Juno and nodded. "She's got her finger on everything that goes on around here. We'll know in a minute."

Juno started to respond, but Clayton held up a finger to indicate that his secretary was back on the line. "That's impossible, Marilyn! Someone had to request it or it wouldn't have been done!" He grinned sheepishly at Juno. "Well, that's just great, Marilyn! Doesn't anybody know what's going on around here? You tell Hansen I want to see him immediately! . . . Where? In Mann's office, that's where!" He slammed down the phone. "Dumb bitch. Can't even keep her work orders straight."

Unable to keep from smiling, Juno could predict the exact progression of the forthcoming events. Everyone would be questioned; no one would know who ordered the room cleaned. Without waiting longer, he walked out and slammed the door behind him. The bureaucracy that permeated the administrative and custodial services of the police department was an ally Reichmann had not anticipated. Juno knew he had better cut through it quickly.

Stopping at the phone booth in the lobby, he called Commissioner Davis, told him what he wanted, and asked for a meeting later that afternoon.

The personnel and records division of the New York Police Department comprised the entire second floor of the new administrative office building. Carefully constructed to make simple and efficient use of the available space, its major work force now consisted of banks of computers. The clerk who waited on Juno was the prototype of the new look: young, attractive, and effective in her job but still aloof. She was visibly annoyed by Davis's call directing her to attend to the detective's needs. Handing him the data, she gave him a cool stare and showed him to a row of comfortable booths.

Each page he turned convinced him more and more how far Thaddeus Reichmann's power extended. The system had been programmed to prevent personnel records from being altered; once an error was entered, it could be corrected, but both the original and the subsequent alteration were always there for examination. There was no way anything could be doctored without that very act becoming a permanent part of the record. Yet the things he had come for—the certified documentation of

Joseph Mann's curriculum vitae and his fingerprint records—were not there! They could not have been omitted carelessly or by chance—the pathologist could not have obtained a New York State medical license without the former and could not have gained entry into the United States without the latter; someone had removed them from a computer whose integrity was supposedly inviolable. The absence of this pertinent material further supported his contention that in Joseph Mann's death lay a vital clue to the Gordian problem confronting them.

Juno motioned to the clerk with whom he had spoken. "There are a number of items missing from this record . . ."

"I noticed, but the commissioner said to get it ready for you *without delay.*" The sarcasm in her voice was unmistakable. "I'm trying to fill in the gaps from other sources. I've telexed Albany and Washington. In fact, some of it just came in."

She turned the teletyped sheet in front of her so that both of them could read it. "As you can see, Dr. Mann graduated from Heidelberg Medical School in 1938. Character references could not be substantiated." She looked up. "That's par for the course. There were so many foreign physicians coming to the United States after the war that most references were accepted at face value; there were too many to check." She turned back to the sheet. "He *did* present his original diploma as evidence of graduation, and he passed the New York State Board examination in 1947. That was enough to grant him a license. Most doctors who got caught in the war didn't even have that much. Exceptions had to be made."

"Could you verify his diploma?"

"We've sent a wire to Heidelberg requesting verification. It may take a couple of days."

"And the Immigration Service?"

"I've asked them for copies of *all* of his records—including fingerprints. They're usually way behind, but I made it a priority check. I should have that information for you by tomorrow afternoon—sometime after two."

Juno gave her an admiring glance, thanked her, told her that he would return the next day, and headed for the elevators to take him to Davis' office. What he wanted from the police commissioner would hardly be granted as readily.

* * *

Juno grasped the arms of the chair to keep his hands from trembling. The void in the pit of his stomach spread rapidly until he felt numb. He had come to see Davis with a request that he knew would evoke surprise and resistance, and he was ready to argue his case and *demand* it be granted if no other tactic was successful. What he wanted was neither irresponsible nor improper; it was a reasonable step in the logical solution of a complex murder investigation, and there was ample precedent for it in the law. He had expected Davis to balk, but he was totally unprepared for the reply he had just received.

"Cremated!" Juno's exclamation was barely audible.

"That's right."

"But why?"

"I'm sorry, Pete, but I don't understand your reaction. Cremation is fairly common these days."

"But by whose authority? If I remember correctly, Mann had no relatives."

"True. But he left very specific instructions."

"How?"

"A certified letter was found in his desk; it was all very legal, believe me. Besides, why the hell would you want his body exhumed? I read the autopsy report; it seemed quite in order."

"I've been to the record room at the morgue. That authorization wasn't in his file."

"Christ, Pete, you know how things get misplaced. What are you getting at?"

Juno's voice was chilling. "It was just a thought. It doesn't matter now. . . ." Standing up and nodding his good-bye, he turned and left without bothering to close the door behind him. Reichmann again, he thought. He wanted to see that authorization.

"Lieutenant Juno"—the secretary's tone was more cordial than usual—"the switchboard operator has been looking for you; but I didn't want to interrupt." She handed him a message slip and returned to her typing. "You can use my phone if you'd like."

Juno pressed the buttons and listened.

"Lieutenant Juno?"

"Yes?"

"Mike Clayton. Remember me? I'm the chief custodian at the medical examiner's—"

"Yes, Mr. Clayton, I know who you are."

"Look, can I see you right away—it's important."

Something in the man's voice concerned Juno: alcohol mixed with fear, he thought. "I guess so. How about meeting me in my office in half an hour? I'll wait for you."

"Could you come down here, Lieutenant? I don't think I'm in any shape to drive." Clayton laughed nervously.

"I'll be there as soon as I can."

Clayton's office was the size of a large broom closet; but it was neatly furnished with a steel gray desk, two simple chairs with worn red plastic cushions, a bookcase partially filled with catalogs against one wall, and a scheduling chart on the other. The custodian's suit coat was draped over one of the chairs, and a half-empty bottle of bourbon stood open on his desk. The luster was gone from his eyes, now bloodshot and darting nervously from side to side. Waving his arm, he motioned Juno to sit down, poured himself another drink, and tossed it down in one gulp.

"Thank you for coming. You left so quick before, I didn't have a chance to introduce you to Mr. Hansen. But no matter—you couldn't have met him anyway. He's dead!" Clayton covered his face with his hands and sobbed.

Juno was simultaneously annoyed, surprised, and puzzled. "Would you like to tell me about it?"

The custodian reached for the bottle again; Juno caught his wrist firmly. "Talk to me first. Then you can have another."

Frowning, Clayton wiped his mouth with the back of his hand. "Like I said, Hansen is dead. I didn't know until I started to look for him after you left. . . ."

"When did he die?"

"This morning."

"How?" Juno felt himself tense.

"A heart attack, I think. You can check upstairs. One of the docs did his autopsy."

Juno chose his words carefully. "I know you must be pretty

close to the men who work for you, but do you usually get *this* upset?"

"No, but Charlie Hansen was a buddy of mine." The slur had disappeared from Clayton's voice. "We were in Vietnam together way back. I got him the job here. We kind of looked out for each other. When his wife and kid were killed in an automobile accident a year or so ago, me and the wife took him in—tried to be a family to him."

"I'm sorry." Juno started to get up. "Why don't you stow the bottle and go home?"

"Please wait. I didn't call you all the way down here just to wipe my nose. There's something else."

"Go ahead. I'm listening."

Clayton lit a cigarette with shaking hands. "Something crazy's going on. Charlie shouldn't have died. There was no reason for it. He wasn't sick a day in his life. He never had any trouble with his heart." He hesitated and looked around. "I don't think he had a heart attack. . . ."

"But people *can* appear perfectly well and then suddenly die of a heart attack."

"Sure, sure. I know that. I wouldn't have given it another thought if it weren't for a couple of other things."

"Such as?"

"Such as you coming around here asking about that empty office. Charlie was responsible for that part of the building, but I'd swear in court that he never touched that room. And there's no record on his work sheet that he did. The guys have to keep pretty good records of their workday, you know—I insist on it." Clayton smiled. "Also, *I* checked myself—there's no record of a work order or a verbal request or *anything* that that office was to be cleaned."

"What are you getting at?"

"I think somebody *swiped* the stuff and Charlie caught them in the act."

"Why do you say that? Did he tell someone?"

"No . . ."

"Then what makes you think so?"

"The look on his face, Lieutenant. The look on his face. No heart attack killed Charlie Hansen—he was scared to death! I don't know what in hell could have scared a bull like Charlie; but you go and take a look at his face, and then tell me it ain't so!"

By eight o'clock when Juno left, traffic had thinned out considerably. As he drove uptown to meet Mikal, he reflected on the dead ends. Instead of finding answers, he had encountered only more questions, one of which was: Where did Charles Hansen, a custodian at the morgue, fit into the puzzle?

At first Juno tried to convince himself that there was no relationship between the Swede's death and the rest of the case, that the fear he had seen on the face of the corpse was the result of sudden death. But he knew better. Hansen worked in the vicinity of Joseph Mann's office, and the pathologist's personal effects were missing. Hansen *had* been in superb health—there was no evidence of heart disease or a heart attack. In fact, the autopsy had revealed *no* abnormalities; the cause of death appeared to have been a sudden, fatal irregularity in the heart rhythm; and that, the pathologist who had done the autopsy agreed, could have been caused by sudden, overwhelming fear.

What had Hansen seen or heard that had scared him to death? Could it have been the same thing that Golding and Goldstein had? If so, at what terrifying point did the different worlds of these three men come together? And why?

Juno glanced again in the rearview mirror and stiffened. The car had been behind him for several blocks. Turning right on Forty-eighth Street, he found the eastbound traffic surprisingly sparse and stepped hard on the accelerator, passing a garbage truck on the right and then slowing abruptly behind a red Corvette in search of a parking place. The car behind him followed suit; as it came into the lights of the truck, he could see that it was a late-model maroon Plymouth sedan. The driver was its only occupant: a man wearing a hat pulled forward over his face.

Juno gunned the car to sixty, sped across Seventh Avenue, and ran a yellow and red light at the intersection of Forty-eighth Street and the Avenue of the Americas; but he could not shake his pursuer. At least one rule had been established: the man behind him had been willing to sacrifice surprise in order not to lose him. Slowing slightly, Juno kept one hand on the steering wheel and with the other took his .45 from the special bracket he had had built for it in the glove compartment.

He decided he would make his move between First and Second Avenues where Forty-eighth Street would be even more deserted—he wanted no interference in what he had to do, and he had to be able to do it unencumbered by the fear of hitting a pedestrian. He considered calling for backup, but that would mean exposing much of what he and Mikal had striven so hard to keep secret. Confident that he could handle this situation alone, he decided that nothing at present justified more outside interference than he already had.

He crossed Second Avenue. As predicted, the sidewalks were empty and only a few cars were parked at the curb. The street was wet and slick in spots where the melted snow had had a chance to freeze; a billow of steam rose through a manhole cover, dissipating rapidly in the wind from the East River. It was an ideal setting. He slowed gently, then jammed his foot on the brake. The car skidded forward and spun around; its front wheels bounced off the curb, and it screeched to a halt, blocking the road. Sliding across the seat at the exact moment the car stopped, Juno jumped out, braced himself against the passenger door, and crouched forward behind the front fender, the automatic held firmly in front of him.

For a split second only, his pursuer remained in the rectangular sight at the end of the barrel. Juno fired. There was a sudden flash of light. He found himself being hurled off the ground. A blast of air singed his cheeks and a deafening roar exploded in his eardrums, driving pain through his head and into the back of his throat. For a moment, everything went black as he stumbled backward; his legs collapsed beneath him, and he sat hard on the asphalt.

Staggering to his feet, he shook his head and arms to brush off the debris and turned back toward the source of the blast. Nothing remained of the maroon Plymouth except a barely visible skeleton of steel engulfed in a ball of flame. Either his bullet had hit the car's gas tank or an explosive device had been detonated. No one could have survived the inferno that continued to blaze.

He put the gun in his coat pocket, walked back toward his car, got in, returned the automatic to the glove compartment, and turned on the ignition.

He sensed the cold steel of the muzzle before he felt it being pressed against his skull.

"Do not turn around, Mr. Juno. Back out of here and drive exactly where I tell you."

16

Lori was packed and ready to leave. Somehow Gerald had made good his boast. She had a ticket for New York on El Al; and the American Secretary of Health, Education, and Welfare had acknowledged the ten-million-dollar gift with gratitude and had personally invited her to come to the United States to participate in the reestablishment of Joshua Fields's genetic research program.

The thought of seeing Peter Juno excited her. Since the death of her parents, she had dealt with being alone by burying herself in her work and her association with the Dom. Now, neither outlet sufficed. She needed someone. Perhaps Juno . . .

The knock on the door startled her. "Come in!"

"I see you've finished packing." Gerald seemed uneasy.

"Not quite. Any word from Mikal?"

He disregarded her question. "I have to talk to you for a moment."

"It must be important. You look upset." She sat down.

"Joshua Fields's research laboratory at Columbia was destroyed by fire a few hours ago."

"My God! And his research notebooks?" Lori sat forward.

Gerald shook his head. "Everything was lost."

"Reichmann?"

"It couldn't have been anyone else."

"Damn!" Swallowing hard, she fought to hold back her tears. She stood up and continued packing her briefcase.

"What are you doing?"

"Packing. I'm still going to New York."

"Are you sure you want to go now?" Gerald reached out and covered her hand with his. "Reichmann's dangerous. It would be almost impossible to keep your trip a secret. He'll be waiting for you."

Lori squeezed his hand. "There's no other way. The disease is progressing. It doesn't look like we'll find Reichmann in time; I'm convinced our only chance is a genetic manipulation. I can't do it here; I told you that before. I need additional laboratory facilities and better-trained personnel—Israel has neither."

"Perhaps you should wait. We know that every young Nazi punk who's been waiting for a new Hitler is flocking to Reichmann. He's getting bolder and more powerful every day—the attack on an institution in the heart of New York City is proof."

"Mikal and Mr. Juno will take good care of me."

Gerald noted the gleam in her eyes and the rising color in her cheeks. "You're adamant then?"

"Absolutely."

Gerald thought for a moment. "Then I'm going with you. You're *my* responsibility." Her reaction had convinced him that the Greek detective was even more of a problem, and in a far different way, than he had anticipated. He was not going to New York because of Lori. Mikal was more than capable of protecting her and attending to Reichmann if the Nazi came after her. The purpose of his trip was to face once and for all the problem Juno posed for the Dom, and he would entrust that mission to no one but himself. He had already sent Mikal a message that they were coming.

The man in the back seat remained silent. With unwavering calm he kept the muzzle of the Luger pressed against Juno's head, maintaining a position directly behind the detective so that his face could not be seen.

Following instructions, Juno drove uptown toward the George

Washington Bridge. He was certain that he would be dead now if his passenger were Reichmann or one of his assassins. That left the Dom. The more he thought about it, the angrier and more concerned he became. It was unlike them to violate a truce—even a temporary one. But then again, Mikal had spoken only for himself; and whether or not he was aware of the actions of his colleagues might determine just how long such a truce would endure.

"Where to?" They were on the ramp leading to the upper level of the bridge.

"Just keep going until I tell you to stop."

Juno shrugged his shoulders and guided the car into the oncoming traffic.

"Where's Mikal?" It was more of a demand than an inquiry.

Juno relaxed slightly. "At the hotel, recovering from a flesh wound in the side. We had a run-in with some of Reichmann's men."

"Is he okay?" The agent increased the pressure of the gun against Juno's skull.

"He's just fine," Juno answered. "Now put that goddamned Luger away or I'll shove it down your throat!"

The man laughed. "Gerald was right about you. And I must say I admire the way you took care of that Nazi. Sorry about the gun."

"Why the hell were *you* following me?"

"I wanted to speak to Mikal. I worried when I saw he wasn't with you and that you were being followed."

"What'd you think I did with him?"

"I don't know you at all, Mr. Juno. My job is to look out for my colleagues."

"I'm supposed to be one of them—at least temporarily. Remember?"

"A man is my colleague when he proves it." The Israeli's voice was cold.

"I'll try to keep that in mind. Now what about that message for Mikal?"

The man did not respond.

"I'll drive you to the hotel if you'd like."

"Too risky."

"Then tell me where to get in touch with you. I'll have Mikal call you."

"Don't be annoyed. We can't be too careful." The agent hesitated. "Tell Mikal that Gerald and Dr. Davide will arrive from Israel on an unscheduled El Al flight into Kennedy tomorrow evening at eight twenty-three. Arrange to meet them. Tight security all the way."

"Jesus Christ! Why bring her *here?*"

"She needs a place to work. That's all I know."

"Anything else?"

"Just a piece of advice: be careful!" The man slid to the opposite side of the car. "Slow down at the next break in the railing, and please don't look around—if you've never seen me, you won't have to lie about it."

As the car slowed, the Israeli jumped out and was gone before Juno could maneuver out of the traffic.

Alone again, Juno had only one thought: Lori Davide. He was looking forward to seeing her again. It was too soon to think of a relationship with another woman. Still, when he thought of Lori . . . He would have to sort out his feelings and deal with them.

He gave Mikal the message, then stretched out on the bed, his hands folded behind his head. "Any luck today?"

"None. No one could tell me anything that would explain Baldini's death. You were right: Reichmann killed him because of his close association with Dr. Joy." He poured himself a drink. "And your day?"

Juno told him all that had happened. "I'm convinced that Mann's the key. There's a reason for those thefts. Someone's gone to a great deal of trouble to hide something. It's Reichmann's M.O., all right, and that ties him and Mann together. But how and why? Mann was a Jew who had been in a concentration camp . . ." Juno sat up on the bed. "Which one?" He answered his own question, "We don't really know which one. We don't even know for sure whether or not he had a scar on his left side. . . ."

"But his autopsy report described a scar similar to the ones we've seen in some of the inmates from Dachau."

"Who knows how valid that report is? Don't you see, *that's* why the tapes were stolen! Joy would have noted the exact numbers on the left forearm, not just their presence. That would have given us a means of finding out which camp Mann had been in. . . . So would exhuming his body and seeing the numbers for ourselves. That's why Reichmann had to have Mann's body cremated. First thing tomorrow, I'm going to see if I can find that authorization; I should have done it sooner." He pulled up a chair next to Mikal. "What are the possible reasons Reichmann killed Mann?"

At first they reconsidered their initial theory that the pathologist had been killed because of his involvement in the investigation of the murders of Golding, Goldstein, and Ben Levi; but both agreed that it had to be more than that. The probability that Mann had had the scientific talent or expertise to stop or cure the disease seemed remote. If Mann had been in Dachau, however, he might have been able to identify Reichmann. Mikal said he would contact authorities in Jerusalem to see if the name alone might tell them when and where Mann had been interned.

"Anything else?" Mikal asked.

"Yes. Mann's office. Remember I told you that even the walls had been stripped? If I'm right, Mann and Reichmann should have been about the same age. They were both Germans. Mann attended Heidelberg—it's in his file. What if Reichmann also had been at Heidelberg? It's a little farfetched, but not impossible, that they might have known each other. . . ."

"And if that Nazi bastard had found out that his old schoolmate was the acting medical examiner of New York—"

"—he wouldn't have taken the chance that his name might come up in the murder investigation. Let's take it one step further. Many people keep mementos from high school and college—class pictures, for example. Wouldn't it be ironic if a picture of Thaddeus Reichmann had been hanging in Mann's office all along and we never knew it? . . . But if Reichmann knew it—or at least thought of the possibility . . ."

"It makes sense."

"Still, one thing bothers me: how could Reichmann know so much about Mann? Even if they had been friends at school, it takes a lot more than that to know the kinds of things about a person that Reichmann seems to have known. Even good friends don't know what pictures a man keeps on his desk or hangs on the walls of his office . . . unless he or someone he had planted in Mann's laboratory had been there . . ." He stopped abruptly, reached over, and clamped his hand over Mikal's mouth. He nodded over his shoulder toward the door, then indicated that the Israeli should keep talking. Silently Juno crossed to the bedpost where his gun hung in its holster. Mikal took his Luger from his jacket and approached from the opposite direction. The two men positioned themselves on either side of the doorway and listened; a manila envelope slid under the door.

Juno pushed back the chain and rushed into the corridor.

"Relax," Mikal said. "Just some details about tomorrow."

Juno rejoined Mikal at the table to watch him decode what appeared to be a flyer advertising a Turkish bath on East Forty-second Street. It took the Israeli fifteen minutes to rearrange the words into a paragraph that almost filled both sides of a piece of hotel stationery.

"Finished?" Juno asked.

"Yes. It says there'll be no other passengers on the plane except Gerald, Lori, and about twenty handpicked agents."

"At least Gerald's smart enough to guard her well."

"Don't underestimate Gerald. He's a top agent with a lot of experience. He knows what he's doing." He continued with the instructions. "Just you and I are to meet them. Gerald wants as little activity as possible. Feels it's less likely to arouse suspicion. Even if Reichmann learns of their arrival, chances are he'd only send a small force if he thinks just the two of us are meeting them."

"I suppose so. But I'd feel better if we had a few more men on our side until everyone was off that plane. We could have problems."

"Gerald's in charge. We'll follow his orders."

Juno didn't like the tone of Mikal's voice. "Whatever you say." He bit his lip.

Mikal continued. "We're supposed to find someplace where Lori can work—she doesn't have sufficient facilities or personnel in Israel. She's got an open invitation to a number of laboratories here in the United States. We'll have to pick one where she can be safe."

"What about Josh's lab at Columbia? I'd like to keep her here in New York."

Mikal looked away.

"What is it?"

"Your brother's lab was destroyed by fire."

"What?" Juno screamed. "When?"

"Sometime early this morning."

Juno felt sick. Somehow it was like losing Josh all over again. Everything Reichmann touched died. And now the Israelis were about to drop Lori Davide at the bastard's doorstep.

"I'm sorry, Pete." Mikal looked up and smiled sympathetically. "Any ideas about another lab?"

"Let me think about it. There must be someone at NYU or Cornell who owed Josh a favor. I'll look into it. . . ."

"Gerald's crazy!" Mikal shouted as he continued reading. "Wants you and I to keep tabs on her by ourselves. Figures that way Reichmann will show his hand and go after her."

"That son of a bitch! He's using her for bait! We may be good, but not *that* good. Reichmann can pick the time, the place, and the way he'll come after her. You lose her, and you may lose your only chance to beat this damned disease. Dangling her in front of Reichmann's nose is sheer suicide." He paused. "What the hell is Gerald going to do in New York?"

"He's got other business here."

"Such as?" Juno asked suspiciously.

"The message doesn't say."

"Very convenient."

"Something's bothering you, Pete. What is it?"

"I don't like the whole setup. But what bugs me most is Gerald. The man primarily responsible for Lori's safety drops her in our laps and then goes sightseeing. He doesn't trust me, but he's willing to entrust Israel's top scientist to my care. Is that logical?"

"Sometimes the most illogical plan is the most logical. Besides"—he smiled—"I'll bet Lori's pleased about the chance to see you again."

"Well, she's not the most unpleasant company I can think of

either." Juno yawned. "Better get some sleep. We've got one hell of a day tomorrow."

The day began badly. A telephone call from Mikal told Juno that Joseph Mann's name appeared nowhere on the fragmentary records that had survived from Dachau; there was nothing even remotely similar to it. The news was not surprising; he did not expect they would find anything. But the second call contained a shock.

"Lieutenant Juno? Mike Clayton. What the fuck's going on? What kind of bastard are you, anyway?"

"What are you talking about?"

"You know damn well what I'm talking about! I told you everything I know about Charlie Hansen and that stuff in Dr. Mann's office . . ."

"I know you did. Now what's wrong?"

"What's wrong? Get your fucking watchdog off my back! I'm warning you—if that son of a bitch scares my wife again, I'm going to break his fucking neck. And then I'm going to come down there and break yours!"

"Look, you dumb bastard, I did *not* send anyone to follow you. Why would I?"

"To see if you could catch me with Mann's stuff. Well, I don't have it! That's the God's truth!"

"I know you don't. If I thought you did, you'd damn well hear about it!"

"Then who is that fucker?" Clayton's voice had lost its fury.

Juno bent forward over his desk. The back of his neck ached, and he felt himself enveloped by that vague mixture of fear and anger that had become an almost constant sensation for him. "Now listen, Mike, and listen carefully. Where are you now?"

"At home. I live on Staten Island."

"Do exactly as I tell you. Don't ask any questions. Just do it!"

"Sure, sure, but—"

"Are your wife and kids home?"

"Yeah, they're right here."

"Keep them there. Don't let anyone in, and don't any of you go out. I'll be there in about half an hour. Keep an eye out for me. And remember, don't open the door for anyone else!"

* * *

It was a small one-story house painted white with forest-green trim—the type of home, Juno thought as he circled the block a third time, that a man like Clayton would choose.

Assured that there was no one watching, he parked the car in the driveway, checked the revolver under his left arm, and mounted the steps.

He rang the bell three times, but no one answered. His fear mounted. Clayton was the kind of man who would not thwart authority without a good reason. Trying the door, he found it locked; a quick walk around the outside of the house told him that the rear door and all of the windows were also securely fastened. If the Claytons had left, he would have them picked up and then read them the riot act; if not . . . He had to know.

With little difficulty he unfastened the lock on the front door, slid back the safety bolt, and stepped into the small entry hall. An eerie silence permeated the air. With his revolver drawn, he checked each of the rooms and found them empty. There was no sign of a fight. Two cups half-filled with coffee sat on the kitchen table. He decided to call Davis to request that an all-points bulletin be put out for them. He was about to dial when he noticed for the first time the partially open door at the far end of the kitchen.

He found them in the garage. Mike Clayton lay face down on the oil-stained concrete floor. The back of his head had been blown off, and the impact of the bullets had destroyed his spine and skull so that a part of his face was almost perpendicular to the bloody pulp that remained. Beneath his left arm, held as if he were still trying to protect her, was the frail body of a little girl with blond curls that floated in the pool of blood flowing from the two bullet holes in her forehead. Mrs. Clayton and their son, a lad of about ten, were sprawled in a corner near the garage door. Juno did not bother to count the number of bullet holes that had taken their lives.

As he surveyed the insane scene, images of Morris Golding, Avram Goldstein, and Charles Hansen flashed through his mind. The remnants of the custodian's features, too, were distorted by more than the fear of death: it was a terror above and beyond human fright, as if the man had been peering into hell at the exact moment he had died. But what superseded even that was the *absence* of that look on the faces of Mrs. Clayton and the children. What horrifying apparition linked these four men together but had spared the other members of the Clayton family? Juno was certain that when he had the answer to *that* question he would have the answers to the others as well.

"What the hell is going on?" Winthrop Davis was livid. "I want to know where you've been, what you've done, and why you have withheld information from me. And make it good, buddy, or I'll have your ass!"

Juno felt his temper flare. He was in no mood to submit to the ravings of a man who placed his own ego above the safety of those he had been appointed to protect. Being called on the carpet was one thing—it was a part of every man's professional existence that he learned to tolerate; being bombarded with verbal abuse was something else—it was a privilege reserved only for those who had earned it.

"What are you getting at, Commissioner?"

"You're no closer to solving this case than you were when I first gave it to you." He hesitated. "Okay, *that* I can understand. It's a bitch of a problem. I'm not sure any of us knows just how big it is. But, by Christ, you're the hand of death! Everywhere you go, death follows you. First your brother and that doctor in Chelsea; then Dr. Mann, Dr. Joy, Roger Baldini, and Sergeant Tracy . . ."

At the mention of Josh and Renée, Juno could feel his anger threatening to erupt; but Davis continued, totally oblivious of the feelings of the man seated before him, ". . . and now this Dr. Ludwick, that Clayton fellow and his family, and the Bridges girl. . . ."

"Who?" Juno was startled by the mention of the unfamiliar name. "I don't know any 'Bridges.'"

Davis flipped open a folder on his desk. "Bridges, Shirley. Twenty-seven years old. Unmarried, female, Caucasian. Computer clerk, division of personnel, NYPD—the girl you spoke to yesterday, the one who got you Mann's record." He threw a photograph across his desk.

A single glance was all that was needed. The picture showed

the woman draped across her desk. A ragged bullet hole had entered her skull just above the bridge of her nose. Death had been instantaneous. Through the streaks of caked blood, the familiar look of utter terror stared back at him.

"And Mann's record?" Juno could barely speak.

"Gone."

Juno swore at himself. He had been so preoccupied with Clayton that he had delayed picking up the information Shirley Bridges had requested from Albany and Washington.

17

Juno and Mikal arrived at Kennedy Airport just after six P.M. They operated independently. Mikal walked twice through the arrival and departure areas of El Al and the several other airlines that shared the same terminal building. Juno drove through that section of the airport, checking the drop-off and pickup zones, the bus and taxi stops, and finally each floor of the adjacent parking garage. They met at the terminal cafeteria for a sandwich at seven P.M. and separated again at 7:30 to repeat their procedure. At 8:10 Juno picked Mikal up; they drove through a small gate that the Israeli had arranged to have opened for them and parked the car in the shadow of the shed used for loading and unloading baggage near the main El Al runway. The flight carrying Lori and Gerald would stop about a hundred yards from them; the Israeli airline preferred not to run the risk of scheduled arrivals at predetermined gates.

As they waited, they reviewed their activities. "Anything unusual?" Juno asked.

"No. Things are quiet. Maybe Reichmann doesn't know Lori and Gerald are coming in tonight."

"Believe me, he knows. He's either decided to make his move elsewhere or his men have done a damned good job of hiding."

"There it is." Mikal pointed toward the flashing wing-tip lights of the jet emerging from the darkness into the halo of light over Kennedy Airport.

Juno reached forward to turn on the ignition. "We'll pick her up right at the door as soon as it lands." He wanted no delay. Lori would be most vulnerable during the few moments it would take her to emerge from the plane, descend the stairs, and enter the car. He would feel comfortable again only when he had her safely in the back seat between Mikal and Gerald and they were out of the airport and on their way back to the Park Lane.

Juno heard Mikal's scream at the moment the plane rolled to a stop; he saw three unmarked vans emerge from where they had been hidden in the darkness at the end of the runway and head for the plane. Still the scope of what he saw did not fully register in his mind until the sound of shots and the flash from an automatic weapon protruding from the window of the first vehicle shattered his inertia. Watching in horror as the first two figures who emerged from the forward door of the plane were cut down, Juno jammed the accelerator to the floor and swung the car sharply to the right to cut off the vans, all now spraying the airliner with bullets.

"Keep them away from the plane!" Mikal shouted. He fired at the tires of the vehicle closest to him and swore as it swerved away undamaged.

"Why the hell don't they stay in the goddamned plane?"

"That's exactly what they should *not* do," Mikal hollered back. "Those bastards aren't trying to shoot the damned thing to death—they're going to try to blow it up with Lori on board. It's *her* they're after! We've got to get her off!"

"Where the fuck are the airport police?"

"Dead or unconscious. These bastards couldn't have gotten this far without getting them out of the way first."

In frustration Juno watched the three vans separate, circle away from the plane, and begin their approach for a second attack. "How close do they need to get?"

"They'll probably use satchel charges. If they hit the fuel tanks, the fire will do the rest."

In the momentary lull in the battle, several men had jumped from the plane and were firing at their attackers from behind its wheels; more were firing from the exits that now stood partially open.

Watching the first van slow down and then accelerate toward the plane, Juno realized that the few men who had succeeded in getting out had little or no chance of repelling the attack. All they could hope for was to keep the attackers far enough away from the plane to prevent an accurate attempt at its vulnerable underbelly. He estimated the defenders could hold off one—perhaps two—more advances.

"Head for the first van! Maybe if we can stop it, we can stop the others." Mikal leaned out of the window, took careful aim, and fired.

"This is no damned good, Mikal!" Juno cut the car to the left and headed back toward the front of the plane. They had one chance. . . .

"What are you doing?" Mikal roared.

"The only thing we can do."

Juno aimed the car toward the plane. At the exact moment that he brought the car to a halt at the foot of the stairs, he and Mikal jumped out. Leaving the motor running and the doors open, they raced up the steps and into the plane. Bullets peppered the doorway they had just entered; the sounds of fire being returned from the men on the ground added to the racket that shattered the air around them.

While Juno grabbed Lori by the wrist and pulled her with him into the galley closest to the exit, Mikal explained to Gerald what his men's roles would be.

"No!" Gasping in horror, Lori watched the men in the plane follow Mikal's orders and line up on either side of the staircase leading to the car. "I won't let them do it!" She swung her briefcase at Juno's head. "Let me go!"

Warding off the blow, Juno spun around to face her. "You'll do what I tell you! Some of those men are about to die for you. Don't waste their blood." Turning back to face the exit, he waited another instant, then put his arm around her and pushed her head down on his chest. "When I say 'Go,' just keep down and run with me. Whatever you do, don't stand up."

"Now!" Mikal's bark was a sharp retort above the gunfire.

"Go!" Pulling her with him as he leaped for the exit, Juno started down the stairs.

It seemed interminable. With one arm tightly around Lori Davide and the other burying her face in his chest, he dragged her down the steps between the two rows of men firing in unison. He maneuvered between the bodies of men falling backward and the hands of their comrades pulling them upright to maintain the human wall that protected him and Lori from the bullets that came in bursts from the distance. It was like racing through a tunnel of bleeding humanity. He slipped once and realized his shoes were covered with the blood that now trickled in rivulets over the steps. He raced forward until he collapsed against the car at the bottom of the stairway; then he grasped Lori under the arms, pushed her forward onto the floor of the back of the car, and slammed the door. "Don't budge!" Moving cautiously to the front door, he pulled it shut after him, crawled along the seat, turned so that his feet were on the floor but his trunk and head were barely above the dashboard, put the car in drive, and jammed his foot down on the accelerator. The car shot away from the plane toward the open runway.

"Gerald! Where is he!" Lori started to sit up.

"Goddammit! Keep down!" Juno pulled himself up just enough to reach behind him and push her head down.

"Where are Gerald and Mikal?"

"They're still at the plane. Now stay down!" He flung himself down on the seat as bullets shattered the back window. Another pierced the windshield near the rearview mirror. He kept going. Pulling himself up again, he peered over the steering wheel and looked around. In front of him was empty concrete. The blurred image of a wire fence was barely visible. About two hundred feet to his right, one van hesitated and then headed toward him. To his left, utter confusion appeared to paralyze newly arrived groups of airport security personnel. Behind . . . Juno felt sick as he watched the scene unfold in his rearview mirror. He wanted to scream, but he could not make the sound; he wanted to weep, but tears failed him. Yet his eyes remained riveted to the mirror and the carnage it reflected.

The stairway was a montage of the dead and the dying. A few men still stood at the railing and fired at the two vans. He searched for Mikal in the smoke, but the distance was too great. He thought he saw the Israeli tending the wounded and trying to pull those exposed back under cover, but it could have been anyone. Juno felt a wave of sorrow surge through him. He liked Mikal. There was something about the Israeli besides his looks that reminded him of Saul. . . .

"What's happening?" Lori's voice pleaded with Juno to tell her.

"I can't see. We're too far away. Stay flat on the floor. I've got to get you out of here. Gerald and Mikal know what they're doing—they can take care of themselves. They'll meet us at the hotel later."

"Dear God, please take care of them!" She stifled a sob and then suddenly shrieked, "Turn around! I must go back for them. They're all I've got!"

"Not on your life! Now shut up and keep your face against that floor! I haven't got time . . ." Juno stopped. He understood. His voice became softer. "They'll be okay."

His attention varying from the wire fence in front of him, the single van chasing him, and the scene in the mirror, Juno contemplated his plan. With him he carried the hopes of the men strewn on the runway behind him and the people they represented, and he pledged not to forsake their trust.

"Lori?"

"Yes?"

"We're going to have to crash the fence. Just lie flat, remain loose, and let yourself give a little on impact. You should be okay. I'll tell you just before we hit."

"What's going on back there?"

"I think they're . . ." Juno glanced into the rearview mirror. A cold shiver raced through him. His mind braked as if to allow his eyes to record the movements in slow motion. Both vans headed for the plane; neither slowed nor turned nor . . . He saw the instant of impact, blinked at the sudden flash of white and yellow and orange, and watched the explosive force expand in concentric circles moving outward from the center toward him. The car shuddered, and he heard Lori's scream mixed with his own. The plane was gone . . . Mikal was gone . . . Gerald was gone. There was only fire.

Juno wept, his tears as much in anger and rage as in sorrow. Then the last of his inhibitions left him: fear deserted him, hesitation vanished. All that remained were anger and hate.

"Now!"

He braced himself, shielded his face with his forearm, and crashed through the wire fence. There was a shattering of glass and a grinding of collapsing steel; the car stopped.

The van was only a hundred yards away. Juno jumped from the car and rolled to his left. He pulled his revolver from the shoulder holster beneath his left arm. Landing on his knees behind the open door, he held the gun in his right hand, steadied it on the back of his left, and took careful aim. Without breathing, he centered the outline of the driver's head at the top of the sight and watched it come into focus through the windshield of the van racing toward him. The rest of the world was a blur; all he saw was the sharp horizontal edge of the metal at the end of the barrel and the now visible features of the man above it. He waited until it seemed as if he could reach out and touch the face, and then he waited an instant longer and squeezed the trigger. His hand jerked, and the crack rebounded against his eardrums; he squeezed again, and he heard and saw the glass shatter. The van careened to the right, then to the left. The explosion and his next shot shattered the air simultaneously. As the blast flung him backward, he saw the body of Lori Davide being hurled into space.

18

Her head ached, her eyes hurt, and she could taste the blood in her mouth; but there was a cool moistness on her forehead.

"Lori?"

The voice was soft, the sound soothing. The image it conjured up in her mind invited her to return to life. Opening her eyes, she blinked painfully at the light and brought the face of Peter Juno into focus. A sense of being lost frightened her; she made one attempt to get up, failed, and collapsed backward.

"Where are we?"

He applied another moist cloth to her forehead. "Don't talk. We're in your room at the Park Lane."

She started to speak again.

"Don't talk, I said." Sensing her unspoken questions, he took her hand. "The plane . . . Gerald . . . Mikal . . . all of them— they're gone." His voice was a whisper. "My last shot must have hit the gas tank of that van, and the explosion set off our car. The impact threw you almost fifty feet. No broken bones, thank God; just a lot of cuts and bruises and some bad burns. You're going to be fine."

"And you, Peter?"

"I'm indestructible." He smiled and squeezed her hand.

"I'm glad . . ." She pulled him toward her and hugged him. Her tears wet both their cheeks as she clung to him.

He turned out the light, collapsed into the armchair, and put his feet up on the stool he had set against the door frame separating Lori's room from his own. From this vantage point he could survey both rooms.

He had gone over the two rooms to look for listening devices but had found none. He had then moved several pieces of heavy furniture against the outside door of her room; it would take a man of immense strength to dislodge them. He had set several glasses on top of them so that the slightest tilt would cause them to fall. His own door was locked but not blockaded, so that they would have an emergency exit. On either side of his chair he had placed a small end table on which he had laid out his armaments: on his right was the .45 automatic from his car, a box of shells, and a flashlight; on his left, his service revolver, shells, and a package of signal flares that could be used as weapons as well as for light. If they survived the night unmolested, then he would carry on as he and Mikal had planned. . . .

Juno thought of the Israeli again and felt a tightening in his throat. Despite their conflicts, he had really liked the man. At another time they might have become good friends; they were alike in many ways.

He watched Lori sleep and listened to the sound of her breathing. He was beginning to put his grief into its proper perspective—Renée would not have wanted him to mourn indefinitely.

The image of Renée when he had found her body flashed through his mind. Her facial expression haunted him. Somehow it was different from that of Golding, Goldstein, and the others. But how? He rubbed the ache in the back of his neck.

He was convinced that the look on the faces of Reichmann's victims at the moment of death was somehow significant. He focused on them one by one, dividing them into two groups: those who had seen something at the time of their deaths that had terrified them, and those who had not. Only Joseph Mann fit into neither category; his face had been destroyed by the bullets that had killed him. But where did Renée fit? She was foolhardy in her *lack* of fear. At times it had resulted in a nearly self-destructive defiance of danger that had threatened both of them; still, it had been an important factor in their success as a team. If anything, she had been even more aggressive than he was; and this had helped to cement a close professional relationship that might otherwise have floundered—

Someone was pounding on the door to his room! Lori screamed. Juno grabbed his .45 and bounded from his chair. He glanced at Lori—she was sitting upright in bed, trembling. He rushed to the door and positioned himself to one side of it, his gun poised.

"What is it?" Lori was standing now in the doorway between their rooms.

Motioning to her to keep silent and to join him, he waited until she stood beside him, her back pressed against the wall.

The pounding continued, but it had lost some of its force.

"Who is it?" Juno demanded.

"Mikal . . . Please, I'm hurt."

Juno stiffened and pulled Lori back; she had started for the door.

"It's Mikal. Let him in!" she commanded.

Juno tried to think. He had seen the plane explode; still, there might have been survivors. Mikal knew where they were staying; Reichmann's men would have attacked before if they had known.

"I'm bleeding . . . let me in . . . please." It was a weak, raspy voice.

Juno held Lori firmly against the wall.

She tried to pull away. "For God's sake, Peter!"

Juno shut his eyes tightly and gripped his gun. It could be Mikal. If the Israeli had escaped from the plane and were bleeding, he'd have lost a lot of blood by now. It would be hard to recognize the voice of someone in shock. He fought to keep himself from opening the door—it could be a trick. He wrestled with the decision. If he were alone, he'd risk it; but he had no right to gamble with Lori's safety. He could not permit his own feelings to negate the sacrifice of all the men who had died at Kennedy, but he knew he could not live with his conscience if he let Mikal bleed to death on his doorstep.

Handing Lori the .45, Juno told her what he wanted her to do. "Talk to him in Hebrew. And no matter what happens, let no one in but me."

The man spoke Hebrew. Juno picked up his service revolver and hurried into Lori's room. He moved the furniture away from the door and, with the revolver in his hand, pulled open the door and rushed out into the hallway. He saw the shadow of the man and felt his presence as the blow caught him behind the ear. Pain rebounded in his head, his vision blurred, and then everything faded into blackness.

Consciousness returned with pain. Juno took a moment to evaluate his surroundings; he was on the floor facing the wall in the corner of his room. His head hurt, there was throbbing behind his eyes, and his hands and feet were numb except for the burning sensation from the ropes binding them. Two men were talking behind him. He recognized one immediately: the man who had attacked him on Fifth Avenue.

"I won't take a chance with this bastard again," the man called Max said. "We'll kill him here."

"And the woman?" the other asked.

"Reichmann said to kill them both."

Juno rolled over—he saw Lori. She was tied to a chair; the robe he had given her had been torn from one shoulder. An ugly bruise marred her left cheek, and her bottom lip was swollen and bleeding. Her head hung limply on her chest as she watched her two captors with hate-filled eyes.

"You miserable lousy bastards!" Juno shouted.

"I owe you, Jew lover!" Max snapped back. He kicked first at Juno's head, then at his stomach and groin.

"Stop!" Lori screamed, but her outcry was cut short as the other man's fist caught her on the ear.

Ignoring the blood running from the gash in his forehead, Juno tried to get his breath. He struggled with his bonds, but his movements only caused them to dig deeper into his flesh.

"Not so smart this time!" Max kicked at him again, but Juno parried the blow with his shoulder. "You didn't expect us to speak Hebrew, did you? Some of us speak it fluently. It's a necessity for us now; this is a war, and this time we shall win!" Max turned to his comrade. "Let's be done with them."

An evil grin crossed the man's face as he stood over Juno. "What do they say? 'Does the condemned man have a last request?'" The Nazi's ugly laugh ended abruptly. The door burst open. . .

Gerald fired from the doorway and then dove behind an armchair for cover. His first bullet hit the man in the shoulder, hurling him back against the wall. His second caught Max in the face; he was dead before he hit the floor.

Grasping his shoulder, the wounded man fired once at the Israeli; the bullet grazed Gerald's temple, momentarily throwing him off balance.

Juno was already moving. With unbelievable strength he threw himself at the Nazi who had spun around and was now aiming at Lori. He hit the man just below the knees, causing him to topple forward. But the German recovered immediately, regained his grip on his weapon, kicked Juno away with his heels, and swung the gun toward Lori again. Gerald's volley cut him down before he could fire.

Trying to smile through his tears, Juno watched silently as Gerald untied Lori and carried her to the bed.

It was not until Gerald had untied him, helped him into a chair, and was cleaning the wound on his forehead that Juno recovered sufficiently to speak more than a few words of gratitude. "I thought you were killed in the explosion at Kennedy."

"I was lucky. I was thrown clear." In addition to the wound he had just sustained, Gerald's cheeks were cut and bruised; and his left hand was wrapped in a crude bandage.

"Mikal . . . ?"

"He didn't make it." He paused. "Neither did anyone else."

"I'm sorry."

"Lori's safe. They knew what the risks were."

It seemed like a cold answer, Juno thought; but he knew Gerald was right: there was always a price.

"How do you feel?" the Israeli asked.

"Fine now." Juno held out his hand. "I owe you one."

"No. We're even. I saw what you did for Lori at the airport."

Lori sat up slowly, supported herself on one elbow, and smiled at Juno through swollen lips. "I'm sorry about the way I acted. I know you wouldn't have let Mikal die. I guess if I hadn't pushed you, we might not have gotten into that mess."

"No apologies necessary. I decided on my own. I should have been smarter."

"You made a near-fatal error," Gerald said. "Never sacrifice the primary objective for the sake of a secondary one. Next time, I might not be there."

"That's unfair!" Lori interrupted.

"No. He's right. I made a foolish mistake."

"Two," Gerald added. "The second was assuming that Nazis don't speak Hebrew. Never make assumptions about the enemy; you'll be wrong as often as you're right."

"I'll keep that in mind." With Mikal gone, Juno was now at the mercy of Gerald and the Dom. Their defeat at Kennedy would make them increasingly cautious and belligerent; he knew they would not hesitate to neutralize anyone who stood in their way. "How did you know where we were?" he asked.

"Mikal kept me informed."

Juno knew that a showdown with Gerald was inevitable. It might as well be now, he decided. "Look," he began, "the three of us have had a close call today. Don't you think this would be a good time to clear the air?"

The Israeli looked hard at him. "Say what's on your mind."

"First, I'd like to know just where I stand. Since you're now the leader of the Dom—"

"How did you—?"

"Mikal told me about the Dom. With Asher Ben Levi dead, a new leader had to be appointed. Only that person would have had the authority to do what you've been doing; bodyguards don't set policy."

"Go on."

"Second, I'd like to know why you're here. Certainly not to protect Lori; Mikal and I could have done that."

"You didn't do a very good job of it."

Juno suppressed his anger. "You came for a showdown with me, didn't you?"

Gerald sat forward. His face showed no emotion. "You seem to know the answers."

"I don't understand," Lori interrupted.

"You will," Juno said. Then he turned back to Gerald. "Do I scare you that much?"

"Scare? No. But you do concern me."

"You think I'll keep you from taking Reichmann back to Israel to stand trial. Is that it?"

"He killed your brother. It's not unnatural for you to want him to be tried here."

"I'll admit I did at first."

"And now?"

"A lot more's at stake here than individual differences. I got to know Mikal, I saw what your men did at Kennedy, I know what you just did. My father died of the disease. He *and* my brother were very important to me. It's taken me a while to understand that your motives are as important to you as mine are to me—maybe even more important. I've lost my family; you stand to see your entire people destroyed. I think your claim to Reichmann supersedes mine."

Gerald held out his hand.

Juno took it and held it firmly. "A *real* truce this time?"

Gerald smiled and nodded. "What now?"

"We get the hell out of here. Reichmann knows where we are; he'll try again when those two don't come back."

Only Juno heard the sharp click. Automatically he jumped up, dove for his .45, aimed, and fired at the door until he had emptied the clip. Before the last bullet had splintered what remained of the upper panel of the door, he was vaulting through the air toward the bed. With his arms outstretched to protect them, he landed on top of the two startled Israelis at the exact moment of the blast.

19

As soon as he felt the building shudder, Reichmann returned the magazine to the rack and hurried from the small newsstand in the lobby of the Park Lane. He saw the desk clerk trying to make his way through the excited crowd gathered at the bank of elevators and heard the head bellman shout for the police and the fire department. Ignoring the angry look of a fashionably dressed woman as he pushed her aside, he rushed through the revolving door at the back entrance and headed west toward the Avenue of the Americas.

Halfway up the block, he tapped on the window of a taxi parked near the curb and bent down to speak to the driver. "The bomb just went off. Max and the others have not come down yet; something must have gone wrong. Wait two minutes and then pull up near the hotel. If Juno and the Israeli doctor leave by the back door or the delivery entrance, just find out where they go. I'll take care of them myself this time."

Reichmann made his way through the pedestrians and paused to speak to a tall, heavyset man at the next corner. "Get your men into the lobby and around the front of the hotel. There's been a change in plans. Just follow them; I'll do the rest." Then he hailed a cab to take him uptown.

He got out three blocks from his apartment. It was beginning to snow, and the wind was increasing as he stopped in a phone booth and called his apartment. When he heard the maid's voice, he hung up and headed home.

Using the back door and the service elevator as usual, he got off two floors above his own, attached the silencer to his Luger, and walked down the stairs. Quietly letting himself into his apartment, he heard the maid in the kitchen, called to her, and pulled the trigger as she appeared in the doorway—she, too, was a threat to him now that he was so close to success. Then he dragged her body into the hall closet, covered it with an old blanket from the top shelf, and called to make arrangements to have it disposed of.

He lit a cigar, sat down at his desk, unlocked the bottom drawer, and took out a folder marked "Phase II."

The bomb had destroyed the doorway and had blown out the window. The rest of the room was a shambles: splinters of wood and fragments of cloth were everywhere; the walls were pockmarked with tiny craters.

Gerald surveyed the destruction through the acrid smoke. "My God, what happened?"

"Implosion bomb . . ." Juno sat up slowly and shook his head. "Type used by a few of the terrorist groups that still operate in New York. Plastic explosives, steel nails, and a timer—that was the click I heard." He pressed on his ears and swallowed to relieve the pressure.

"I didn't hear anything."

"If you've heard it once, you never forget it. When it's used correctly, the bomb's placed outside a door and the blast is inward. The timer is set to give the person who's arming the detonator about thirty seconds to get away."

"That's why you fired."

"I hope I got the bastard." Juno got up from the bed. "The explosive is just the propellant; the nails do the rest." He waved his hand to indicate the results.

"Nasty."

"Very."

Lori looked at him and stifled a scream. "My God!"

He looked down. He was covered with blood from a multitude of small lacerations. The blood ran in tiny rivulets from his back where he had been most exposed. He had felt nothing because the local shock had numbed the nerve endings—the pain would come later. If he had been standing rather than prone, he would probably be dead.

"Just a few cuts . . ."

"I'll clean them."

"No time." He reached forward and gently pulled her to a sitting position. "We've got to get out of here. Reichmann's men will be back. Those two Gerald killed must have been the advance force; the bomb was a backup. There's sure to be more. Besides, in a few minutes this place will be crawling with police."

He felt lightheaded and nauseated, but he steadied himself and made his way through the debris to the closet. As he slipped into his raincoat, he felt the first pangs of pain. His skin was raw, and the slightest pressure was excruciating. In his present state, the prospect of what lay ahead worried him. Gerald would be able to care for himself. It was obvious, however, that Lori would be unable to walk—she had a nasty gash on her left leg from the blast. Juno knew he would have to carry her. She started to argue but took one look at the determination on his face and without another word allowed him to pick her up in his arms.

He paused just long enough in the shattered doorway to view the body of their assailant, a young fair-haired man now covered with blood.

"You're a good shot," Gerald commented.

"I take no pride in killing young fanatics." Juno kicked open the door to the stairwell.

"It's a long way down."

"We have no choice," Juno said. "It's too dangerous to take the elevator. Reichmann may have men stationed in the lobby."

"How did he find us?"

"Had us followed from the airport."

"But how do you know that?"

"If Reichmann had known where Mikal and I were staying, he would have come after us here before this." He paused to catch his breath and to adjust Lori's weight in his aching arms; the inside of his raincoat was wet with a sticky mixture of blood and sweat.

"Where are we going?" Lori asked.

"I'll tell you when we get there."

By the time they had reached the first floor, Juno was feeling the effects of the loss of blood. His arms and legs were dead weights that seemed detached from him, and he moved mechanically. He was winded, and his head and chest pounded mercilessly. He took the stairs to the first subbasement, then made his way up the back staircase to the street, hailed a cab, and told the driver where he wanted to go. He had not been to Josh's apartment in some time; at the thought of it, painful memories flooded his mind but then were blotted out—he had collapsed across Lori's knees as the taxi turned and headed uptown.

Her injured leg dressed and propped on a pillow, Lori tended to his wounds. Watching her, Juno liked what he saw. The smudges of soot on her chin and along one side of her nose somehow gave her an appealing, earthy look that complemented rather than detracted from her beauty. The touch of her breasts as she leaned against him to wipe the dried blood from the side of his head caused a stirring that he had not experienced since the night he had left for Zurich.

Gerald came and sat at the foot of the couch. "How do you feel?"

"Better, thanks. No medicine like a pretty doctor."

Lori blushed. "Do you think we'll be safe here?"

"We should be okay. I haven't been here for some time; if Reichmann knows me as well as he seems to, he should be convinced by now I wouldn't come back."

Gerald outlined his plan for guarding Lori. Two agents would be in the apartment at all times; another, disguised as a painter, in the hall; one on the staircase; two in the lobby of the building; and one each in cars in the underground tenants' garage and across the street from the canopied entrance. "When you find her a place to work, we'll set up the same kind of surveillance there."

"And in the evenings?"

Gerald grinned. "I think you and I might share that shift. I'll tell my men; if they do their job well, you shouldn't notice them anyway."

Juno hesitated. "Let me ask you about something."

"Of course."

"You obviously have tremendous connections here and abroad. Why haven't you asked for help? Israel's an important ally to the Western world. Why do you insist on going it alone? Certainly you can do better than one New York City cop."

"Try to appreciate our position. We're a small country surrounded by volatile neighbors. If it were known that we were facing total annihilation—even ten years from now—we would fail to survive as a viable nation *in months!* Treaties, trade agreements, our voice in international affairs, and even our word would be worthless the moment the news leaked out. Nobody gives a damn about a 'lame duck,' as your American history books call it. In addition, our enemies might decide to attack us now—when we're vulnerable. Our only hope of surviving is to find Reichmann and force him to tell us the cure and to keep quiet while we do it. And that's another reason we've got to find Reichmann fast: as soon as he's sure we don't know how to stop the disease, he'll announce it—for the glory, and because he knows damned well what would happen to us if the world found out."

Juno rubbed the back of his neck. "I see. And now I see, too, the reason for our conflict. I was the fly in your ointment."

"Exactly."

"But why didn't you take me into your confidence?"

"Would *you* have in a similar situation?"

There was no need for Juno to reply. The Israeli was right. "Then why deal with me at all? You could have easily neutralized me."

"People with a cause—especially a good one—are not easily dissuaded or 'neutralized,' as you put it; they do not give up. By manipulating things so that you joined us, we were able to keep an eye on you. Much safer from our point of view than to permit you to proceed on your own. You were right when you said we were afraid of you, and for two very good reasons: in your desire to help us, you might well have revealed the very secret that we wanted kept hidden; too, if you found Reichmann and either killed him or put him on trial, you would have robbed us of the one man who has the information that will save us."

"Do you think we'll find him in time?"

Gerald looked away. "I have to, or I'd go mad."

Lori briefed Juno on her findings and told him what she would need to complete her work. It took him just forty-eight hours to get her the laboratory she needed. With the help of the Secretary of Health, Education, and Welfare, one of Josh's friends at Columbia convinced the medical school administration to permit her to use a vacant laboratory in their Clearwater complex. The old research institute, closed for years because of waning research grants, was otherwise unoccupied. Gerald and his men could seal off the floor she was on and thus protect her effectively. They could come and go without attracting attention since the entrances and exits were almost a mile from the nearest major road.

Lori stood in the center of the laboratory and viewed it with amazement. What would have taken months in Israel had been accomplished in two days. . . .

She felt dizzy. The vision in her right eye blurred. She could not feel her feet, and the numbness was spreading upward. She tried to think, but the thoughts would not focus. She tried remembering—dates, places, things she had done—but even the memories came and went before she could hold on to them. Leaning against a laboratory bench, she maneuvered awkwardly toward a chair, stumbled, and slipped to the floor. Before she lost consciousness, however, she was overcome by fear. Although this attack would pass in minutes, she knew it would happen again.

Juno laughed to himself. The value of bureaucracy was in the eye of the beholder. For years he had complained about filling out reports in numbers he was convinced provided a copy to almost every precinct commander in the five boroughs of New York. But today he had found the first legitimate reason for the tons of paper consumed yearly by the New York City Police Department: a funeral home had to have an authorization to cremate a body. He was on his way to pick up that authorization from the one that had cremated Joseph Mann.

A meticulous examination of the letter had verified the authenticity of the signature. Joseph Mann had also provided for the disposition of his ashes; and, as he had directed, they had been scattered over a pond on a small estate he had owned near Bernardsville, in northern New Jersey. He had ensured that his remains would yield no clues to the secrets that had died with him.

The thought plagued Juno as he walked down the ramp to the garage beneath police headquarters. His frustration was somewhat assuaged, however, by his anticipation of seeing Lori at dinner that evening. He got into his car, took out his notebook, and contemplated his next move: to check with Heidelberg to document Mann's medical education and test his theory that Reichmann, too, might have attended the famous medical school at the same time. His next stop: the International Telephone Exchange Building on Fifth Avenue.

When he reached forward to insert the ignition key, he stopped, his eyes riveted to the hood of the car. A small area at the front of the hood reflected the overhead fluorescent lights more than the rest; someone tampering with the hood release had wiped away any fingerprints that might have been left in the coat of dirt and grime that was deposited over the entire body of the car. Reichmann or his henchmen would have left no such clue to an explosive device under the hood—the trap had to be something other than that. He turned and examined his surroundings in the garage. No one was in sight. He considered the alternatives. If he got out of the car, he would be vulnerable, wedged in between the front bumper and the wall. But the risk of an attack in a location where it could attract the attention of dozens of armed policemen was immense; Reichmann and his men would have wanted better odds.

He decided not to remain in the car—there could be a *timed* explosive device. Slipping down in the seat, he reached for the door handle . . .

"Bastards!" He sat up quickly, rolled over into the back of the car, tore out the back seat, crawled into the trunk, released the lock, and jumped out.

Whoever had set the bomb had been not only expert but also ingenious. Juno had seen this type only once before—it had killed two of his colleagues on the force. The device itself and its mechanism were simple; detecting it was nearly impossible: only his determination not to underestimate Reichmann had saved him. The explosive was attached to the chassis of the car immediately beneath the driver's seat. Opening either front door activated it; opening it a second time detonated it. If he had gotten out to check under the hood, he would have been blown to bits.

He called the bomb squad and left to find a taxi.

It was quiet in the apartment. Lori and Gerald were asleep, and he had about thirty minutes before the Israeli would relieve him. For the first time since Renée's death, Juno was again at peace with himself. He had found a purpose for his life other than revenge: finding Reichmann and protecting Lori and her work could save the Jews; if it did, it would help him repay the Fieldses for what they had given him.

"Would you like some company?"

Looking up, he saw Lori silhouetted against the light in the bedroom. She wore no robe, only the simple nylon nightgown that one of Gerald's men had purchased for her.

"Sure." He motioned her to the chair beside him. "Trouble sleeping?" He tried to keep from staring at her.

"A little."

He got up and walked to the window. "How's your work going?"

"Slowly. It's hard to get started in a new lab."

"Do you have everything you need?" He turned to face her.

She ignored his question and held out her hands. Reluctantly he came and sat beside her.

"I want you, Peter." Her voice was firm.

Juno's heart pounded, but he said nothing.

"Talk to me."

"I don't know what to say." He hesitated. "Please stop and think for a moment. You know nothing about me; and I, even less about you."

"Why are you fighting so hard?"

He ran his hand lightly over her cheek and marveled at its softness. "You're one of the loveliest women I've ever known. It would be easy to . . . Is that what you really want?"

"Yes. I can't tell you how I'll feel tomorrow, only what I know I feel tonight. I know I'm rushing things a bit—I mean to. I want to squeeze everything I can into whatever life there is left for me; I want whatever happiness I can steal, and I want you to share it with me." She paused. "Whenever I wanted to put something off as a child, my father would tell me a story: he had a brother named Jacob who wanted to be a doctor, so Jacob left Israel—it was Palestine then—and went to Germany in 1932 to study. In 1934 he was accepted to medical school, but he decided to wait until things quieted down for the Jews. He applied for admission again in 1935 and 1936; by then, the Nuremberg Laws were in force and there were no Jews openly practicing medicine; and any Jew who had been in medical school had been thrown out. Jacob died in a concentration camp in 1942.

"The moral: if you want something, take it now." She took his face between her hands and kissed him on the lips.

The taste of her obliterated any reservations that remained. Her lips were soft, and the tongue that darted around his own was sweet and inviting. He could feel her warmth through her nightgown; he felt her nipples harden against his chest and her thighs tense against his.

"The bedroom," she whispered.

Gerald came out of his room and saw them.

"Perfect timing," she said. "Peter and I were just going to bed."

The two men looked at each other and shrugged.

Gerald grinned. "Better do what the boss commands," he said.

Juno listened to the sounds of her breathing and savored the smell of her body. Lori slept peacefully, her head resting on his chest, her arm draped around his neck, her fingers intertwined in his hair. Loving her had exceeded his expectations; he was satiated and content.

The more he thought about it, however, the more uncertain he became. At another time, would they have given themselves to each other? Had she simply reached out to take from life what she could while there was still time? Question after question raced through his mind until the turmoil became unbearable and he forced himself to justify what they had enjoyed together by remembering the story her father had told her. . . .

There was something she had said that disturbed him, something that pertained not to the past but to the *present;* but he could not recall what it was or its relevance.

He sat up suddenly and shook her. "That story your father used to tell you. You mentioned the Nuremberg Laws. When did you say the Jews were thrown out of the German medical schools?"

Still groggy, she gave him a puzzled look. "I think it was 1936." She shook her head, smiled, and fell back to sleep.

He got into his clothes, blew her a silent kiss, and rushed out into the living room to speak to Gerald.

He knew everything had been too pat. There *had* to be answers; no one—not even Thaddeus Reichmann—was infallible. There was always a flaw, and now he knew what that flaw was. He knew where to look and what to look for.

20

At seven A.M., when the Israeli agents arrived to relieve them, Juno and Gerald left to begin the tasks they had laid out for themselves. For security, they worked together.

There were no replies to the three wires Juno had sent to Heidelberg the previous day requesting information about Mann and Reichmann, but he had expected to receive none in so short a time. He called Albany to corroborate Joseph Mann's year of graduation from medical school and then headed for the library.

Lori Davide was correct about the Nuremberg Laws. Issued on September 15, 1935, they deprived Jews of German citizenship, forbade marriage and extramarital relations between Jews and Aryans, and prohibited Jews from employing female Aryan servants under thirty-five years of age. Thirteen supplementary decrees that followed essentially outlawed the Jews completely. But more important to Juno than the content of the laws was their chronological history. In 1933, the first year of the Third Reich, Jews were excluded from public office, civil service, teaching, the theater, radio, journalism, and farming; in 1934, from the stock exchanges. By the time the legal decree banning them from the professions and business was passed in 1938, there had already been no Jews in law or medicine or in the professional schools for over two years. *There was no way a Jew could have received a medical degree from Heidelberg in 1938!*

* * *

Lori felt no remorse. If she had had any reservations, the ecstasy that lingered everywhere he had touched her had banished them. Still glowing from the previous night, she turned her attention back to the experiment in progress.

She had ordered normal human cells from a commercial drug house, had grown them in tissue culture, and was in the process of extracting the DNA as she had done in her laboratory in Israel. Once the DNA was available, the next step would be the hit-and-miss process of finding the fragment suitable for recombination with plasmid DNA.

She was expert in being able to choose the specific restriction enzyme to cut DNA at the desired location. The most critical part of her work would be to make the right choice so that both plasmid and human DNA would be cut accurately and recombination would take place. Then the problem would be to isolate the correctly combined fragments so that substitution on the thirteenth chromosome of every Jew could be accomplished.

She worked so quickly and efficiently that she had fleetingly contemplated not hiring trained technicians because of the time it would take Juno and Gerald to screen them. When she was unable to account for two thirty-minute periods of the day, however, she realized that the number and length of the attacks of the disease were increasing and that it might interrupt her at any point.

Completing the final entry in her notebook, she closed her eyes and tried to escape again into her memory of the previous night.

"Are you all right?" Gerald asked as he walked into the laboratory.

She looked up. "I'm fine. How was your day?"

"Not good. This damned disease is spreading faster than we anticipated."

"More deaths?"

"Many more. I don't know how much longer we can keep it quiet."

She looked past him. "Where's Peter?"

"He stopped at his office. I'll pick him up on the way back to the apartment. I just wanted to make certain you were okay."

Gerald turned to leave. "Don't work too late. It's snowing again, and I want you out of here before it gets too heavy. Besides"—he smiled—"Peter says to be home on time for dinner."

She threatened to throw her notebook at him, but Gerald was already out the door. "Time—it's always a matter of time." She repeated the words to herself again as she began to clean up.

Juno got into the car, unbuttoned his coat, and sat back. "How's Lori?"

"Fine. She's cleaning up. We'll meet her at the apartment. Anyplace else you need to stop?"

"No. Let's go home."

"What are your plans for tomorrow?"

"To follow up on Mann; he's our first concrete lead."

"I'm afraid we don't have too much time left." Gerald paused. "There have been more deaths—a lot of them."

"Then we're just going to have to push it."

"I don't like to rush; it invites mistakes—and we've already made enough."

"Unless you're willing to reverse your decision about concealing the disease, we have no choice."

"I can't."

"Then we'd better move fast."

"Tell me what you want me and my people to do."

"Do you have a good agent in Germany?"

"Several."

"I want you to send three of them to Heidelberg. It'll save us from having to wait for replies to my inquiries. I want one to go to the office of the registrar, one to the secretary of the faculty, and one to the secretary of the alumni association—or whatever they're called at Heidelberg."

"My people will know."

"I want to find out if *anyone*—a student, a faculty member, or even a clerk who was there in the mid- to late thirties—remembers Joseph Mann and/or Thaddeus Reichmann; if they do, find out absolutely everything they know about them: when they entered; when they graduated; who their friends and professors were; but most important, *if* they were there. There has to be a reason for the discrepancy. Mann obtained a license to practice medicine in New York State in 1947 based upon a certified diploma indicating that he graduated from Heidelberg in 1938. *How did he get that diploma?* Did someone make a mistake in entering the date? Or"—Juno hesitated—"could Mann have been working for Reichmann, and that Nazi bastard supplied him with forged documents? That possibility keeps bugging me. It would explain how Reichmann knew Renée and I were in charge of the investigation and why Mann was so anxious to help us—and so upset about Ludwick. But if Mann were Reichmann's stooge, why was he killed? Seems to me Reichmann would have tried to keep him alive: he couldn't have had an informer in a better place."

"Maybe Reichmann was concerned that Mann would panic and confess to save his own skin."

"Mann was an egomaniac, as cool a character as you'll ever meet; I can't imagine *anything* panicking him. And he certainly wasn't the type to own up to anything that might tarnish his image. There has to be another reason." He paused and thought for a moment. "We're forgetting one thing: Mann was a Jew. He'd been in a concentration camp—I saw the numbers myself."

Gerald looked away. "There are all kinds of Jews."

Juno broke the uncomfortable silence. "I want to cable Mann's photo to your agents so that if they do find someone who remembers him, they can get that person to verify it."

"It's been over thirty years . . ."

"People change, but not entirely; you'd be surprised how old friends and teachers remember little things that age doesn't alter. Besides, if someone can identify the face but not necessarily the name, perhaps we'll learn if Mann was his real one." Juno glanced at his watch. "If you'll pull over by that phone booth, I'll call Personnel and Records. There should still be someone there. If I can get them to pull Mann's photo before they quit for the day, we can have it copied and sent out by wire first thing in the morning."

Gerald stopped the car, and Juno jumped out and hurried through the snow to make the call. The Israeli watched him with admiration. Juno was good—damned good. Maybe he could persuade him to work for the Dom. He laughed to himself as he reached over to open the door for the detective, but his mood changed abruptly with one look at Juno's face.

"There is no photo. Joseph Mann never allowed one to be taken."

Juno was excited and disturbed by the vigor of her lovemaking. She gave herself to him with a passion that he had found in no other woman—as if she were trying to fit a lifetime with him into these few hours—and this troubled him.

As they lay together in the darkness and listened to the silence, she told him why. Her voice was calm and soft. "Peter?"

"Yes?"

"Will you do something for me?"

"Sure. What?"

"Marry me."

He laughed. "When?"

"Tomorrow."

He laughed again. "Aren't you rushing things a bit *too* much?"

"Will you?" Her tone told him she was not joking. "Please answer my question! Will you marry me tomorrow?"

Holding her tighter, he knew there was only one answer he could give her. "Yes."

She kissed him gently and clung to him. "I want you to promise not to say a word when you hear what else I have to tell you."

He looked at her questioningly.

"Will you promise?"

"I promise."

"I'm dying, Peter. . . ."

He wanted to scream, but he choked back the sound—he had promised her. He felt sick; he wanted to run and to vomit. Still he could not hold back the tears. He felt his heart hammering in his chest as if it were trying to escape before shattering. He felt himself tremble; he felt her next to him; he felt his world dying with her.

She bent over him, wiped his eyes, and kissed first one lid, then the other. "I love you, Peter Juno . . . more than I have ever loved anyone or anything . . . and I want to spend the rest of my life as your wife. Will you still have me?"

He sobbed uncontrollably and without shame.

She took his face in her hands and smiled at him.

He tried to smile back. "It'll take a couple of days to get a license and the blood tests. Can you wait that long?"

She nodded and kissed him.

For several minutes they lay together without speaking. Finally, propping himself on one elbow, he looked down at her and gently pushed her hair off her forehead. "When did it start?"

"I began having intermittent symptoms a few days before I came to New York, but the attacks are getting longer and more frequent. Today was the worst."

"How long do we have?"

"A couple of weeks—maybe a month if we're lucky."

He felt another wave of nausea spread over him, but it was lost in the rage and the frustration that threatened to overwhelm him. "I'll find Reichmann, and I'll *make* him give us the answer!"

"I'm not convinced he has an answer, Peter." She looked away.

"He has to have one!" Turning her face back to his, he looked at her with a mixture of disbelief and determination. *"I will never give up!"*

21

He had heard Josh and others describe its symptoms, he had seen the bodies of several of its victims, he had been a witness to the barbarous killings that had accompanied its rebirth and development, and he had felt the terrible pain of losing people he loved because of it. Until this moment, however, as he sat by helplessly and watched Lori suffer through one of the symptomatic episodes that were the hallmark of the disease before it killed, Juno had not really comprehended its devastating effects on a living human being.

At first he thought she had fallen back to sleep; but when he bent over to kiss her awake, it was there in all its terrible ugliness. She did not respond to his voice or his touch; she was a prisoner in a horrifying world in which there was no sensation, no voluntary movement, no appreciation of incoming stimuli or impulses, and no ability to generate her own. Only the autonomous function of the heart and the ability to breathe remained.

The first stage—the rapid and progressive development of neurologic failure—had occurred without his knowing it; what he saw now was the visible expression of what the disease against the Jews really was. Her face was gray, her eyes glassy, her body limp with dysrhythmic bursts of twitching that caused her to stiffen and grimace so that her teeth clenched and saliva trickled from the corners of her mouth. Her beauty was lost in contortions that deformed her face, and her body was distorted by spasms so strong they lifted it from the bed.

Suddenly, almost as quickly as it had started, the seizure ceased. He could see her body relax and her face return to normal; and then she slept—the deep, undisturbed sleep that was the predictable aftermath of the uncontrolled episode she had suffered.

Without moving, he watched her and counted every breath; and when he was satisfied that she was all right, he kissed her lightly on the forehead, wiped the tears from the corners of his eyes, and ran for the shower.

Hands by his sides, feet apart, leaning against the cold tile of the stall, he let the spray of water flow over him. Every bone and muscle in him ached, and he knew he was losing control. Rage and hate had displaced all other emotions except fear; he wanted to rush out and tear down New York City building by building until he found Thaddeus Reichmann. Then . . . He smashed his fist over and over again against the wall of the shower until the pain sobered him. Now he knew why Lori had wanted to cram so much of living into so short a time—she more than anyone else was aware of how little was left. He felt his tears blend with the water from the shower, but he was uncertain if they were spent more for her or for himself. He swore at himself and hit the wall again; if he wanted to save her, he would not do it by self-pity. She had one chance to survive: Reichmann. . . . Gerald had been right; if he did not believe that they would find the Nazi in time, he would go mad!

Reichmann clenched his fists to control his anger. Peter Juno's perspicacity had undermined his reawakened confidence in the invincibility of the new breed of black knight, a group of whom now sat around his dining-room table.

"They've made fools of you!" He pounded his fist on the table. "And I won't have it! Juno, Dr. Davide, and this Israeli agent called Gerald must be eliminated! I don't care if it costs all of your lives. If you can't take care of three wounded people—one of them a woman—you don't deserve to live!" He turned to the man who had driven the taxi. "You say they are at Fields's apartment?"

The man nodded.

"And you followed the woman to the old Clearwater laboratory?"

"She goes there every day at exactly seven-thirty in the morning and returns to the apartment each evening at six-thirty."

"Continue."

"She travels to and from the laboratory by car. There are three Israeli agents with her, and four more in the car behind her."

"And during the day?"

"She is well-guarded. Two agents watch the entrance to the laboratory grounds, two are stationed at the only open entrance to the main building, and three patrol the floor she works on."

"Well, at least one of you has accomplished the task I assigned to him. All right, I'll make it easy for you. We'll go after only one of them this time—Dr. Davide. By taking her, we'll force the others to come to us—on our ground. Phase II of my plan begins tomorrow."

Frightened that the rapid progression of the disease in herself would curtail the time she needed to complete her work, Lori had taken shortcuts. As she had with the human cells, she now used a commercial source of the restriction enzyme rather than going through the time-consuming process of preparing her own. As a result, she had condensed into two days the experimental procedure that usually took seven to ten.

Early that morning she had added the same carefully selected enzyme to the preparations of both human and plasmid DNA and had followed the progress of the enzyme's action. The enzyme had made staggering cuts diagonally across the threads of plasmid DNA, leaving ends capable of attaching to those from the other preparation. Every plasmid had been cut at the same point in the DNA sequence; in contrast, the human DNA now was a protean mixture of thousands of genes, of which she needed only one. The problem was how to isolate the one she wanted—in hours, not days or weeks.

She had to gamble. She drew on all the knowledge that her years of experience had provided her. She knew that, under ordinary circumstances, a specific antibody could be used to remove a specific protein from solution by combining with it to make it insoluble. Antibodies to each of the twenty-three pairs of human chromosomes were available; they were used as tools in genetic research. She theorized that if she added antibodies to all but the thirteenth pair of chromosomes, the DNA that composed the genes of the other twenty-two would be precipitated, leaving the material she was seeking.

Now it was done. The antibody-chromosome complexes had been separated. She was ready to evaluate the results of the test she had performed to prove that the human DNA fragment she wanted remained. The answer lay on the photographic plate before her.

"My God!" She started to scream and then caught herself. It had worked! In disbelief she examined the photomicrograph a second and a third time. She had made no mistake! In the two flasks of DNA in front of her—one containing plasmid genes, the other, human genes that would replace the defective equivalent on every thirteenth chromosome—lay the potential salvation of the Jews. All that remained was to mix the contents of the two flasks at low temperature. The plasmid would capture the human DNA fragment; then, at higher temperature, she would add another enzyme to "glue" the pieces together to make recombinant DNA. Afterward she would inject the material into a test subject. There was substantial evidence from her previous experiments on animals to suggest that the plasmid would deposit the piece of normal DNA it carried onto the thirteenth chromosome. As the human body had a distinctly greater affinity for normal than for abnormal DNA, the substitution should take place. There would be only one readout for this last experiment: life or death.

She recorded the results in her notebook and started to write a discussion of her findings.

"Dr. Davide!"

Lori spun around. The guard who was stationed outside the door to the laboratory stumbled into the room and stared at her blankly. He tried to speak, but his words were lost in the torrent of blood that erupted from his mouth. He grabbed at the gaping bullet hole in his chest and pitched forward.

For an instant Lori was paralyzed with fear; then suddenly she was unafraid. She had known that a confrontation with Reichmann was inevitable, but the dread of when it would come and how was worse than the encounter itself. Although she desperately wanted to live, all that mattered now was to ensure that someone could carry on her work. Quickly she scribbled several words at the end of the paragraph she had been writing. Then she tore off her laboratory coat, threw it over the two flasks and her notebook, grabbed the Luger Gerald had left her, and rushed out into the hallway.

Gerald was waiting for Juno at the Telephone Exchange Building.

"Anything from your people?" Juno asked.

"Yes. No luck. No one remembers a Joseph Mann *or* a Thaddeus Reichmann. Whatever records had not been destroyed in the war were lost in a recent fire."

"Reichmann again."

"Probably."

"And your people are certain that *no one*, not an old professor, a laboratory assistant . . ."

"They're certain—they're professionals. If we only had a photograph . . ."

The two men did not speak again until they were in the car. Both hands resting on the steering wheel, head down, Juno sat there as if in a daze.

"What's bothering you?" Gerald asked. "We'll find him."

Without looking up, Juno told him. "Do you know Lori is dying from the disease?"

"My God! No! It can't be!" Gerald stared at the snow beginning to accumulate on the windshield. "I don't know what to say. I guess I don't have to tell you how it feels to love her." He took a deep breath. "Would you like some time alone, Pete? It may help. Why don't you drop me off? Remember, we *all* need you." He grasped Juno's arm firmly. "We *will* find Reichmann!"

"You take the car; I like walking in the snow. I'll meet you back at the apartment at six." He got out and extended his hand to the Israeli. "Thanks."

Gripping it tightly with both of his, Gerald nodded. "Shalom."

"Shalom."

* * *

It was not snowing hard, rather in powdery flurries that blew across Fifth Avenue. Savoring the snowflakes on his face, Juno ambled uptown, his mind and body numb. Finally, deciding he had had enough, he hailed a taxi to take him back to the apartment.

As soon as he stepped out of the cab, he knew something was wrong. The car that should have been parked across the street was gone. Neither the doorman nor Gerald's agents were in the lobby, and the elevators at the far end stood open and empty. Moving cautiously, back against the wall, revolver drawn, he examined each of the elevators, decided not to risk getting trapped in one, and raced for the stairs.

On the fifteenth-floor landing, he found the agent assigned to guard the stairwell; he was draped over the railing with a bullet hole through his chest. Almost without feeling the ache in his thighs or the shortness of breath that caused him to gasp for air, he vaulted up the remaining steps, paused at the door, kicked it open, and rushed down the corridor toward the apartment. Opposite the entrance, another Israeli was sitting motionless on the floor, a trickle of blood oozing from the wound in the middle of his forehead. With the image of Lori before his eyes, Juno hit the partially open door with his shoulder, stumbled into the entryway, and skidded to a halt. The apartment was as neat as when he had left it; nothing had been touched.

"Lori!" He called her name over and over again, but there was no reply. As though he were moving in slow motion, he began to check each of the rooms for some sign of her. When there was only one room left to search, his mind rebelled, and his tired body refused to go on. But he knew he had no choice; with a shaking hand he opened the door to her bedroom.

His scream rebounded throughout the apartment. Fighting to blot out the horror of the images exploding in his mind, he fell back against the wall, slid to the floor, and sat staring at the bed. It was empty. Neatly made and empty—except for the pillow that had been carefully placed in the middle of it, a Star of David and the word "*Jude*" inscribed across it in blood.

He buried his head in his arms, a kaleidoscope of thoughts rushing through every level of his brain. He looked at his watch.

It was six o'clock. Lori always came home at *six-thirty!* Clutching at the one remaining fragment of hope—that Reichmann's men had been there and *not* found her—he jumped up, ran from the apartment, flew down the stairs and through the lobby, and collided with Gerald just as he was about to enter. Grabbing the Israeli by the arm, he summarized what he had found as they ran for the car.

With the red light flashing on the dashboard, they sped uptown. For Juno it meant reliving the moments before discovering the bodies of Josh and Renée and the terrible memory of what he had felt when he had found them.

Stepping harder on the accelerator, he swore at the car, the traffic, the distance, and his inability to transport himself instantaneously to Lori's laboratory; but his outbursts only increased his frustration and his anger. By the time they could see the entrance to the Clearwater grounds, his rage was almost out of control; Gerald had to grab his arm to get him to stop.

Leaving Juno to keep watch at the car, Gerald drew his Luger and made his way cautiously through the shrubbery beside the main gate. He returned a moment later. "Both guards are dead. Shot through the back of the head. They must have been taken by surprise. . . ."

Before Gerald had finished speaking, Juno was speeding toward the laboratory building. He jumped out of the car, drew his revolver, and raced into the lobby, with Gerald close behind. "Shit!" Juno looked away and inhaled deeply to quiet the nausea that rose into his throat. Two Israeli agents were sprawled in the center of the floor in a pool of blood; their Lugers were still in their holsters.

Bending down, Gerald felt the neck of each for a pulse, found none, and rolled the two bodies over to examine the wounds. "Probably a short-range automatic rifle. High-caliber. We'd better be careful." He signaled to Juno to use the back stairs while he headed for the flight off the lobby.

At the bottom of the rear stairwell, Juno found another Israeli. The man had been shot twice in the neck; his distorted posture and bloodless bruises indicated that he had been dropped over the railing from above after he was dead.

With his back to the wall and his revolver poised, Juno

searched the staircase above him and found it empty. By the time he reached the second landing, his anxiety and fear overcame his caution; he raced up the remaining stairs, rushed into the hall leading to Lori's laboratory, and felt his sanity start to desert him as he viewed the scene before him.

Gerald was leaning against the far wall beside the door to the laboratory. His arms hung limply at his sides, and his whole body shook. Behind him, an Israeli agent lay dead; and the leg of another protruded from the room.

"Lori!" Juno screamed and started toward the laboratory. Ignoring Gerald's raised hand, he pushed by him. He stopped abruptly and staggered backward. Scrawled across the door in blood was a single word: *"Jude!"*

"She's not in there. She's gone." Gerald spoke in a monotone.

Together they searched the rest of the building and the grounds. There was no sign of her.

Back in the laboratory, Juno collapsed onto a stool. He needed to put events into perspective. Lori's laboratory coat on the benchtop caught his eye. Aimlessly he reached out for it. There was something under it! He lifted the garment carefully. Lori's laboratory notebook and two flasks filled with brownish fluid were hidden beneath it.

He opened the cover of the notebook and began to read. He was able to grasp the general meaning of some of the words, but the figures and equations were as foreign to him as the Hebrew notations scattered throughout the pages. As he came to the final section, he sat up stiffly. The first part of it had been written in meticulous English; the last several words, in careless Hebrew, across the line rather than on it.

"Gerald!"

The Israeli stood in the doorway staring at the floor. He looked up.

"Translate this for me."

Gerald looked at the Hebrew words and shrugged his shoulders.

"Well, what does it say?" Juno asked.

"It makes no sense. She was probably daydreaming about you and doodling—is that how you say it?"

"Tell me what it says anyway. If you look at the page, those last words in Hebrew are sort of scribbled there—as if she were in a hurry. Maybe that's when Reichmann's men broke in. I think she was trying to tell us something."

Gerald read the words slowly. "'The son of a bitch went to Jericho SOS.'"

"Why would Lori write an SOS? She knew we'd realize she was in trouble." Juno waved his arm to indicate their surroundings. He repeated the letters over and over again. Suddenly he snapped his fingers. "SOS isn't always a distress signal! It's used in medicine someplace—something to do with drugs. One night Josh and I had a laugh over those medical abbreviations; he had a thing about them." Juno started pulling drawers open.

"What are you looking for?"

"A medical dictionary. Every lab has one."

"Try this." Gerald pulled a book off the shelf over the laboratory bench and handed it to Juno.

Juno found the page he wanted and read the definition. "'SOS—an abbreviation sometimes used in hospital orders and on prescriptions to indicate that the drug prescribed may be repeated; *e.g.*, seconal, 100 mgm., p.o. hs, SOS × 1, PRN, which means that the oral seconal given at bedtime may be repeated once if necessary.'"

"Doesn't help much," Gerald said.

"It's got to mean something!" Juno repeated the translation of Lori's words to himself. "Did Lori swear a lot?"

"Almost never. Why?"

"Is there a Hebrew word for son of a bitch?"

"Not really. It's sort of a Hebrew bastardization of the term. 'Son' in Hebrew is 'ben' . . ."

"Ben Levi!" Juno shouted. "Ben Levi went to Jericho. Repeat." He trembled. Saul's words called out to him from long ago: "His name is Joshua, like the man who blew down the walls of Jericho with bugles and trumpets. . . ." He choked back his tears. "Lori's telling us that Ben Levi went to see Josh. We should repeat it."

"What . . . ?"

"Wasn't Ben Levi on his way to see Josh to get help about the disease because Josh was an expert in the field of genetics?"

"Yes, but—"

"Lori wants us to go to see an expert again."

"But why?"

It was so clear to Juno now that his excitement almost prevented him from speaking. "Because somewhere in her notes is the answer—or at least a part of it—to the disease. Don't you see? She must have succeeded up to a point, knew Reichmann was about to get her, and wanted to be certain we'd take her notebook to someone who could interpret it and finish her work."

"And in case Reichmann got the notebook, he wouldn't understand what she meant. Like me, he'd think she was just—"

"Doodling." Juno smiled for the first time. Suddenly he stood up. "She's still alive! I know it!"

"How can you say that? Reichmann kills his enemies; he takes no prisoners."

"He did this time. He needs her for something—I'm not sure what—but if he didn't, we'd have found her—dead, like the others. He'd have made sure we did."

"Go on," Gerald said.

Juno thought for a moment. "Who does Reichmann want most—next to Lori?"

"You, I guess."

"Exactly. And he knows if he has her, I'll come after her. She's the bait."

Gerald looked away. "What will you do?"

Juno stood up. "Go after her, of course! What choice do I have?"

22

Juno and Gerald worked quickly. The Israeli called in a team to remove the bodies and to clean up and secure the laboratory. Not knowing what to do with the two flasks, Juno suggested that, like all biologicals in liquid form, they should probably be refrigerated. They arranged to have them and Lori's notebook taken to the Israeli consulate in New York City for safekeeping. Now they had one task only: to find Reichmann. As they drove downtown, the conflict between their personal motives and what was clearly the common good of the Jews continued to plague them.

"And you still won't change your mind and stop trying to keep the disease a secret?" Juno asked again. "If you would, we could send in the whole works—police, FBI, CIA."

"Dammit, I just can't! It's hard enough for me to have to face sacrificing Lori's life without you badgering me. This is one of those times that people in our profession dread—when we have to do what's right, no matter what the price."

"But what if another geneticist can't complete her work?"

"Right now, let's find Lori and Reichmann; then I won't have to face that problem. Now can we change the subject?"

"Sure."

"Where are we heading?"

"To the record room at the morgue. Mann is our only lead. So far, it's gotten us nowhere, so we look at it from another angle. If Mann is a key, I want to reexamine everything he had a finger in. For some reason, he insisted on assisting at the autopsies of Avram Goldstein and Asher Ben Levi. I want to know why."

Juno swore at the increasing traffic into Manhattan. Every moment that passed brought Lori closer to death either at the hands of Reichmann or of the disease. His impatience and his fear mounted logarithmically as he envisioned what the Nazi might do to her. The image of Renée's body . . . the look on her face . . . He had been distracted from this line of thought by the Nazi attack at the Park Lane. "That's it!" he said excitedly to himself.

A reasonably cohesive mosaic had begun to evolve. Thaddeus Reichmann had the ingenuity to take advantage of the improbable and to carry out successfully a ruse so inconceivable that no one would have believed it. But Juno had to be sure; he had to have proof. He would not risk Lori's life and the future of the Jews on a hastily devised solution.

Turning sharply right as they exited from the Harlem River Driver, Juno headed across town. "I want to see if Davis is still in his office before we go to the morgue."

"Why?"

"I have a question only he can answer."

"Do you think it's wise now?"

"If I get the right answer, it is."

Davis looked up indignantly. "What the hell is this? Don't you ever knock, dammit?"

Juno held his temper. "Sorry, Commissioner. I'm glad you're still here."

"Well, whatever you want, make it quick."

"Just answer one question. Did Renée know about Mann's death? Did you tell her about it?"

Davis seemed uncertain of his reply. "I think so, but—"

"Yes or no, dammit?"

"Who the hell do you think you're talking to?"

Juno took a step toward Davis's desk and glared down at him. "Lives depend on your answer. Did she know?"

"Yes. I distinctly remember discussing it with her because you were away. Now what's so damned important about—?"

Juno was gone before Davis could finish his question.

The fact that the autopsy reports on Avram Goldstein and Asher Ben Levi were readily available strongly confirmed Juno's theory that Joseph Mann's role was far more than a peripheral one. Juno turned at once to the description of the nervous system of Avram Goldstein. The words staggered him. ". . . early evidence of a diffuse degenerative disease . . ." He tore at the pages of Ben Levi's report. The same words! He had found the elusive link between isolated fragments of seemingly unrelated evidence. At last he could explain the chain of events that had started for him with Morris Golding's murder but had started for the Jews over thirty years before in Dachau.

Now he knew where to find Reichmann. He reached for the phone.

Lori's head snapped back as Reichmann hit her again. Her eyes were swollen, and blood trickled from her nose and mouth.

"Where is your notebook? How far has your work progressed?" He continued to hit her as he asked the questions. Finally she lapsed into unconsciousness.

Reichmann turned to the man behind him. "Can you believe it? They wiped out seven Israeli agents and succeeded in bringing her here, but the fools did not find her notebook! It was probably right under their noses." He wiped the blood from his hands with a towel and slipped into the suit coat being held for him. "Take three men and go back and find it!" Turning to another, he asked, "Where's Juno?"

"In the record room at the morgue. You think he'll take the bait?"

"Of course!" Reichmann's eyes narrowed, and he looked hard at the man. "But don't underestimate him. Very few would have gotten as far as he has. If I had a hundred like him, I would need no one else." He paused. "Juno and the Israeli will be here soon, and we must not disappoint them."

* * *

From the pieces of information he had put together about Reichmann, Juno was able to hypothesize where the Nazi was hiding. Gerald arranged to have the men and equipment they would need. Now they waited on the roof of the building across the street for the Israeli agents to report back to them about the number and location of the men Reichmann had dispersed around him for protection.

"Which floor is it?" Gerald asked.

"Tenth, right front."

"Exits and entrances?"

"The only entrance to the apartment is directly into the living room from the corridor; to the building, through the front lobby. It's set up exactly like Josh's building, except there's a fire escape outside the bedroom window, and a rear exit from the building leads onto an alley behind it. Reichmann's apartment has a living room, dining room, small kitchen, bathroom, and a large bedroom in the rear; a balcony opens off the living room."

"How did you get all that information?"

"A building inspector owed me a few favors."

Gerald's men reported in over the two-way radio. They had finished their work with no indication that they had been detected. Reichmann had two men in the lobby, one on the staircase near the tenth-floor landing, two in the corridor outside his apartment, one on the fire escape, and two in cars parked at the curb in front of the building. Juno and Gerald knew what to do.

Juno surveyed the scene as he drove. Ahead of him, on the opposite side of the street, he could see two of Reichmann's men sitting in their cars, one parked behind the other in front of the building. Gerald, his collar pulled up to hide his face, was approaching the entrance; two of his men were strolling on the sidewalk in front of him. Measuring the distance carefully, Juno waited until he was directly opposite the building and then slowed as if starting to make a U-turn. At the moment he saw Gerald nod, Juno rammed the accelerator to the floor, turned the wheel, and aimed for the space between the two cars. He hit the rear of one and the front of the other, driving both up onto the sidewalk. Within seconds Juno was out of the car and racing for the entrance to the apartment building. Simultaneously, the two Israeli agents turned and quickly disposed of the drivers of the cars.

Through the glass door of the building, Juno could see the two guards in the lobby running toward him. He and Gerald had known that the noise of the crash would alert them; they had planned it that way. The moment Reichmann's men came through the door, Juno hit the one nearest him squarely in the abdomen and then across the back of the neck as the man fell. Gerald immobilized the other.

Juno joined Gerald in a doorway at the entrance to the alley. The Israeli aimed a high-powered rifle with a silencer and telescopic lens at the Nazi high up on the fire escape. His shot had to be absolutely accurate or the man would cry out when hit; if not then, certainly when he fell. Juno felt Gerald tense, and then he heard the ugly spit from the rifle's muzzle. An instant later Juno watched the man fall ten floors; he turned his head just before the body hit the ground in front of them.

Juno headed for the ladder to the fire escape while Gerald dashed for the lobby. Reichmann's man on the tenth-floor landing inside the building would be more of a problem: the curve in the staircase would not allow a clean shot from a long distance. Juno would try to get at him from above; Gerald, from below.

By the time he reached the roof, Juno's legs ached, and his chest felt as if it would explode. After pausing to catch his breath, he cautiously opened the steel door from the roof, slipped inside, and started down the stairs. He stopped at the thirteenth floor; he could not see the guard, but he could hear him whistling. Suddenly the whistling ceased.

"Is someone there?" The Nazi's words echoed loudly through the stairwell.

Juno wiped the sweat from his face with the back of his sleeve. Each breath seemed to be amplified a thousandfold by the walls around him.

"Who is it?"

Juno inched his way to the railing. The man was calling *down*, not up. "Jesus Christ! Gerald!" Juno's silent exclamation caught in his throat as he heard a rifle bolt slide into place. Carefully, Juno peered over the rail. The Nazi was taking careful aim, waiting patiently for the Israeli's head and chest to be exposed. Juno's decision was instantaneous. Taking three steps at a time, he bounded down the stairs, firing before his feet hit the landing. He fell, his head and shoulder hitting the floor, and momentarily blacked out.

"You dumb bastard! You could have gotten yourself killed," Gerald hissed.

Blinking, Juno saw the guard slumped against the wall. Blood covered the man's face and chest; he still clutched the unfired rifle in his hand. "Dumb bastard yourself," Juno whispered. "You were sticking out like a sore thumb. That son of a bitch was just about to blow your head off."

Glancing backward, Gerald shivered as he saw for the first time how vulnerable he had been. "Now I owe you one."

"We're even," Juno said.

Their most difficult task was to eliminate the guards in the tenth-floor corridor. The hallway was long and narrow and offered no place of concealment. They had one chance. The apartments on each floor were staggered so that the entrances to those on one side alternated with those opposite them; eight feet in either direction across from the door to Reichmann's apartment were those of the two across the hall. One of the Israeli agents had already phoned each of the apartments and found the tenants were not at home. Juno and Gerald had entered via the fire escape so as not to be seen. The rest depended entirely on timing, marksmanship, and speed.

Exactly at the predetermined moment, Juno rushed out of one door and Gerald the other; both fired simultaneously and each caught his victim in his arms before he hit the floor. Neither guard had uttered a sound; both had died instantaneously from the bullets that had pierced their throats.

Juno and Gerald approached the door to Thaddeus Reichmann's apartment. For an instant they paused and looked at one another. Then Juno stepped back and kicked in the door.

They were totally unprepared for what confronted them. The apartment was empty. Spread out in the center of the bare floor was Lori's blouse—torn to shreds, every fragment spotted with blood.

23

The image of what Reichmann might have done to Lori tormented Juno. Only the belief that she was still alive drove him on. He forced himself to think rationally. Somewhere in all that had happened was the clue to where Reichmann was.

Juno reviewed each of the murders Reichmann or one of his men had committed, but there was no pattern of answers except for the persisting theme of Dachau, the scars, and the Luger. He considered the circumstances surrounding the theft of the data from Joseph Mann's autopsy and his personal belongings from his office. . . . His thoughts raced onward and suddenly braked. Mann's body had been cremated! His ashes had been scattered over a pond on the estate the pathologist had owned in northern New Jersey. . . .

"It's the Manheim estate you want." The clerk at the Somerset County Hall of Records closed the ledger and turned back to Juno. "It was built by old man Manheim just before Prohibition with the millions he'd made from his breweries. Dr. Mann bought it three years ago—"

"Where is it?" Juno interrupted.

"Off Route 202." The clerk reached beneath the counter, pulled out a map, and marked the location and the directions to it in red. "It's a pretty spot . . ." she called after him, but Juno was already out the door.

The Manheim estate comprised fifty acres just southwest of Bernardsville, New Jersey. Juno parked the car about a mile from the entrance, and he and Gerald walked into the woods surrounding it. Reaching a clearing on the top of a hill that sloped down to a broad plain, they crawled to the edge of the tree line. Both men gasped at the scene below them.

"Jesus Christ!" Juno whispered. "I wonder if anyone else knows what's going on here."

The grounds around the main house had been carved out of the wilderness. The landscaped area was almost fifteen hundred yards long and half as wide, bordered on the south and east by a small creek, to the north by low barren cliffs, and to the west by the woods they had traveled. The entire compound was surrounded by parallel electrified barbed-wire fences fifty feet apart; pairs of guards in khaki storm coats with automatic rifles slung over their shoulders and killer dogs on chain leashes patrolled the area between the fences in a pattern designed so that one pair was never out of visual contact with their counterparts on either side. In the southwest corner, two parallel low wooden buildings, obviously quarters for Reichmann's men, lay beneath the shadow of the forest. In the center of the complex, surrounded by neatly manicured rock gardens partially covered by snow, was a two-story mansion with a tower at each of the four corners. Pairs of guards circled the house at hundred-foot intervals. Spotlights were scattered throughout the grounds and along the roof line of the house. It was not a castle, Juno thought; it was a damned fortress!

They sketched a rough diagram of the buildings and the grounds and then made their way back to the car. It was almost four o'clock. They drove back to Morristown and obtained a room at the Governor Morris Inn. He had come full circle, Juno thought to himself, remembering that Morristown had been the home of Morris Golding. He swore that it would end here.

Standing at the window of their room, Juno watched the snow begin to fall again. It was a dark night with mounting winds; the forecast was for snow becoming heavy before midnight and lasting until mid-morning. "Can your men function well in snow?" he asked Gerald.

"They've had little experience in it, but they'll do what they have to."

"Then we go tonight. About eleven. The snow and the wind will give us cover. Those guards of Reichmann's are going to be too busy trying to keep warm to check every twig that snaps. How many men can you get?"

"Six, maybe eight. We've lost a lot, and it would take too long to bring in more."

Juno frowned. He had estimated that Reichmann had at least forty. "It'll have to do."

It took them less than an hour to formulate their plan. Gerald arranged for the men and equipment they needed, then turned to Juno. "You've obviously put at least some of the pieces together," he said. "I think I've got a right to know."

Juno told him.

Juno shivered uncontrollably. The cold penetrated every part of him despite the heavy clothes, gloves, and boots; even the ski mask and the black grease covering the exposed parts of his face did not help. The wind drove the snow against him, accentuating the cold and reducing visibility almost to zero.

Each of them carried the newest model collapsible lightweight M18 semiautomatic rifle, specially greased to protect it against moisture. In addition, they had Smith & Wesson high-impact revolvers in their jacket pockets and Israeli commando knives in their boots. Juno and Gerald carried packs of fragmentation grenades; each of the other agents, white phosphorous bombs. They all had several blocks of plastic explosives.

Juno and Gerald had been lying in the snow at the edge of the clearing for almost thirty minutes now while the other Israelis skirted the clearing to take up their positions. Juno pushed the snow from his eyes and checked his watch. They had two more minutes to wait. He rubbed his hands together and wiggled his toes to ease the numbness and then leaned forward to try to make out the fence and the house through the snow. He could barely see the guards; they walked a few steps back and forth and then huddled together trying to keep warm.

He felt Gerald's elbow in his side. "Time to start." The Israeli picked up his rifle and attached the silencer and the heat scope that would allow him to aim accurately through the darkness. Juno did likewise. Gerald looked at his watch. "Now!"

They fired, aimed again, and fired a second time. Juno peered through the scope; both the guard and the dog lay motionless in the snow.

"Move!" Gerald was already heading down the hill.

Juno could hardly see as he plunged into the darkness behind the Israeli. His eyes and cheeks burned as the snow bit at him, and his chest ached as the wind usurped his breath. He slipped and stumbled over patches of ice on the grass and rocks and collapsed beside Gerald at the outer fence. As each team of men checked in, Juno knew the first part of their plan had worked: no guard or dog between the two fences remained alive.

In less than a minute Gerald had cut through both sets of barbed wire, and they were on the grounds. Rifles slung over their backs, they lay flat on their bellies and inched their way to within ten feet of the outer ring of light from the imposing mansion. Hugging the ground, they raised their heads just enough to be able to see the guards. They had their timing down to split seconds. Once the guards turned the corner, Juno and Gerald would have sixteen seconds to race across the hundred yards and conceal themselves in the rock gardens before the next pair of Reichmann's men appeared.

When he saw Gerald raise his hand to signal him, Juno set himself, dug his heels into the snow, and took a deep breath. The hand dropped. Juno hurled himself forward. His hands were numb as he clung to the sling of the rifle and to the satchel of grenades on his belt. His hips and thighs ached as he drove them onward, thinking of nothing else but lifting his knees high and planting his feet hard, praying that the roaring wind masked the crunch of his boots in the snow. The light blinded him. He fought for every breath. His head spun as panic surged through him—he was sure he was not moving; he thought he heard the guards about to come around the corner of the mansion. But suddenly he was across and slipping among the plants and shrubs.

Shaking his head to refocus his eyes, he saw Gerald land

beside him and signal him with his knife. As he pulled his own knife from his boot, Juno felt a wave of nausea. He had shot men before, but he had never killed with a knife. Killing with a gun was an impersonal act; but to shove a blade into a man's body, you had to be close enough to smell him.

It was over in a moment. A hand across the mouth; the head pulled backward; a knee in the back; and one short, powerful jab of the wrist and forearm upward and backward. The knife met resistance only at the skin, as Gerald had said it would. There was no sound. The horror and the finality of the act did not hit Juno until after they had dragged the bodies into the garden and were all regrouping at one side of the mansion. He turned aside and vomited.

Juno watched the Israelis with growing admiration. Gerald did not speak; all orders were given with hand signals. There were no questions, no hesitation. They all knew what to do and when. They operated like a finely tuned, computerized machine. The others disappeared toward the back of the house; Juno followed Gerald to the front door.

The time for stealth and silence was over. They unslung their rifles and set the levers that converted the weapons to automatic. Juno held Gerald's rifle until the Israeli had packed the hinges and the locks on the massive oak doors with plastic explosives; then both men stepped back, one on either side of the entrance-way, and waited.

There was a muffled explosion; the doors, torn open, fell backward into the entry hall. With Gerald beside him, Juno rushed through the smoke into the foyer and pulled the trigger. The three men rushing toward them fell. He swung his weapon to the left and watched the second burst catch two Nazis as they came through the door at the end of the hall. Then he stepped back against the wall and waited. Gerald had killed two more men coming down the spiral staircase to their right and was now bounding up the stairs to check the rooms on the second floor. In seconds the Israeli was back.

"No one upstairs," he panted.

"No further trouble here," Juno whispered and then nodded toward a set of ornately carved doors partially hidden by the staircase.

Back to back to protect their flanks, their weapons poised and ready to kill, they moved slowly toward the doors. Then, side by side, they stepped back and kicked them in simultaneously.

Thaddeus Reichmann looked up from behind his desk. "Please come in," he said calmly. "I have been expecting you." He stood up, unafraid and in control of himself and the situation confronting him. "I am Thaddeus Reichmann. Good evening, Lieutenant Juno."

"Good evening, Dr. Mann," Juno answered coldly.

"The name makes no difference; but for the record, it *is* Herr Doktor Thaddeus Josef Reichmann."

24

"Where is she?" Juno screamed and was on the Nazi before Gerald could stop him. His first blow bloodied Reichmann's mouth; his second hurled him over the back of the chair and sent him sprawling onto the floor.

"Stop it! You'll kill him!" Gerald tried to pull Juno off as the detective tightened his hold on Reichmann's throat.

"Tell me where she is or I'll break you in half!"

The ruddiness in Reichmann's cheeks gave way to a sick dusky blue; his eyes bulged; the veins in his temples and neck ballooned outward.

Gerald shouted, "If you kill him, he can't tell us a thing!"

Reluctantly Juno released his grip. Whitish froth bubbled from Reichmann's mouth, and rivulets of sweat poured from his face as he pulled himself up, straightened his hair and jacket, and collapsed into his chair. He glared at Juno.

"Where is she?" Juno snarled.

Reichmann smiled. "She is alive. Why should I have killed her? The disease will do it for me."

Juno fought to restrain himself. He knew Gerald was right; they needed answers. Violence would not work. Experience had taught him to identify an opponent's weakest spot and to attack it relentlessly. His target: Reichmann's ego. "You're very sure of yourself for someone who's fucked up the way you have."

Reichmann smiled again. "On the contrary, I knew exactly what I was doing. You were my foremost adversary. When eliminating you became more of a problem than I had anticipated, I decided to make you come to me. I gave you clues in a reasonable and orderly fashion, knowing you would finally put the pieces together. And here you are."

"You gave me nothing! You're an egomaniac so obsessed with details you imagine everyone's mind works like yours. Well, it doesn't. You're an amateur!" Juno saw Reichmann tense. "The theft of Baldini's records and Joy's notes and tapes, switching the autopsy report on Mann, having some poor bastard cremated in your place—"

"An amateur would not have been that clever or that thorough," Reichmann said. "You did not expect me to make it too easy for you, did you? And the signature on the authorization *was* authentic. After all, it was my handwriting, no matter which name I signed."

"Don't be so cocky, you bastard. I realized that after your victims—not you—told me that Thaddeus Reichmann and Joseph Mann were the same."

Reichmann seemed puzzled; Juno stepped up his assault. "The one thing you didn't anticipate was that look of fear that remained imprinted on your victims' faces. Golding and Goldstein had a look of terror because seeing you suddenly made them remember their guilt and the horrors of Dachau. Hansen, Clayton, and that girl in the record room were scared to death—they thought they were seeing the ghost of Joseph Mann. The others had no such look because either they didn't know who you were or they never saw you.

"But it was Sergeant Tracy"—he swallowed hard—"who confirmed it. When I finally forced myself to think about her, the answer was there—in the look on *her* face at the moment you killed her. There was very little that Renée was afraid of. She wouldn't have been frightened by seeing Joseph Mann—she was smart enough to have put it together once she knew Mann wasn't dead; or if she didn't, I'm sure you told her. What frightened her was being confronted by an insane, sadistic butcher! And what I learned from Ludwick—"

Reichmann's left eye twitched. "Ludwick told you nothing," he snapped.

"But he did. He told me that only a pathologist who had seen the disease in its full-blown form could recognize it in its early stages. Where had Joseph Mann seen the disease before so that he was able to recognize it in Goldstein and Ben Levi? In Dachau, of course—not as an inmate, but as Thaddeus Reichmann. You just had to include those minor abnormalities you found in Goldstein and Ben Levi in their autopsy reports, didn't you?"

Reichmann's face was now an angry reddish-purple hue.

"Your fetish for details and accuracy gave you away again on Mann's medical diploma. Although the Nuremberg Laws outlawing Jews from medical schools wasn't passed until 1938, no Jew had attended a German medical school for more than two years before that. Joseph Mann could not have graduated in 1938; but Thaddeus Reichmann did!

"Once I was sure Joseph Mann and Thaddeus Reichmann were the same, the rest was easy. I knew you were recruiting an army. When I found Mann's apartment empty, I figured you'd moved to a larger, more secluded facility. But where? At first it seemed like an unanswerable question; but then I remembered where Mann had directed his ashes be scattered. With Nazi Party headquarters just a few miles from here, it wasn't hard to put it all together. And don't bullshit me that you planned all of that just to get me here. You fucked up!"

Reichmann glared at his two captors. "Enjoy your moment of triumph. It will be short-lived, because you cannot win! *I* have already won."

"You have won *nothing!*" Juno shouted. "Somehow you bungled into this damned disease. Well, if you started it, you can stop it. And I want to know how!"

"Bungled?" Reichmann's eyes were on fire. "I did not bungle into anything! I knew what I was doing! I discovered the existence of slow viruses in 1939—years before anyone else even knew what slow viruses were. Then, of course, I was working with animals. But this was *my* virus! Nothing was left to chance! The war and the concentration camps simply gave me the opportunity to extend my experiments to humans. But at Dachau

I made an outstanding discovery: the virus was specific for Jews; it caused a fatal disease that was transmitted from Jew to Jew. Also, it could be passed to the offspring in the genetic material from either parent! I had the ultimate instrument for the 'Final Solution of the Jewish Problem'! When the war ended, I knew that our defeat was only a temporary one. We would rise again! I had my weapon. As long as I was willing to be patient, I knew I could finish what we had started: to finally rid the world of the Jews!"

"You fucking animal!" The muzzle of Gerald's rifle slashed across Reichmann's cheek.

Wiping the blood from the side of his face, Reichmann smiled. "It makes no difference what you do to me. The Jews are finished! Just before the war ended, I injected *every* Jewish inmate in Dachau with my virus. I told them it was a vaccination against typhus. The fools actually believed me!" He sat forward. "I made sure that even after Germany lost the war, the 'Final Solution' would continue. What I did not know, however, was when the disease would occur and spread. And I had to survive to see it!" He paused to catch his breath.

"So you had numbers tattooed on your left forearm and posed as a Jewish doctor who had been in a concentration camp," Juno said.

"Brilliant, wasn't it? I have waited all these years . . ."

"It was *not* by chance that this disease occurred? You created this evil purposely?" Gerald's voice was filled with disbelief and rage.

Reichmann wiped the sweat from his face. "Of course I did!"

"And you've been waiting more than thirty years . . . ?"

"Yes. Everything I did was simply to stay alive to see the culmination of my efforts. And from what better place to monitor the deaths of Jews than from the medical examiner's office?"

Fists clenched, jaw set, his anger and hatred on the verge of erupting, Gerald said, "Tell us how to stop this disease or cure it or—"

Reichmann's words were preceded by an ugly, guttural burst of laughter. "Don't you understand what I have been telling you? *There is no cure! There is no way to stop it! Nothing can interfere with* this *Holocaust!*"

Juno took a step toward Reichmann. "You're a goddamned liar! Golding and Goldstein had the disease when they were in Dachau, and you cured them."

Reichmann laughed again. "They only thought they did. They had some sort of dysentery that I treated with bismuth solution. I told them that they had the disease and that I cured it just to keep my hold on them. *There is no cure!*" Reichmann looked past them. "You two are already dead men!" He pointed behind them.

Slowly stepping through the doorway were four young Nazis, submachine guns held tightly in their hands.

"Put down your guns," Reichmann commanded.

Without speaking, Juno and Gerald dropped their rifles. One of the men stepped forward and picked them up while two others pushed the detective and the Israeli against the wall, searched them thoroughly, relieved them of their other weapons, and then threw them onto the couch near Reichmann's desk.

"Now where were we?" Reichmann said. "Oh, yes. You wanted to see Dr. Davide." He gestured to one of his men.

Only the butt of the guard's submachine gun thrust into his belly kept Juno from destroying everyone and everything in sight. Doubled over and gasping for breath, he watched as Lori was dragged into the room and dropped at his feet. She hovered between coma and semiconsciousness. Her face was covered with welts and bruises and smeared with dried blood, and her lips were cut and swollen.

Gerald gripped Juno's arm to keep him from negating in one uncontrolled, irrevocable burst of rage everything for which Lori had suffered.

"There is your great scientist. Now you have what you came for: Dr. Davide and your answer about my having a cure for the disease. You have also had a brief glimpse of the birth of the Fourth Reich." Reichmann indicated their surroundings with his hand. "As for me, I do not have the hysterical hatred of the Jews that Rosenberg and Heydrich did. To me, the Jews are simply a means to an end. I will prove to the world that Germany—"

Reichmann's words were lost in the sound of gunfire that ended as abruptly as it had begun. Six more young men dressed in fatigues and carrying automatic rifles filed into the room and stood beside their comrades. The last to enter, a tall, slim man who appeared to be their leader, marched directly to Reichmann, clicked his heels, saluted, and smiled triumphantly. "The Israelis are dead. They were caught in our trap, as you predicted." He saluted again and turned to join his men at the far end of the room.

Juno felt himself covered by sweat as he glanced at Gerald's face. The Israeli's lower lip trembled, and his eyes were filled with hate. Without warning, he lunged for Reichmann. The silence was shattered by a single shot. For an instant, Gerald seemed to stop, suspended in midair, before he pitched forward and crashed to the floor. Blood streaming from his neck, he lay motionless, sprawled across Lori's legs.

Reichmann walked around his desk and stood over him, the smoking Luger held firmly in his hand. "Fool!"

Numb, Juno stared at Gerald's body as Reichmann turned and barked orders at his men.

Juno tensed. He felt his pulse racing. Gerald's right arm moved. Slightly. But he did move! In front of Gerald's outstretched hand were the weapons and the grenades Reichmann's men had taken from them.

Gerald needed time—a single moment unobserved . . .

"You didn't think we'd come unprepared, did you?" Juno asked.

Reichmann turned slowly, his sullen smile waning at the unexpected interruption.

Juno continued. "The gene that was to have been your accomplice has betrayed you. Dr. Davide came up with a cure before you got her. Her data's locked up in the safe in the Israeli consulate. I'm sure your men told you we'd been there. . . ."

Reichmann's hand shot out, the Luger tearing across Juno's face. "Now *you* are lying."

All Juno saw was a blur. Gerald reached forward, grabbed a grenade with each hand, tore at the pins with his teeth, and . . .

Reichmann spun around and fired. Two bullets tore into the Israeli's back. With a weak smile Gerald rolled the grenades into the group of Reichmann's men. His hand reached for Lori's as he died.

Juno heard the blast and saw the flash of light, but that was all.

The bodies of the Nazis had absorbed the blast. Only Juno, Lori, and Reichmann remained alive amidst the carnage, the flames, and the smoke. Gerald had known what he was doing: he had evened the odds; he had bet his own life—and those of the Jews—that Juno could carry on alone.

Swallowing hard to relieve the pressure in his ears, Juno turned back to face Reichmann. The Nazi's face was distorted with rage.

"Now it is just you and I." Reichmann raised the gun.

Juno felt no fear, only the burning compulsion to make Reichmann's victory a hollow one. "The whole world knows about you now; they will hunt you down and destroy you!"

"I do not believe that Dr. Davide has found a—"

The sound of the gunshot and Reichmann's scream pierced the air almost simultaneously. The back of the Nazi's head shattered. He slid to the floor, the Luger still clutched in his hand.

Lori looked up at Juno through glazed eyes. The Smith & Wesson Gerald had passed to her fell from her hand.

25

A team of plastic surgeons, former colleagues of Josh at Columbia Presbyterian Hospital, had spent more than three hours repairing Lori's wounds. She would recover with almost no permanent evidence of the beating she had suffered; but after awakening momentarily several hours ago, she had lapsed into a coma, following the progression of neurologic symptoms caused by the disease. She was still unconscious—this was the longest attack she had had. To support her respirations and to watch her heart function, another team of doctors at Columbia had transferred her to the intensive care unit; she was now on a respirator and a cardiac monitor. The disease was approaching its final victory.

In the darkened waiting room next to the intensive care unit, Juno felt himself slipping into the depths of despair. Thus far he had been unable to find anyone willing to assume the responsibility for the human experiment Lori had planned. Trying to alter the genes of animals was one thing; to attempt it in man was another. Her fate and that of the Jews was all but sealed. She had come so close. If only she had had the time, he knew she would have succeeded. . . .

"You may see her now." The nurse at the door interrupted his thoughts.

Although still weak and pale, Lori looked better. She was off the respirator, and the alarm on the cardiac monitor had been turned down. He kissed her and pulled up a chair beside her bed. Tears welled up in the corners of his eyes.

"I'm not dead yet. If you're going to sit there and mourn, I'm going to have you thrown out of here."

"Sorry."

"You should be. Actually, I feel rather good. I'll probably be asymptomatic for eight to ten hours. Want to take me out to dinner? Or would you rather do something else?" She winked playfully and ran her finger over the back of his hand. "On second thought, I think we'll have to settle for a short walk in the corridor. They told me I could get up for a few minutes." He did not respond. "Peter, have you been listening to me?"

He hadn't. He had been formulating his own plans for the way in which they would spend the next few hours. He fired questions at her, and her ability to answer them clearly gave him a flicker of hope.

"How about it?" he asked.

"I'm willing to give it a try if you are."

He kissed her gently on the lips and then ran for the nurse.

Everything Lori requested, including the flasks and her notebook, was neatly piled on the workbench in the small laboratory near the intensive care unit. She nodded her approval as Juno pushed her wheelchair close to the countertop. They both realized the huge dimensions of the problems facing them: they had to condense several days' work into a few hours. She knew the risks but had accepted them without hesitation.

They worked quickly and efficiently together. He was her hands and feet, and she talked him through each step of the procedure that might result in recombinant DNA.

In the darkened laboratory, glasses protecting their eyes from the ultraviolet light used to demonstrate the fluorescent DNA stain, evidence of success slowly emerged. Lines of DNA, one of which represented recombinant DNA, began to appear as a series of thin and thick bands in the acrylamide gel used for the final separation.

"My God, we've done it!" Lori trembled and felt tears fill her eyes. "That band"—she pointed to a glowing line in the gel—"it's what we're looking for! Normal human DNA attached to the DNA of a plasmid. This test proves it!"

Juno did not totally understand; but in her excitement, he felt a part of her success.

Suddenly Lori was quiet, and she stared at the tubes in front of them in disbelief. In the pattern of fluorescing bands was the hope of the Jews . . . and her hope.

She picked up one of the tubes containing the milky white combination of the two flasks and examined its turbidity against a bright light. "I still don't believe we've been able to do it! All that remains is for you to call the doctor to inject this into my vein." She looked up at him and ran her hand lovingly over his cheek. "Whatever happens, Peter, always remember me as I am now. And never forget that I love you more than . . ." Her words were lost in the foam welling up in her throat. Her hand fell from his cheek; her other hand trembled but continued to hold the tube. Coma overtook her.

As if he had spent his entire life preparing himself only for this moment, Juno wrenched the tube from her spastic hand, filled the syringe, found a vein in her arm, pushed the needle through the skin, waited for the blood to return, and then pressed the plunger.

As he had promised her, he did not take her back to the ICU.

"Please, Peter," she had said, "if I'm to die, let me die with you—just the two of us alone."

He kept his word. He held her in his arms in the darkness in the private room he had requested. There were no tubes, no alarms, no machines—just the two of them. She was barely alive. He could feel her body heave with each breath.

For two days he had watched her at the brink of death. He had no more prayers, no more tears; he just held her and waited.

"Peter . . ."

At first he would not believe he had heard his name; he was certain the sound came from somewhere in a dream. But then it was there again.

"Peter . . . ?"

"Yes?" His voice was no more than a whisper; he did not want the sound to shatter the dream.

"I love you, Peter."

Tears rolled down his cheeks. She would live.